Cradle in the Back of the Hall

Lenward E. Thomas

Cradle in the Back of the Hall

Copyright © 1998
Lenward E. Thomas

All rights reserved. No part of this book may be reproduced in any form, except for the inclusion of brief quotations in a review, without permission in writing from the author or publisher.

Library of Congress Catalog Card Number: 98-90180
ISBN: 1-57502-763-1

This is a work of fiction, a product of the author's imagination. Any resemblance to actual events or persons, living or dead, is entirely coincidental.

Printed in the USA by

MORRIS PUBLISHING
3212 East Highway 30 • Kearney, NE 68847 • 1-800-650-7888

For Rebecca
for her encouragement,
patience and understanding

ACKNOWLEDGEMENTS

My deep appreciation is extended to funeral directors for their assistance and their anecdotes.

Thanks, also to my writing instructor Patsy Baker O'Leary and the students of her class whose encouragements made this novel possible.

Special thanks to Janet Johnson for her computer abilities and to Mike Bennett for his artistic talent.

CHAPTER 1

Mary had long honey blonde hair that glinted with golden light in the sun. Her eyes were the color of a mountain lake, blue, green or gray according to her mood.

In the eyes of her father, she was a well-behaved ordinary girl until the day he saw his daughter and Jeffrey partially naked in the far end of the vegetable garden. Stunned, he could only stare at his daughter as her body moved in rhythmic motion under the boy for whom he cared so little.

He tried to call out to them, but no sound came forth. Seth dropped his cane and grasped the bean pole at the end of the row of butter beans. The wire-racked stake shook and the dried seed pods at the bottom of the vines sounded like a rattlesnake's warning. Mr. Ridley fell face down into the green vegetation, breaking the pole off at the ground and tangling himself in the wire and vines.

Mary heard the commotion above Jeffrey's shallow panting, and looked in the direction of the house. She saw her papa lying on the ground. Had he been standing there watching? Why had he fallen? Shoving Jeffrey away, she hastily got up and pulled her dress down, brushing the dirt away.

Jeffrey's pants lay nearby. Mary kicked them to him and he pulled them on and buckled the belt. He rushed to Seth and stooped, placing his ear to the man's pale purple lips.

"We must get help! We must get help!" Mary kept saying as she stood beside them fumbling at her skirt, trying to brush more dirt away.

"Go have your mama phone the doctor while I try to get him breathing. Hurry!" Jeffrey managed to speak softly, not wanting to further excite her. She turned toward the house, yelling, "Mama, Mama!"

The late autumn sun had sunk behind the trees casting up its last rays to underline the clouds in a rosy tinge. Ida Ridley was lighting the kerosene lamp when she heard Mary calling. She gathered up the apron that covered her oversized body and rushed to the kitchen back door, just off the side porch. "What on earth is wrong, girl?"

"It's Papa! He fell in the garden. I don't think he's breathing. We've got to get help!"

"I'll go to him. You run and call Doctor Grady. Hurry!" She reached for her glasses and they fell behind the table. She didn't bother to reach for them and rushed out the door, knocking the picture of President Hoover from the wall.

In the garden, Ida immediately saw Jeffrey standing over her husband at the end of the row. Jeffrey stood and shook his head. "I think he's gone, Mrs.

Ridley."

"He can't be," she said as she stumbled over the vines and fell full weight across her husband. He coughed. She rolled off and managed to raise his head to her lap and called out, "Seth, can you hear me? Speak to me, Seth!" she pleaded.

His gasps became rapid as guttural sounds came from deep in his throat. With half opened eyes, he stared at his wife.

"Let's move him to the house," Jeffrey suggested.

"We can't move him until the doctor comes! Do you want to kill him?" Ida slowly shifted Seth's head and loosened his light-weight jacket and shirt collar. "Run out to the lane and see if Mary's on her way back from the store. She went to call Doctor Grady. Oh, I do hope he comes soon." She watched Jeffery walk slowly past their white, two-story frame farmhouse to the middle of the dirt road. "Why don't you hurry up?" she yelled.

The country store had the only telephone in the community and was only a few hundred yards from the Ridley farmhouse. Ida could see the store from her front porch but not from the garden. As she sat behind the bean row she heard an automobile approaching, wishing it to be Doctor Grady's car. A surge of guilt gripped her. Rarely did she ever leave Seth alone. The stroke he had last year left his right side paralyzed and his speech impaired. If he survived this time, surely she would be able to learn what brought on his collapse.

The doors of Doctor Grady's 1932 Ford automobile slammed and he rushed toward the garden with Mary by his side. Jeffrey followed and stood apart from them. He saw that Seth's eyes were closed. He approached reluctantly and stood behind Ida Ridley.

"You were smart not to move him," the doctor said, opening his medical satchel. He removed a needle and syringe. He stooped and forced his patient's eyelids open. "I'm afraid he's had another stroke. We must get him to the county hospital."

"Thank you for coming so quickly, Doctor," Ida said as her hand caressed the fallen man's forehead.

"I'm glad I was at the store and not so far away," the Doctor replied. He administered a shot into Seth's arm and the man's head fell forward on Ida's lap. "Keep holding his head and I'll go call for help to carry him into town. I shouldn't be more than a few minutes," the doctor said.

Doctor Grady followed Farmer Jone's rickety pickup truck to the edge of the garden. Mary had gathered bed covers from the house and placed them on the truck. The three men lifted Seth carefully and placed him crosswise on the flatbed. Ida pulled herself onto the back of the truck and sat beside him, holding his head in her lap. Mary rode on the front seat with the driver while Jeffrey got in the back to help Ida.

"What in the world was he doing in the garden with you two?" she asked. "He could hardly walk. Being way over there must have taken too much of his strength. I've warned him repeatedly not to venture so far from the house. What was he thinking 'bout?"

Jeffrey did not respond.

"Did you all take him there with you?" She waited for a reply, but Jeffrey didn't speak. "Well, did you?"

"No."

"Did he follow you out there?"

"That's what he did. We didn't know he was there."

The sick man's head fell back and his lips parted. In the dim twilight Jeffery saw his lips move but wasn't sure if the vibration of the truck caused his lips to tremble or if the old man kept trying to tell his wife something. Jeffrey saw Seth struggling to speak and moved nearer as Ida held her ear close to her husband's mouth.

Jeffery purposely tapped the metal truck bed to keep her from hearing the words he thought the man was trying desperately to say to his wife.

"Be quiet," she nearly shouted. "He's mumbling something."

"I just wanted to see if he would respond to sound."

When Jeffrey lowered his ear to Seth's mouth, she pushed him away with her shoulder. For a long time she stared silently into Jeffrey's eyes. What if Seth had told his wife about him and Mary? The way the woman stared at him, Jeffrey felt certain she understood something. When he couldn't stand her stare any longer, he turned away so she couldn't see his face. He could never hide his guilt, anyway, but he could ward off the staring and feel more comfortable looking into the distance.

CHAPTER 2

Ida knew the trip over the bumpy dirt road was uncomfortable for Seth. The truck wove its way through the dark parking lot of the county hospital and stopped at the back entrance with a jerk. Ida pulled Seth close to her loose bosom.

Jeffrey jumped quickly from the back of the truck and while he stood in the lighted area, Ida noticed the fly of his pants was not buttoned. She kept watching and rocking Seth in her arms as Jeffrey rushed through the rear door to bring help.

As the stretcher bearers arrived, Mary hurried out of the cab of the truck to assist the others.

Ida struggled to pull herself to the side of the flatbed to make sure Seth was being placed on the stretcher carefully. The truck tilted to the left as she shifted. "I must get some of this weight off," she said aloud.

"What did you say?" Mary asked.

She pretended not to hear. Mary had been

pestering her for months to lose weight. Ida knew her problem was growing worse and she didn't need to be told that she was too large. For months, her arthritis had been killing her slowly. Now it took all her energy to pull herself upright on the tailgate. Promising herself that she would try to satisfy that nagging stepdaughter and lose a few pounds, she struggled again to get off the truck. She promised her Maker that if He would let Seth survive this attack she would cut back on her eating - - no more than two full plates of food during each meal. I just can't think about my weight anymore right now, not at a time when my poor Seth may be dying. Maybe in a few days when my mind is a little clearer and I feel a little closer to the Lord, then I'll truly decide.

Everyone rushed into the hospital behind the stretcher, leaving her to get off the truck all by herself. She managed to swing herself off and in the dim light at the emergency entrance she hiked up her bloomers, pulling her dress high. Her reflection in the dingy outside glass panel of the back door looked back at her and she saw a large woman whose flesh billowed like waves in deep water as she walked. She fingered her greying, windblown hair, trying to smooth it down. Grabbing the handle of the door, she found it had locked automatically behind the others when they entered. She pounded on the glass with clenched fists and yelled "Come open the door!"

The lights went out at the back entrance, leaving her in pitch darkness. After waiting for her eyes to adjust, she fumbled her way around the unpainted building to the front door, wishing she had brought her glasses from the kitchen. As she stepped off the paved area surrounding the unloading strip, she stumbled and fell into an oversized bush.

As she crawled out, her breath was short and her face felt flushed. "Lord, don't let me be having a stroke. I'll get this fat off. I promise," she muttered.

When she arrived at the front, the door was propped open to let in fresh air. Mary was in the waiting room when Ida entered the lobby.

"What in the world happened to you?" Mary asked.

"What happened to me? I'll tell you what happened to me. Had you brought my glasses this wouldn't have happened." She caught a glimpse of her wrinkled clothes and messed up hair in the large mirror hanging over the couch. She grabbed her head and rushed out the door. Mary followed. The people sitting in the lobby began to giggle. Mary looked at them and smiled.

"What's so funny?" Ida asked, pulling the door closed behind them. "If you had been looking after me, I wouldn't be in this mess. Why didn't you bring my glasses?"

"You didn't ask me to bring them."

"I did so!" she snapped. "I think you have completely quit doing things for me." She reached to pull up her stockings and realized one of her slippers was missing. "Go behind the building and look for my shoe," she demanded. "It's somewhere out there around them bushes some fool planted at the back entrance." She motioned Mary away. "I don't care what people think, I'm gonna go back in there and see poor Seth. He may be dead by now for all I know."

She kicked the other shoe off, picked it up then jerked the door open and waddled through the lobby of waiting people, glaring at them so fiercely they fell silent as she went into the hall. The small dilapidated county hospital was in such need of repair it was nearly at the point of being condemned. Tattered notices were posted on the walls. Jeffrey stood reading a notice about pregnancy.

"Where is he?" Ida demanded to know.

He pointed to the last door on the right.

"Your fly needs buttoning", she said abruptly.

Jeffrey fumbled at his fly as she rushed down the hall, her head twisting from one side to the other, looking in every open door. Outside Seth's room, two doctors were removing their stethoscopes when Ida approached. One took her hand and sadly shook his head. She gave a loud scream and ran into the room. Jeffrey tried to follow, but she slammed the door in his face. "Go away," she yelled. He backed against the wall, turned and saw the doctors staring at him in disbelief. Jeffrey lifted his hands as if to say, "I give up."

"Don't worry about her," the doctor said. "We know how Mrs. Ridley is and in a few minutes we'll give her a sedative to quieten her. Let her get it out of her system. She'll soon be all right." Jeffrey nodded and left. In the waiting area Mary rushed toward him with Ida's shoe still in her hand.

"He died, Mary." Jeffrey placed his hand on her shoulder, then whispered, "It isn't always fair when the good have to go."

"I know." She put her arms around him and rested her cheek against his. Ida's shoe knocked against his back. "He had suffered so long - - not being able to really be himself with all the restrictions Ida placed on him." Jeffrey heard her resentment. "She really doesn't like me. The only thing she ever seems to appreciate is the fact that I call her Mama once in a while." She held him close. Jeffrey looked around to see if they were being watched. Mary thought his shyness in public prevented him from showing his true feelings. She saw him blush and felt him relax his arm as a shapely redhead in a nurse's uniform passed by.

Ida's sobs carried well down the hall. "I don't want to go to her, but maybe it's best if I do," Mary said. She left him standing alone. As she approached the room she slowed her pace. The doctors opened the door and she disappeared inside the room.

Jeffrey saw the redhead coming toward him. He stepped to the center of the hallway just as she arrived. In one hand she carried a large box and pulled another by a small rope, her generous breast bouncing with each step. His heart throbbed as he looked at her tight uniform with her breast straining to be free. "May I carry that for you?" he asked while taking the one from her hand.

"That would be nice." She smiled and handed the rope to him as well.

He lifted the box from the floor and followed her. The nurse stopped in front of a door marked Supplies and unlocked it. He stepped inside the dark room behind her. She fought the air above her head in search of the pull string to the overhead light. He set the boxes down and reached for the string, too. While they grabbed in the darkness above their heads, he deliberately bumped into her. When the light came on they were standing so close her hands fell to his chest. She turned, stooped to pick up the boxes, and he leaned into her arched body. She looked up and smiled. He licked his lips and managed to say, "Ah, ah, have you worked here very long?" He knew he was stammering, but he couldn't control himself.

"No. Anyway, not long enough to have had you as a patient. Does a strong healthy man like you ever get sick?" she inquired, placing her hand on his shoulder.

"Only from the excitement of a pretty woman touching me. Then my heart starts pounding like it's doing right now. Here." He took her hand and placed it on his chest. "Do I need medical attention?"

"Oh, you wouldn't get excited over a little overhead light being turned on, would you?"

There was a teasing note in her voice. She raised her left eyebrow and blinked her blue eyes several times. As he stepped toward her, she didn't step back. Instead, she pushed the door closed with her foot and reached for the light string dangling above their heads.

CHAPTER 3

Mary and the doctor steered Ida down the hall and into what appeared to be a makeshift lab. She sat on a bench and stretched out her legs, crossing them at the ankle and rested her head against the wall behind her. She wasn't wearing a brassiere and her large breasts seemed to mold into her stomach. In her lap she held her shoes. All sounds were shut out of her mind and she thought of Viola. She would ask her to help with the funeral arrangements because she knew just what to do. She had buried three husbands since Ida had known her and a fourth was buried somewhere in Tennessee.

"I've gotta have something for my nerves," Ida kept mumbling. She opened her eyes. "Dr. Grady, where are you? I've gotta have some medicine," she moaned.

A nurse approached holding a syringe above her head, squirting liquid from its needle. Ida pulled her large legs out of the way when the nurse crossed to her right side and forced the needle into her plump arm.

For the first time Ida had the same feeling she did when they gave her twilight sleep just before she gave birth to the child no one knew about. She thought about the baby and began counting on her fingers. She couldn't think about it now. She had to make arrangements for Seth to be buried. She cried out for Viola. She didn't know if she could get through this with just Mary being with her.

She became groggy and leaned her head against the wall, her hands relaxed on her lap. She needed Viola. After all, she was her best friend.

Seldom did they go to funerals together anymore. Long before she stopped attending them, she found so many funny things to make her laugh during the eulogies that Viola was embarrassed and told her she should be more serious and quit laughing at everything, or she would never attend another one with her. Somehow, Ida just couldn't keep quiet. "I want to get the very best out of living," she said and continued laughing.

Now that Seth was dead, she needed Viola's friendship and support more than ever. Their friendship went way back and she recalled how she and Viola had walked together for their health in their earlier days. The funeral home was on the other side of town. She remembered the last time they went by there before she went to live with Seth. It was the evening Horace had invited them in for coffee.

The funeral home was operated by two bachelor brothers who lived in the back rooms of the old deteriorating building. The outside color had long faded to a dingy gray. The windows swung low on the back of the structure and were easily accessible to anyone walking on the side street or on the narrow street behind it.

Viola told everyone their trips by the Funeral

Home was Ida's reducing walk and that she went just to keep her company. The truth of the matter was they would make sure their rounds included the back street, hoping to see the undertaker brothers.

Early one crisp autumn evening when the sky was a pewter gray and leaves were crunching underfoot, they noticed the curtains were open to the embalming room. The overhead lights were brighter than usual and they decided to take a peek inside. Viola was hesitant, but Ida insisted they approach the window together. The instant they looked in they saw two naked men lying side by side on porcelain enamel tables.

"Have you ever seen two naked men at the same time?" Ida asked Viola.

"Not two dead ones," she replied, her eyes glued to the corpses.

"Why are they left alone right here under all these lights?"

"What difference does it make if the lights are on or not? You know they can't see."

"Well, why are that man's eyes still open, then?" She pointed to the table nearest them. Ida tried to shield her laughter. With her hand held tightly to her mouth the air made a noise as it was forced out through her fingers. Trying to laugh and speak at the same time, Ida said, "Sounds like one of them may still be alive. I bet it was the one with his eyes open."

"That's not very funny." Viola chided.

Ida thought it was and doubled over with laughter. Before she had a chance to controll herself, the back door suddenly opened and the attendant saw them as they turned from the window. He recognized them and asked in a rather loud voice, "Are you ladies enjoying your walk this evening? I see you are looking at the men. Do they interest you all?"

"They are not exactly what we're looking for, Horace," Ida said trying to hold back her laughter. "Viola, here, is desperate. She told me only last week if she only had one, she could care less if there wasn't a speck of life left in him."

"Ida, I do know you are the most insulting woman I've ever seen." Viola's words were harsh and mean, but Ida had grown accustomed to her insults and just kept laughing.

"Ladies, ladies. Let's not get angry. There are still some good men left around in this community with a spark still left in them. Take my brother, for instance. He's only fifty and just might be interested in one of you." Horace was almost shouting.

Ida pushed Viola in the direction of the man. "She'll take him. Where is he?"

"Well, he's supposed to be off duty tonight but, with these two on the slab, he'll be coming in shortly. Would you like to come in and wait?"

"Well, we are sorta in a hurry right now. Maybe another time," Viola said.

"Shucks, Viola," Ida whispered. "You'd better go. It might be your last chance. If you wait too long, he may be cold as those in there on the slab." She pointed to the embalming room.

"What did you say, Ida?" Horace asked.

"Oh, nothing. Just insisting that Viola stick around and talk to your brother."

"Both of you stick around. He's down at Macks

eating stewed chitlins. It seems every time we have a corpse in here, he likes to go down and eat 'em."

"Viola makes a fine pan of chitlins."

"What did you say?" Horace asked, his hand to his ear.

"Viola makes a good pan of chitlins. Let her know the next time you have a body in here and she'll fix your brother right up, won't you, Viola?"

"You just tend to your own business," Viola whispered, hardly moving her lips.

"Eh. What you say? Gotta do your business?" Horace asked, still cupping his hand around his ear.

"Just mind yours," Viola said without looking at Ida.

"Sure you can use mine. Just come on in this way," He held the door open for them to enter.

Ida grasped her friend's hand to lead her inside but Viola resisted her tugging and pulled her hand away.

Horace stepped into another room and turned off the outside light at the moment the heavy screen door slammed. Viola grabbed Ida's arm and said, "Good Lord! Let's get out of here!" They rushed toward the lighted area at the end of the hall.

"You're inside now," Ida whispered, "and you can't leave until his brother arrives. It just wouldn't be the thing to do after you accepted his invitation."

"I didn't accept. You did."

"Well, we can't leave now."

"I will if I want to," Viola said.

"Well, you just go ahead and leave. One of them men back there on the table just might have that spark of life left in him that Horace mentioned, and then I bet you'd be sorry. At least he wouldn't have to waste time taking his clothes off." Ida hit Viola on the backside and laughed aloud.

Horace entered another room and turned on the light. "Come in here," he beckoned. "and I'll make us some coffee."

Ida would have preferred a cool soft drink since they had nearly completed their hiking and she was still hot and perspiring. Dark wet circles spread under the arms of her flimsy voile dress and tiny drops of water dripped from the ends of her hair. She noticed how calm Viola seemed to be while primping her hair. The room was dimmer than the hall so maybe the wet circles wouldn't be so noticeable, Ida thought. A long table extended the full length of the small room and was pushed tightly against the wall. Ida noticed a hump under its white covering. The table had been moved to make more space for them but Viola bumped it as she squeezed past Ida.

Horace handed them an empty cup. There were dark coffee stains in the one he gave Viola and Ida tried to take it to remove them with her fingers, but Viola snatched it from her. Horace saw the struggle and took the cup himself. He walked over to the table and picked up the covering and began wiping the stains. Viola caught a glimpse of a body and rushed from the room, slamming the door behind her. When in the hall, she saw Horace's older brother entering the hallway.

"What's wrong?" he asked. "Has anything happened? Not any of your folks, is it?"

"No, but I'm sure I'll be the next one stretched out here. I've been scared out of my wits." She was breathing heavily and her voice choppy. "To... to be scared that bad, I, I might as well be dead."

"I'm Dudley," he introduced himself.

"I know," was all she said before Ida entered the hall.

"Viola, you're such a child. I guess we'd better go." She took her by the hand, nodded toward Dudley and said good-bye to Horace as they passed the door.

"You ladies don't have to leave, you know. My handsome brother Dudley just got here."

Ida turned and looked at the brother again. He was handsome, with his grey temples, a full sculptured jaw and muscular arms and thighs. Although his chest wasn't very broad and his shoulders were a little slumped, he certainly was nicer looking than his younger brother. Horace's pale skin made him look like a corpse. There were dark circles under his eyes and Ida knew he must have tried to used mortician wax to cover them up. The brothers didn't look anything alike and the older they got, the more Ida believed the rumor she heard years ago that they didn't have the same father. Seeing them together under bright lights seemed to confirm her belief.

Mary shook Ida to awaken her. She raised her head, looked around and asked, "Where am I?"

"We must go home now. The undertaker will come for Papa. They want us at the funeral parlor tomorrow. You must get some rest."

Ida stumbled several times when she got to her feet, so Jeffrey helped Mary get her in the truck and they rode on the back. As they drove from the parking lot they saw Ida crying and looking back at the hospital.

CHAPTER 4

Viola gave Ida all the help she asked for, but she wasn't pleased with the burial clothes and the cheap coffin Ida had selected. Viola never did care for black, particularly the coffins that were covered with felt. Viola knew how chintzy Ida was when it came to spending money and thought she would have had someone make the coffin. Ida constantly expressed to Viola her strong feeling about "not throwing money away" and "staying out of the hole," and she wasn't going to spent her money foolishly and was quick to warn everyone who appeared extravagant to do the same.

Viola remembered the day several years ago when she went shopping with her and how Ida had argued about having to spend ten dollars to buy the only suit Seth ever owned. It was a black one and was still hanging in the back hall closet. Ida had told her that Seth hadn't attended church since his first stroke and that she was saving the suit for his burial clothes. She had also told her that Seth had lived for so long after his sickness, she was wondering if she should sell it or keep it for his burial?

"The last time you saw it hanging there, you said it had already turned a greenish-brown," Viola reminded her.

"But I can't see spending extra money to buy a new suit just to put it in the ground, and I'm going to use it. I worked for hours last night trying to get the mold out of the fabric." Ida took a deep breath and walked to the window to examine it again. "Look. I've ironed it several times and the lapels kept rolling up around the edges. What can I do about that, Viola?" She threw the coat to Viola and picked up the pants to press them again.

"Surely, you can afford a new suit to bury him in. It's the last thing you can do for him," Viola said while working feverishly to remove what looked like a large tobacco juice stain on the lapel.

Ida picked up the flat iron from the homemade ironing board, licked her finger and tested the heat on the bottom. She stared at her friend and said, "I've done all I can for Seth and I want you to understand that. What I do today I'm doing for myself and I'm not gonna feel bad about it. Furthermore, I'm not gonna spend money foolishly on something I'll never see again. Seth wouldn't want me to do it." She began pressing the black necktie.

"But think what people will say."

"I don't give a hoot what others will say." After a moment of hesitation, Ida continued, "Remember how Margaret put her husband away?"

"Yes, and I remember how long folks talked about

how stingy she was, too."

"What do you mean, too?" Ida snapped back. Before she exchanged the cool iron for the hot one on the cook stove, she scratched a gravy spot from the tie. "Sometime, I wish you'd keep your thoughts to yourself and not pay so much attention to the things I say and do. Everybody don't think like you, Viola. I know what I'm doing."

"I thought you wanted my ideas and my help. Why did you ask me to be with you if you can do it all by yourself?"

"Sometimes I wish I could do everything without anybody's help."

Viola sat at the table a long time listening to Ida fume about the condition of Seth's clothes. She pushed away from the kitchen table in disgust. Folding the suit coat, she laid it on the back of a chair.

"Don't just throw the coat across the back. I just finished ironing it." Ida paused, her voice became soft and apologetic. "Spread it out on the table and I'll find a hanger to put it on."

Ida had Viola to drive her to the funeral home to deliver the burial clothes after they combed their hair and put a little rouge and powder on their faces. They said very little to one another on the way and Viola kept wondering if she should ask about Mary and how she was taking her daddy's death, but she remembered that every time Mary's name was mentioned, Ida had nothing but criticism and spoke it freely.

Finally, Ida broke the silence. "I'll never forgive Mary for bringing on Seth's stroke and..."

Viola interrupted and asked, "Mary? What are

you talking about?"

Ida stared straight ahead. "You'll never know what his dying words were to me. I really couldn't make them all out because Jeffrey was making so much noise on the back of the truck. I laid awake all night trying to put his words together." Neither spoke to one another until they came in sight of the funeral home. "After the funeral I don't think I want to see my step-daughter or that bastard friend of hers ever again."

Viola straightened her back, sat up higher and pulled to the edge of the road and waited for a vehicle to pass. When she pulled back to the center, her car hit a deep rut and Ida nearly bounced off the seat. The hanger of clothes fell from Ida's lap and became wedged between the car door and her thigh. She shifted and her legs knocked the car out of gear, but she managed to pull the suit free without causing Viola to lose control of the car.

The lapels of the coat were rolled even more and she busily rolled them in the opposite direction, hoping they would lay flat before she delivered the suit to the undertaker. When she looked up, Viola was driving on the wrong side of the dirt road. Since there was no other vehicle on the road, Ida said nothing.

The old Model A Ford had been driven for years, but still ran despite traveling over the rough country roads. Viola swore that the worst thing about her car was the seat Ida had worn out.

"You must tell me what Seth said to you. Tell me and I'm sure you'll feel better. You can't keep things bottled up inside at a time like this."

Ida hadn't shown emotion since leaving the

hospital. She wished she had another shot of the medicine she was given last night. She swallowed hard and said, "He told me something just before he died and I must keep it a secret, Viola. You're the only person I've ever shared my secrets with and, maybe someday, I'll feel like talking to you about it."

Viola caught the hint and didn't speak or look at Ida anymore until they came in view of the funeral home.

"I've never been one to show my emotions, Viola, and that stepdaughter of mine shows even less. She hasn't shed one tear. She has left me with the full responsibility of caring for her daddy these last few months. All she talks about is Jeffrey. I get so sick..."

They approached the funeral home and Viola interrupted and asked, "What entrance do you want to take?" She didn't wait for a response, but instead wheeled the old Ford up to the front door.

"Just stop here and you sit in the car. I won't be a minute. I'll drop the clothes off since I can't see Seth. I'll be right back." She opened the car door and struggled to get out, pulling some of the stuffing from the worn car seat as she managed to get her feet on the ground. Viola reached to pull the car door closed and heard Ida grunt as she swung the clothes hanger across her shoulder. She watched her rush inside.

Ida returned to the car, out of breath, and told Viola, "I didn't schedule a "settin-up" at the funeral parlor and I don't want to have anyone to sit with the body at the house all night, either. It's just too much trouble."

Viola wasn't pleased at all when she learned of

the plans. "You mean, no one will sit up with him his last night? Not even you?"

"No." She looked away and asked, "Why should I? He's dead."

"I can't believe you, Ida. There you are gonna be left a nice place to live for the rest of your life, and it all came from him, and you're not even gonna be with him his last night on earth? I just don't understand you, Ida. I really don't."

"I've done all I can for that man. I told you that earlier." Ida pulled the car door shut and stared straight ahead.

They remained silent as they rode the two miles back to the house. Ida had time to think, but Viola had confused her so she couldn't remember if she left word for Horace to bring the body to the house about six o'clock. She wanted him to come alone as there would be someone there to help him unload the body. Usually, lots of cakes and pies would be delivered to the house of the deceased and she could offer him something to eat and have a chance to socialize with him if the timing was right. Most of the callers would be gone by that time, anyway.

Ida had no idea what time it was, but when they arrived home they saw several automobiles parked in the yard and along the roadside near the house. A few people were standing on the back porch and Ida waved her hand for Viola to walk around and greet them.

Ida entered the front door. A variety of smells drifted from the kitchen and she heard laughter when she reached the hallway. She saw the door to her bedroom open and closed it. Mary's room door also stood open and she noticed her prized handmade crocheted bedspread covering her bed. Her first impulse was to snatch it off, fold it and put it in the back hall closet. "Mary just won't let my personal things alone. I'll talk to that girl when these folks leave," she mumbled to herself.

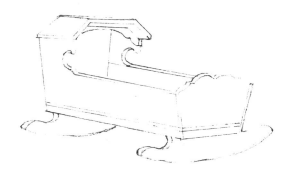

CHAPTER 5

As the mantel clock struck six, Ida glanced out the window while saying goodbye to some of the last afternoon visitors. Seth's body would be arriving at any time now. She remembered leaving instructions for Horace to drive the hearse to the side porch between the main living quarters and kitchen. The door was wider at that entrance, making it easier to maneuver the coffin into the parlor.

Viola had helped Ida shift the furniture to make room at the front window for Seth's body. The window shades were pulled and the tiebacks from the thin organdy curtains were removed so they would hang straight, creating a backdrop for the black coffin.

The hearse arrived much later than expected. It was nearly sundown when Horace drove up. Ida met him at the front of the house to remind him where to park. Viola was still following her around and asking questions. "Are you gonna put him next to his first wife? Is that new preacher at the Methodist Church going to preach his funeral?"

Ida tried to avoid as many questions as she could without hurting her friend's feelings again, but Viola continued, "The preacher over there really didn't know Seth well and I don't see why you can't call in the one from over at the Baptist Church. He knows the family and maybe can find a few good words to say about him."

"Just what do you mean? Seth was a good man and everybody knew that. Furthermore, there's nothing to the rumors that he was courting that skinny little hussy in town when he had his first stroke." Ida was almost bitter with her words. She left to meet the hearse at the back door.

Carless, the undertaker's helper stood on the back porch listening to the conversation as Horace opened the back doors to the drab black hearse. "Come help me, Carless," Horace called, looking around for some more men to help remove the body. Seeing Ida, he asked, "Where are the menfolk you said would be here to help with the unloading?"

"Oh, they had to leave. But don't worry, we have several strong ladies still here who are capable of lifting. They can give you some assistance." She was disappointed that he brought his helper. She turned toward the kitchen and called out, "Viola. Beaulah. Irma. Lena. Isabell. Y'all come out here a minute and give us a hand."

All the ladies gathered on the back porch and when Horace saw them he whispered to Ida while patting the top of the coffin. "Is there enough strength among them for the task." Turning to them he asked, "Do you ladies know how heavy this coffin is? Are there some others here?"

"I can help," Ida told Horace, then whispered to Viola, "I've drug him around all this time, surely I can do it one more time." She surveyed the scene then stepped toward the back of the hearse and motioned for the others to come.

Horace and his helper pulled the coffin partially out of the rear doors of the hearse. Leaving his helper to keep the coffin balanced, Horace stepped back to give instructions. The ladies lined up along the sides of the coffin and grasped the handles as the coffin slowly slid through the back door of the hearse. "It's heavy," Horace said. "Walk slowly and carefully," he ordered and went up the rickety wooden steps and motioned them to come forward.

Ida stood at the head of the coffin opposite Carless. She heard the ladies behind her straining and groaning. She looked over her shoulder and saw wrinkles plowing through Viola's forehead and heard her softly whisper to Isabell, "I'm carrying more than my share of the load."

There were a few more grunts as they heaved and stumbled trying to get up the steps. Guiding them, Horace said, "You all be carefull when you set the coffin down on the porch."

The old boards in the porch creaked when the coffin was placed on the floor. Not waiting for further instructions from Horace, Ida opened the screen door and held it against the wall with her foot. She stretched to take hold of the coffin handle and gave orders for the ladies to, "Come over and take hold" and watched carefully as they lined up again and began slowly lifting the coffin. She heard a thud and suddenly the coffin became very light. "Oh, my God!" Ida yelled, releasing her hold.

Horace had just entered the parlor and rushed to Ida. Her knees had buckled and she was on the floor just inside the room. He saw Seth's body lying beneath the shell of the coffin and quickly closed the door to block Ida's view.

Irma was horrified when she turned and stepped on the dead man's arm. She pulled her other foot from under the dead body, released the coffin handle and ran down the steps. Viola squeezed through the partially opened door to help Horace pull Ida to the couch. The other ladies stood gazing at Seth, wondering what they should do. Beaulah, the bravest of the group, squatted and removed the portion of the satin lining covering his face and straightened his necktie, then backed against the wall.

Fannie Mae, the negro woman who had finished her duties in the kitchen, came to the porch to ask if someone could take her home. She was busy untying her huge white apron and was unaware of the accident. When she saw the corpse lying at the feet of the women, she ran back into the kitchen and crawled through the open window. The others heard her scream and watched as she ran across the field to her shack on the back of the farm.

Carless grabbed the top part of the coffin and pulled it to the end of the porch. Isabell rushed into the kitchen and brought out a table cloth and a kerosene lamp. She spread the cloth over the body and called Horace.

When he opened the door, he saw Beulah trying to place Seth's arm back on his chest. "We'll take care of that, Mrs. Weatherspoon. You go inside and help comfort Mrs. Ridley," he said.

Although it was not yet dark, Lena held the kerosene lamp high as the two men struggled with the stiff body. Finally, they got it to the edge of the porch and Horace asked Carless to direct him while he backed the hearse close enough to the porch to load the parts of the coffin and the body. Before his helper yelled "Stop", the steps were knocked from their foundation. The hearse was near enough to slide the bottom of the coffin and its shell inside and against the draped window, leaving enough room on the side to place the corpse. Horace climbed inside the hearse and pulled while Carless pushed the body. They heard the nails rip Seth's suit.

The women were in the parlor and Beaulah hovered over Ida as long as Ida felt she could stand her. Ida got off the settee, leaving Beulah, and moved to the homemade piano bench. Viola slipped down and Ida sat next to her. Ida heard the hearse driving off and quickly stood up. Viola slid to the floor when the bench tilted. Ida turned, saw her sprawled in the floor, chuckled and said, "I told Seth when he made that bench that he was putting the legs too close together."

Mary and Jeffrey passed the speeding hearse on its way back to town as they drove toward home. They had placed the coffin spray of daisies, fern and chrysanthemum on the back seat of Jeffrey's old Hudson and he was driving slowly to avoid spilling the water from the flower container. Mary had paid for the flowers herself, and from time to time checked the rear seat to make sure they were riding safely. Somehow, she knew Ida would not approve of them, but what did she care--Jeffrey liked them.

The florist told them the trough in which the flowers were arranged was constructed to fit the top of the coffin and all they had to do was place it carefully on top, making sure it was firmly positioned.

When they arrived home she heard several versions of what happened while they were away and why the hearse was in such a hurry to get back to town. She was glad she and Jeffrey were not there when all the commotion took place.

Mary held the flower spray as Ida examined each blossom to make sure they were not old blooms. She pulled several of the large chrysanthemums out and rearranged them as Mary looked on. Neither said anything. When they were fixed to her satisfaction, Ida took the flowers from Mary and gave them to Jeffrey. "Take these to the back porch where it's cool and put them on the pump shelf. Be sure to add more water to keep them fresh," Ida said in her usual domineering voice.

Mary followed Jeffrey and as soon as they reached the porch, she changed the flowers Ida had shifted and placed them as near as she could remember in their original place and then returned to the parlor.

"Will they bring Papa back out here tonight?" Mary asked her stepmother.

"They're supposed to," she responded nonchalantly.

"About what time?"

"How should I know?" Ida said.

"You didn't ask?" Mary inquired. Ida gave her a hard look and left for the kitchen.

Viola moved closer to Mary and whispered to her, "I told her she shouldn't have bought the cheapest coffin they had. It was absolutely terrible, Seth falling through the bottom of that coffin, and right here among all her closest friends."

Mary's eyes filled with tears. Embracing Viola, she began to cry. "I just don't know what to do. I can't seem to do anything right, not even buying the right kind of flowers. Did you see Ida rearranging them?. When all this is over, I think I'll just move out."

"Now, honey, you stay right here and hold your ground. Things will work out." She pulled Mary closer and whispered in her ear, "There are things I will tell you later. Just be patient, will you?" Viola felt Mary's head nodding against her face as she grieved for her papa. Viola tightly embraced her.

CHAPTER 6

"We'd better put him in a more expensive coffin, or we'll be sued," Horace said after they unloaded Seth and placed him on the porcelain table in the embalming room. "Look at his suit. We'll never to be able to repair it so we'll just have to get him another one. Whattcha think, Dudley?"

"Do you think we could use the one old Mrs. Crabstein brought here years ago to bury her husband in?"

"Was that the old man whose body was given to the embalming school?"

"Yeah, and we kept his clothes before we shipped his body up North. She moved back down here, you know, and never came for the suit."

"Hadn't thought of that job in years. Do you know where the suit is?"

"Folded away in some box in our living quarters. I'll go see if I can find it."

Dudley returned, holding up a light tan-colored suit made from a shiny fabric that was popular some years back. "It isn't a very good color, but I think we could explain to Ida, don't you?"

"We never would be able to find one like she had him dressed in, even if we searched every attic in the area. Here, hand it to me."

Horace threw the suit across the corpse. "It'll fit if we roll the sleeves up and tuck the excess material under the body. Don't think the gravy spotted tie will match though, so we'll just use one of ours. Go pick out one, but don't get a good one." Horace ripped the coat seams open and drapped it around the body to make it fit.

The necktie Dudley picked was a slightly burned toast color and didn't look too out of place with the tan suit. "Here. Try this one." He held it until Horace finished buttoning the shirt collar.

"That looks fine. Let's slip him into another coffin. Do we have one in the same price range?"

"We have the new grey one that come in last week. We'll lose money on it, though."

"But she didn't like the grey one."

Horace placed the base part of the coffin on the top of another table and rolled it next to the embalming table holding Seth's body. "Don't you think we could replace the bottom on this with screws? We can certainly do a better job rebuilding it than the manufacturing company made it." He rubbed his hands over the bottom of the coffin and asked Dudley to get the hammer and remove the nails from it.

They screwed the bottom on firmly, flipped the coffin over and covered the screw holes with wax.

"Luckily, most of the scratches are on the backside and not too noticeable. There", Dudley said as he put the hammer aside. "What the heck? She's getting a bargain. She'll get the suit and the tie and they won't cost her anything. She should be happy."

"Don't count on it," Horace said.

The women stayed at Ida's house until the undertaker returned with Seth's body. Horace brought a very short and sickly-looking older man with him. When Ida saw him, she was glad Jeffrey had stayed around to help unload the body, but she was also glad he'd stayed in the barn and out of her sight until the hearse arrived.

Everyone seemed cautious and very quiet as they were given instructions on how to lift the coffin. Not until it was placed in front of the window did everyone seem to relax.

The undertaker's helper, a little sprout of a man, moved one kerosene lamp to the foot and the other to the head of the coffin. The glow made Seth look more like he was asleep, rather than dead. "Did I see some flowers on the back porch when we arrived?" the little man asked.

Jeffrey went for them and when he returned, the man took the flowers and moved gracefully toward the coffin. He stood on tiptoe and when he stretched to place them on top of the coffin, the container tilted and water poured onto the body. Horace saw what was happening and quickly stepped forward and closed the coffin lid. He was centering the spray of flowers when Ida came and stood by him.

"Aren't you going to leave the lid open?" she asked.

"There's no need if no one will be sitting up with him all night. If we keep it closed tonight, he will look fresher during the funeral tomorrow."

Ida couldn't understand the logic, but she made no comment.

"Now that we have closed it, it mustn't be opened until we return to take the body to the church. Bodies have a way of discoloring when they are exposed to light and humidity for long periods of time, you know." Ida had never heard of such a thing. "Oh, there'll be no need to open it," she said.

"In that case, everything will be fine." Horace turned and said, "Good night, Ladies." Ida held the door open for the men to leave and watched until they reached the hearse.

Viola got mad over the hour set for the funeral and left before bedtime. She thought it was selfish of Ida to schedule the funeral so early in the morning, accusing her of not wanting many people to attend. "Nine o'clock is just too early, and frankly, I don't know if I can make it at that hour or not," she told Ida.

"Well, if you can't attend, you just can't attend. I'll try to understand, so don't you worry. We'll get him buried," she said, trying to reassure Viola of her ability to handle it by herself.

After Viola left, Ida and Mary were the only ones in the house with Seth's body. Mary went upstairs to bed. Ida centered the flowers on the coffin again and blew out the lamps. She rushed toward the door, afraid to look back in the darkness.

When Ida was undressing for bed, she felt a chill in the room. She pulled her gown over her head, got in bed and pulled the sheet over her. She felt a little ashamed of the way she had spoken to Viola and her recent attitude toward her. Seth was gone now and she began making promises to herself that she would change her disposition and try, as best she could, not to snap back at anyone when they told her something she didn't particularly like.

Her thoughts were interrupted when she heard the stairs creaking. The clock had just struck two and she hadn't been to sleep. The sounds on the steps stopped suddenly and she wondered if Mary was on her way to the parlor? She slid from underneath the light weight covering and crept to the door. The full moon cast its dim glow through the sheer window curtains, lighting the room enough for her to see that the lamp had been removed from the hall table. She went quietly to the parlor door and saw Mary silhouetted in the lamplight, kneeling at the head of her father's coffin. She had never seen Mary praying before. Ida backed all the way up the hall to her room, went inside and closed the door softly.

Two rows of folding chairs were placed by the graveside for the family. The sun was making its way in the sky and a flock of pigeons wheeled overhead. Ida squinted, hoping they wouldn't drop anything. She sat next to Mary and a few of Seth's kinfolk filled the remaining seats. Ida wasn't too happy about them being late, particularly when they had to squeeze between her and the coffin while everyone looked on.

When the group was seated, Ida hadn't noticed the preacher moving toward the crowd to begin the graveside portion of the service. She stood and stretched to center the flower arrangement one last time. She realized they were a little out of reach and stepped closer. Her weight caused a slight cave-in at the edge of the grave where the artificial grass had been laid. Her right foot sank and she reached for the handle of the coffin. The sudden jolt caused the flowers to fall across her shoulders and slide down her back.

Several of the men rushed to assist her and after pulling her free, she noticed one of her Sunday shoes had come off. She whispered, "Would one of you please reach down there and get my shoe?" Elmer, the man with long gorilla like arms, reached into the hole beneath the coffin, but raised up without the shoe.

Embarrassed, Mary covered her face with both her hands.

Ida got Horace's attention and beckoned him to come. He pushed his way through the crowd and leaned toward her. "Don't you dare bury my Sunday shoe," Ida whispered. "When everybody leaves the graveyard, you figure out some way to get my shoe and bring it to me. I'll be waiting at home." Horace nodded and wove his way back through the crowd. Ida waved to the preacher to begin.

The graveside service seemed short. When the final prayer was said, the preacher went to Ida, shook her hand and moved slowly down the row of family members, speaking to each and saying, "God bless you."

Ida noticed Viola standing apart from the crowd talking to several ladies. She placed her hand on Mary's shoulder and pushed herself upright, nearly turning Mary's chair over.

Viola saw Ida coming toward them and went to meet her. "Ida, dear. It was a lovely service".

Ida knew her loud greeting wasn't for her, but for

the benefit of those standing around. The other ladies simply smiled.

Viola took hold of Ida's arm and they walked toward the waiting car the funeral home had provided for the family.

"I told you plainly that you should have gotten the preacher from the Baptist Church. Not one thing was said about his personal life."

"He said a plenty," Ida responded as she opened the door to the car.

"I hate to tell you this, Ida, but you have a harsh tongue," Viola said and started walking toward the crowd.

Ida moved to Viola's car to wait for her.

When she was seated, she saw all the people around the grave staring at her as a young chubby boy ran in her direction.

CHAPTER 7

*I*da sat in the front seat of Viola's car with her arms propped on the open door, dangling her feet outside the car. The young boy ran to the car and said. "My name's Leander, but my folks call me Lee for short. I've been looking at you a long time."

His round face was beaming. The chubbiness around his jaws and the little rolls of fat around his neck seemed childlike. Ida knew he couldn't be more than a dozen years old and thought he was big for that age.

"Don't worry about your shoe, I'll git it before they put dirt in the hole," Lee said, swinging on the opened car door.

"Why did you come to the funeral, Lee?"

"My papa and mama is kin to the man they just buried. They told me you're one of his wives. I wanted to come over and tell you how sorry I am that he died and that I'll get your shoe." He looked at her foot now propped on the running board. "Don't you have two pair? I have. A brown one and this here black pair."

Ida didn't look at his shoes, but kept watching the folks who were staring at her. "Do you know a lot of the other people here?"

"I don't know nobody 'cept my folks. We just got here this morning."

"Where do you live?"

"In Tennessee."

"Did you drive all night to get here?"

"We ain't drove long. We just come over from Scottsboro this morning."

"Is that where you spent the night?"

"Yeah, and Papa said I ain't gonna stay here long. They gonna take me back to Tennessee before school starts."

"I wonder why they came to the funeral? Did they tell you?" Ida asked, testing the dampness of the grass with her stockinged foot.

"Papa said that his Uncle Seth might have some money and he might be in his will."

Ida tightened her jaw and shifted on the seat, pulling her foot back to the running board. "Did he say anything else?"

"Him and Mama talked about something else and I think it's got to do with Uncle Seth's first wife, but I ain't sure what they said." He paused, then asked, "Did he have a lot of money?"

Ida didn't reply and the boy kept swinging on the car door, waiting for an answer.

"They think he left a lot of money and it sounds like he did, 'cause they said his second wife was so stingy that she never spent any."

"Well, you just run along and tell your folks I'm

glad he left some money."

The boy turned and ran off toward the grave. Ida watched him searching the crowd. She saw him pull the sleeve of a man who looked about fifty years old and whisper into his ear. The man looked around for his wife, took her arm and guided her toward Ida. Lee followed. Ida didn't bother to get out of the car when they approached and said nothing until they introduced themselves.

"We're Seth's cousins, Jasper and Fannie. This is our son, Lee."

"I just met Lee. I didn't know Seth had cousins in Tennessee. He never mentioned you."

"Well, it's been a long time since we were in the area. Perhaps it's because Uncle Seth has been an invalid for so long, he forgot to mention us," Fannie said.

Ida observed her visitor's smiling faces, their fine-looking clothes, and Fannie's fancy hair style. Her shoes matched her short gloves and cloche hat.

Jasper asked, "May we come by to see you this evening? The undertaker asked Lee to stay after everybody leaves the graveyard. He wants him to retrieve your shoe." Jasper ran his hand through the boy's thick head of hair. "We thought you might like for us to bring the shoe to you and visit awhile."

"Thank you, but Horace, the undertaker, has made plans to bring it to me himself," Ida said, feeling sure it was their excuse to get to the house in time to hear the will read.

"But it's right on our way back to Scottsboro," Fannie said, fidgeting from one foot to the other. She pulled Lee off the car door.

People were beginning to move away as Ida glanced toward the graveside. Some waved as others zigzagged through the headstones on their way to their automobiles, occasionally stopping to read the epitaphs on old lichened stones that leaned drunkenly.

"We would like to talk to Mary since we arrived so late and didn't have a chance to speak with her," Fannie remarked. "My, how she has grown. And she's such a pretty young lady and so charming. She must be about seventeen now?"

"She's twenty," Ida said, knowing full well Mary wasn't charming and certainly not pretty.

As the crowd began to move from the graveside, not one person came to say good-by to Ida. Those remaining gathered around Mary, hugging and kissing like she was a movie star, or something. Ida couldn't stand all the attention Mary was getting, so she looked Fannie in the eyes and said, "I must go to be with Mary."

Jasper and Fannie stepped back as Ida grabbed the door frame of the car and pulled herself up. She kicked the other shoe off and said, "Excuse me," leaving them standing by the car.

Mary was too embarrassed to look at Ida as she stood beside her in her stocking feet. After a few minutes, Ida took Mary by the elbow and whispered, "We must be getting home now. The lawyer will be there and we don't want to keep him waiting too long."

Mary slowly but forcefully pulled her arm away when she felt Ida squeezing it firmly. "Why don't you go on? I'm sure you can manage quite well without me," Mary said, trying to sound pleasent. "I've met some new relatives and must get acquainted. Go on, I'll be on shortly."

Lee was standing next to Ida. She placed her arm around the boy's shoulder and said, "If the undertaker insists that you bring my shoe, you and I will have some cake. You look like you're hungry." She patted his little round stomach, nodded to the others around her and walked toward Viola's car.

Viola put Ida out at home. "I'll see you later when the company has left," she said and drove off.

Ida was the first to arrive and she sat on the slightly leaning, nearly worn out porch waiting for Horace. An hour and twenty minutes later he drove up in the hearse, followed by the car from Tennessee. Before the car stopped, Lee had the car door open and jumped out as soon as it came to a halt. He ran to Ida smiling, holding the shoe in front of him.

"See, I brought it. Mama said I could. Now can I have my cake?"

Ida knew they had delayed getting to her house so they could be there for dinner.

"Can I eat my cake now?"

"Yes, and anything else you want to eat, but let's wait until the others are inside." She stood on the top step and waved reluctantly for Fannie, Jasper and Horace to come in.

Fannie dusted the porch chair with her lace handkerchief before she sat down. Horace sat on the edge of the porch with Jasper, and Lee chased the rooster around the yard.

"Lee's ready to eat but we'll wait until Mary and the lawyer arrive. There's no point in cleaning up twice," Ida announced.

Mary and the banker arrived without the lawyer and followed the crowd into the kitchen. As they ate, Ida wondered if there would be anything left over. She didn't like to cook and was grateful for all the victuals neighbors had brought to the house. At Fannie's insistence, Jasper ate like it was going to be his last meal.

Lee was not about to get the biggest piece of cake. "That big piece is for me," Ida said, "but you can have that slice with all that yummy icing. Doesn't that look good?" Ida said, trying to convince the boy.

"But I don't want that piece with all the icing. You got the biggest slice and I'm your company, and I think I should have it," Lee said as he poked his lips out and pushed the plate to the center of the table. He went to the window and stared out. "I'm not going to eat it."

"Here. I'll take it," Jasper said. "Don't offer him any more. He's much too large anyway."

Lee darted back to the table and grabbed the plate from his daddy.

Fannie made herself busy about the kitchen collecting the plates after everyone finished eating. Ida felt she was trying to take over. "You don't have to do that, Fannie. I'll put the remaining food away." Lee watched Ida take the plates of leftover food and set them on the sideboard. She opened the doors to the storage area and shoved the leftover food inside and closed the compartments. "There. That should keep until suppertime." Once the food was out of sight, she glanced at Lee and wondered if it would be safe.

Mr. Crusade, the banker, pushed himself from the table and brushed the cake crumbs from the oil cloth onto the cracked linoleum floor. He removed papers from his inside coat pocket.

Ida thought, "What a fat slob he is, brushing the crumbs on my kitchen floor."

Crusade moved closer to the table, thumbed through the pages, them laid them out in front of everyone.

Mary slid her chair next to the banker as Fannie stood leaning over his shoulder. Ida counted the sheets in the document.

Chapter 8

The pages Mr. Crusade spread on the kitchen table looked too complicated for Ida to understand. Why was there a need for a map? Why all the red lines drawn across it and why did everyone have their heads so close together as the banker rearranged the sheets?

"How personal is all this?" Ida asked Mr. Crusade.

"It's strictly a family matter. Everyone here family?" he asked while removing a cigar from his inner coat pocket and placing it on the table in front of him.

"Well, if it's very personal, only me and Mary are the family. Me, of course, is his wife."

"I know that, so if the two of you would like, we can go to another room to discuss this matter."

"I prefer that," Ida said as she watched Fannie get up, snatch her purse from the table and asked Lee and Jasper to follow her to the back porch. Lee did not go and continued to sit at the table. Fannie slammed the door behind her.

Lee sat staring at the banker. They looked at each other for a few moments and finally, when Lee didn't attempt to follow his parents out, Mr. Crusade said, "Maybe we should go to the Parlor." He gathered the papers and they left Lee sitting by himself. From the doorway of the parlor, Ida waved to Lee, signaling him to go to the porch, but he remained.

Ida went to the window and hooked the tiebacks and raised the shade to let in the afternoon sun. She watched the dust motes dance in the air. Mary moved some of the furniture to its original place then sat on the settee with the banker. Ida pulled the small library table in front of them and went to the kitchen door to close it. She saw Lee take the cigar and put it in the deep pocket of his shirt. Returning, she sat on the other side of Mr. Crusade. The settee creaked.

The papers were spread out in front of them again and Mr. Crusade asked, "You know this is not the will. Mr. Pepperell has that and will be getting in touch with you later today. I told him that I needed to talk with the two of you before he delivered the will." He paused long enough to thumb through the papers. "Here. This is what I want to talk to you about." He held up the map marked in red.

Ida leaned closer, adjusted her glasses and asked, "What's the map all about?"

"Shortly before Seth had his last stroke, he took out a sizable loan on the farm. It's our custom..."

"What?" Ida almost screamed. "He mortgaged the farm?"

"Yes. Our policy is to ask our customers for what purpose, or reason, do they need the money. Seth was reluctant to tell us. Rather than question him further..."

"I don't believe it!" Ida interrupted. She angrily got up and stomped around the room.

Mr. Crusade continued. "When he didn't want to tell us, we went ahead and approved the loan. The area of the farm marked in red now belongs to the bank."

Ida came back to the table. "You mean all the area you have marked in red? Why, that's everything except the house and this little piece of woodland," she shouted.

"I know. He didn't want us to include the living quarters so we agreed to reduce the amount he wanted to borrow against the farm."

"What in the world did he do with the money? What did he need it for? He never mentioned anything to me." Ida, her eyes filled with tears, went to the fireplace and leaned on the mantel. The acrid smell of the ashes left from the early springtime fires filled the room. Her world was beginning to collapse around her. What must she do? She rubbed her sweaty hand on her hips. Turning toward Mary, she saw her shrug her shoulders. The expression on her face convinced her that Mary knew about the arrangement Seth had made with the bank. "I'll never get over this." Her voice became soft and shaky. "To think I have waited on him hand and foot, all this time by myself, and he pulled such a stunt on me as this." She shook her finger in Mary's face and said, "You'll pay for this, Mary Ridley. You'll pay for this!"

Trying to appear calm, Mary's attention went from Ida's finger shaking to the map in front of her. She moved closer to Mr. Crusade and nervously traced the red lines marking the wooded area a short distance from the house.

Ida raised her voice. "What are y'all doing? You're plotting against me. I know you are!" She loomed toward Mary.

The stout man stood and raised his hand in front of Ida. "Just wait a minute. I insist we just calm down. Let's discuss this situation without getting angry."

"Don't you tell me to calm down. You're in my house!" Ida wasn't sure that she should have made the statement, but as always she spoke before thinking. Why I may not even have the house anymore, she thought.

Mary said softly, "Mr. Crusade, maybe we can settle this at a later time?"

Ida searched Mary's face and wished she could be calm and more like her, but this time she knew for certain they had planned their strategy and she had to stand her ground. She didn't care how much she insulted them now. No one was going to rob her of her entitlement and she would see to that. She knew she didn't know the law, but wanted both of them to understand she wouldn't stand by and watch everything she had taken from her. "Oh, no, we aren't gonna wait 'til another time. We're gonna settle this right now." Ida's voice was harsh. "Do you hear me, Mary Ridley?"

The door opened and Fannie and Jasper entered the room.

"Just what do you two want?" Ida asked sarcastically.

"Oh, nothing. We heard the racket and wanted to see if there is anything we can do." Fannie's words sounded more inquisitive than like an offer of help.

"Then just get out. I know you're here to hear the will read. Well, I can tell you that the lawyer hasn't arrived yet. This is another matter and I would appreciate it if you'll just leave!"

"That sounds more like a threat than a request," Mary calmly said,

Fannie and Jasper left the room and, before the noise of the back door slamming faded away, they heard a loud knock on the front door.

Chapter 9

*I*da opened the front door to find a tall, fat man whom she had never seen. He was dressed in a light brown suit and tie. The suit looked familiar, resembling the one Seth was buried in only a few hours earlier.

"Come in," she said, still sniffing and trying to hold back the tears.

The stranger shook Ida's hand, smiled at Mary and seemed surprised to see the banker still there.

"I'm Stacy Pepperell, your daughter's lawyer."

Ida snatched her hand away forcefully.

"Hello, Albert. Am I too early?" he asked the banker.

"We are not quite through, but..."

Mary interrupted. "Come. You may sit here," pointing to the seat opposite the table.

"I'll just sit here if you don't mind." he said as he moved a small rocking chair near the window. "Is this all right, Mrs. Ridley?"

Ida sized the lawyer up and wondered if he would fit in the chair.

"Sit anywhere you like", she snapped, "except this antique rocker." Ida never sat in the chair for fear it would break. She tugged at it until the lawyer released it.

The lawyer looked at Albert and raised his eyebrow.

"I'll be leaving," the banker said as he began gathering his papers.

Ida regained her composure and spoke with authority. "Oh, no you won't. You just sit right there until you explain to me in detail why you let Seth mortgage the farm and what he did with the money."

Reluctantly, Mr. Crusade stood and backed against the wall behind the library table, fumbling for the doorknob. Mary went and stood beside him.

"We can finish at another time, Mr. Crusade," Mary said, leading him toward the front door. She opened it and whispered, "Everything will work out. I'll see you tomorrow at the bank."

Albert glanced at Mr. Pepperell as if to ask his approval of his leaving. "Maybe I should be the one to come back later?" the lawyer said. The statement was directed to Mary, but Ida was quick to respond.

"No! You stay right here. I'm sure you can best explain the scheme the bank is involved in and I may need you to help me sue the hell out of them!" Ida said.

"I'm afraid I don't know what you're talking about."

"You're a lawyer, aren't you?" her abrupt question rang out.

"Yes, but I have no idea what seems to be your problem."

"Don't try to fool me. All of you are just alike. Trying to grab every dollar you can get your hands on. Well, you won't get by with it this time."

Mary took the banker by the hand and led him back into the parlor. "Can't you keep quiet Ida, for just a few minutes; at least until you hear what they have to say to us." She released the banker's hand and walked swiftly toward her stepmother. Ida backed away from the chair and moved quickly to the window.

Mary said, "Come over here and have a seat, Mr. Crusade. We might as well get all this over with right now." Mary's voice was trembling as she took her seat beside Mr. Pepperell. "First, Mr. Crusade, will you tell Ida when and why Papa mortgaged the farm?"

Mr. Crusade cleared his throat and shifted several times in his seat. "Well, Ida, Seth was a compulsive gambler and six years ago he deeded everything to Mary."

"What!" Ida yelled. "What do you mean,`deeded everything to Mary'? Well, we'll just see about that!" her eyes darted at Mary, then back to Mr. Crusade.

"Perhaps an explanation is in the will," the banker suggested. "Let Mr. Pepperell read it to you."

The lawyer unfolded the papers and began to read.

"`I, Seth Ridley, being in sound mind...'"

Ida took two sudden steps toward the lawyer and snatched the papers from his hand. "You just wait a minute. I want to see it for myself." Mary rose and snatched them from her, leaving a torn corner of the document in Ida's hand. She handed the papers back to Mr. Pepperell as Ida plopped into the brown mohair settee, jarring the floor. A figurine rocked on the homemade what-not until it fell. In an almost inaudible voice Ida said, "I wish the whole damn house would fall apart."

"What did you say?" Mary demanded.

Ida didn't bother to answer, but sat with her head thrown back, her eyes closed.

The lawyer began reading again. "*I, Seth Ridley, being in...*"

"I don't want to hear it right now," Ida said scornfully, struggling to raise her plump body from the settee.

"You must listen, Mrs. Ridley," the lawyer said calmly.

"I'm not, I'm not, and furthermore," Ida paused and took a deep breath, lowered her voice and said, "I'm not Mrs. Ridley. We were never married."

"What?" The lawyer stared at Mary. She sat undisturbed by the surprise on the lawyer's face. He turned to Ida and asked, "Not married to him?"

"That's right," the banker said. "That's why she didn't know anything about the money. She wasn't required to sign the papers for the loan Mr. Ridley took out with us."

Mary was quick to respond. "The secret has been kept from everyone, even our closest friends."

Ida sat errect and asked Mary, "And you knew?"

"Yes. Papa deeded me the farm and the woodlands and left you the house. He borrowed money to pay his gambling debts and when they were paid off, we struggled to make the mortgage payments but couldn't manage to keep them up. We agreed to let the bank take the farm if Papa could have a life estate on it."

Mr. Crusade added, "When we heard of Mr. Ridley's death, the bank officers decided to give Mary two options. She may catch up on the payments, which totals about four thousand dollars, or we will pay her three thousand more, which we consider to be a fair market value, and proceed with the foreclosure. We want to make it as easy as possible on her; therefore, we'll give her ten days to decide."

Mary stared into space as Ida paced around the room wringing her hands. "We gotta do something, Mary," Ida said, her voice loud and resentful.

"It's my decision," Mary snapped. "I don't have to decide today. Just let it rest for now, will you?" She moved closer to the lawyer.

"Mr. Pepperell," Crusade said, "why don't you read the will?"

The door opened and in stepped Jasper, Fannie and Lee.

Chapter 10

"Well, you might as well come in. The whole wide world now knows our business." Ida snarled, as Fannie rushed for the seat nearest the lawyer. The banker sat next to Ida on the settee. Lee, big for his age, settled in his papa's lap in a chair in front of the lawyer.

"Get over here on the stool," Ida ordered Lee as she reached for the stool with her foot, pulling it in front of her. "You're a little big to sit in his lap, aren't you?" she asked, trying to sound pleasent. Lee stared at her for a moment, looked at his papa, then moved to the stool.

"I don't see any need to introduce y'all," Ida said. "These are supposed to be cousins of Seth's. I'm really not sure, but I am sure they were just outside the door listening to every word." Silence engulfed the room. "Before we get started, I want to ask Jasper how in the world did he know Seth had died."

"Let me tell you," said Fannie, eagerly.

"I didn't ask you. Let Jasper answer."

"Well, we were on vacation when we heard..."

"No, we were not on our vacation, dear," Fannie interrupted, "we were just bringing Lee to his grandparents to..."

"What's wrong? I know why you're here. Didn't you two decide on a story before you arrived?" Ida asked. Fannie looked away as Jasper struggled for something to say.

"Well, it just so happened that we were shopping in town when we saw the hearse pull up at a filling station across the street."

"No, darling. It was on our side of the street," Fannie injected. Jasper threw her a disgusted glance at her and continued.

"When the driver got out to pay the attendant, I went over and merely asked him if he was the local undertaker. He told me yes and that he was Horace Dunlock. We had a long chat and before he drove off he told me he was taking Seth Ridley back to the funeral home." Jasper paused for a moment and looked at Fannie, knowing that any time she would interrupt and finish the story, but she sat quietly.

But before he had a chance to speak again, Ida spoke up. "Well, get on with your story, can't you see you're wasting time? These men have something else to do other than sit around here listening to your explanation." She swallowed hard. When Jasper failed to speak, Ida went on, "Who gives a rip, anyway, how or when you got here? Forget I asked." She put her hand on Lee's head and tossed his hair. Lee looked up, smiled and cushioned his head against her stout leg. She felt him relax as she fumbled with the curl on the nape of his neck. His blonde hair was parted down the middle and when he glanced up at Ida, everyone saw her smile briefly for the first time.

Mr. Pepperell asked, "Are you ready for me to read the will?"

"That's what you came for, isn't it?" Ida words were harsh, but barely audible.

"You understand that Seth's will is a holographic one. He wrote it himself, dated it, and I'm sure it will be validated by the probate court. We only need proof that it is in his handwriting and I think I can prove that with the papers I have in my office signed by him." He turned to the last page and said, "It was written and signed September 2, 1927. Let's see. That will be six years ago next week." The lawyer paused. "Are there any questions before I start reading?"

Ida began counting the years on her fingers. It was September 26, 1924 when she had come to live in the Ridley house.

The room suddenly became stifling hot. Ida wiped her forehead with her handkerchief and blotted the corners of her mouth. She longed for a breath of fresh air. Getting off the settee to raise another window, she pushed Lee aside and stepped around him. Lee saw that her dress was damp and plastered to her hips. He slightly pulled it loose at the time she reached to unstick it. She patted Lee on the head, smiled and softly said,"Thank you." Fannie blushed and pretended not to see. Ida raised the window and returned to a chair opposite the banker. All the eyes on the lawyer shifted to Ida. Fannie moved to the edge of her chair and stretched her neck to get a glimpse of the papers. Mr. Pepperell waited until Ida was seated, then asked again if there were questions.

The banker rustled the map on his lap and without looking at anyone asked the lawyer, "Why don't you begin?"

The lawyer bowed his head and Ida saw the fat around his neck pile up and bulge around his chin. She thought how little he looked like a lawyer and how much he looked like a bullfrog.

"Please bear in mind that this will was written only six years ago." He fixed his pale eyes on Ida and continued. "Since Ida said she hadn't married Seth, I want to explain something to everyone so there will be no misunderstanding". The lawyer got to his feet, and began marching back and forth in front of the fireplace.

Jasper saw the shocked expression on Fannie's face. He watched her eyes dart first to Ida, then to Mary and finally they became fixed on him.

"For a long time men and women have lived together for a period of time without taking the trouble to get married. These arrangements are called common-law marriages because English courts recognized that by living together the couple voluntarily assumed rights and obligations to each other that society should protect and enforce."

Ida interrupted, "We don't need a history lesson. Get on with the reading of the will."

"But I want to tell you that several states still recognize common-law marriages." He paused and looked at each person. Staring at Ida, he said, "Maybe you have a question."

Ida became fidgety, but said nothing.

Fannie was quick to respond. She pulled her chair

closer to the lawyer and leaned her arm on the settee and said "Yes, I have a question. Isn't it true that when two people live together it has to be for seven years before it can become a common-law marriage? I know it must," she said, and emphasized, "I've heard it all my life."

Ida knew what Fannie was driving at and thought if she didn't keep quiet she would make sure the woman wasn't going to have much of her life left.

"The courts will have to decide such matters," Mr. Pepperell said. "Now, let's hear the will." He began reading:

'I, Seth Ridley, being in sound mind, do hereby make this my last will and testament.

"Ida has been good to me and has provided me with her services and I'm gonna leave her the house. She can live in it for the rest of her life, or if she gets married, it will go to Mary."

Trying to compose herself, Ida wrung her hands and shuffled her feet.

For a moment Mary watched the twitching muscle in Ida's neck. When she heard Jeffrey's car pulling up in the side yard, she stood and asked Mr. Pepperell, "Would you excuse me for a moment?" Not waiting for his approval, she quickly left the room. The lawyer sat down. Ida went to the open window and watched as Jeffrey drove to the edge of the back porch.

"Where in the world is she going at a time like this?" Ida asked in a hushed whisper. No one bothered to respond, and she continued. "I'm sure she is up to no good. She's always had a scheme." She rushed to the door. "I'll be back in a minute," she said, opening the screen door with her foot. She leaned forward and called, "Mary, why don't you get yourself back in here?" Ida pulled at her dress which had hiked up again in the back and nearly sloped to the floor in the front. All eyes focused on her giant-sized legs and hips. Everyone waited for a reply from Mary. Just before Ida called the second time, she saw Mary cross between the kitchen and the house, leading Jeffrey. She held his hand tightly. He followed behind, seeming reluctant to join the group gathered in the parlor. Reaching the door, she found Ida had hooked the screen.

"There's no need to bring him in. He has no business in here."

"Open the door, Ida," Mary demanded.

"There's no reason for him to be here. Have him go away."

"If you don't open the door, we'll just snatch it open," Mary said, jerking at the handle. Ida unhooked the screen door but didn't bother to open it for them.

When they were inside, Jeffrey leaned against the wall near the doorway. Mary, still holding his hand said, "Jeffrey must hear the rest of Papa's will. It wasn't easy persuading him to come, but he'll play an important part in solving the problems that will surely come up." She led Jeffrey to a chair and released his hand as he sat down behind the lawyer. "I'm sorry to have stopped you, Mr. Pepperell," she said, "but it's important to have him here."

Ida wanted to hear an apology in Mary's softly spoken words, but knowing her attitude, she only heard resentment.

Mary cleared her throat and asked Mr. Pepperell, "Why don't you finish reading the will?"

The lawyer stood, unfolded the sheets and said, "These continue to be Mr. Ridley's words," and began to read.

A little more than four years ago, I arranged for the farm to be deeded to Mary, realizing the financial problems which were building. I'm solely responsible for the mess I've found myself in. My gambling debts have become so bad, I felt I could be sent off to jail. Mary suggested selling the farm to pay the debts so the family would not be shamed. Without her encouraging me to quit gambling I would have never been able to lift my head again."

Mr. Pepperell folded the will and handed it to Mary. He removed a handkerchief from his side coat pocket and blew his nose. Fannie saw Jasper's jaw tighten while he stared at her. Lee looked at his papa, then at his mama and at his papa again. Mr. Crusade dropped his head and tucked his feet under the chair.

When Mary cried she never made a sound. Only tears rolled down her cheeks. Ida's heart softened when she saw Mary's face and she felt the anguish that her step-daughter must be going through. She pulled a handkerchief from her pocket and held it out to Mary, then slowly placed her hand on her shoulder and gave it a faint squeeze. Mary put one arm around Ida's waist.

CHAPTER 11

Mary felt Ida's body lean on her when Ida placed her hands in hers. Her hands were damp and cool as she held them against her cheek. Ida's pulse quickened and suddenly, all of her weight was against Mary. Ida's body slowly started to collapse and Mary, unable to hold her up, let her slide slowly to the floor. Before Jeffrey could get to them, Fannie and the banker moved from the settee to make room for Ida to be laid down.

"I'll go for the doctor," Jasper said and rushed toward his car.

Color returned to Ida's face within minutes and she rallied, whispering, "Don't let him go for the doctor. I'm all right. Go to the funeral home for Horace. I want to see him".

"She must be dying, calling for the undertaker like that!" Fannie said. She had an almost happy tone in her voice.

Ida raised her head and said, "Don't get your

hopes up. I just want to see someone that seems to care for me."

Fannie's mouth fell open. Mr. Crusade moved over to assist Mary in lifting Ida to an upright position. The map and legal papers Mr. Pepperell was holding in his lap scattered on the floor as he stood. When Lee started gathering them, Fannie rushed over to him, grabbed his arm and jerked him toward the door. Lee struggled, trying to pull from her grasp and when she let go of his arm he fell backwards against the what-not. Several glass pieces crashed to the floor.

Ida immediately stood up, rushed over and stood in front of Lee. She spread her arms wide to protect him from his mama's threats.

Mary now wondered if her weak spell was a put-on.

"You will not touch him," Ida exclaiming loudly.

Lee listened intently. "That's nothing but junk." Ida continued, "Mary's mess. I've been trying to get rid of it and now we don't have to worry about some of it any more, do we?"

"I'll see that he replaces every piece of it," Fannie said, placing her arm around Mary to assure her.

Ida said, "You'll do nothing of the sort. If Lee wants to break everything in this house, he can do it. Why be concerned? I don't have anything left, so why should Mary?" she asked, flailing her arms about the room.

"You're an asp!" Fannie screamed.

Lee peeped from behind Ida and saw his mother's red face. "Why are you saying ugly words when you punish me when I say 'em?" he yelled.

Fannie paid him no attention. "Go spread your venom elsewhere, Ida Ridley, or whatever your last name is. You'll not contaminate my son any longer. Come, Lee, we're leaving!"

Lee didn't move. Fannie turned her face from Ida and quietly said, "You vicious woman." She grasped the boy by both arms, but he pulled away as Ida continued to shield him. Ida's dress was hiked up, riding high on her hips. Fannie reached between Ida's plump legs and, grabbing Lee's feet, pulled him forward. Ida tightened her knees around the child's neck, determined not to release him. Fannie kept pulling until Ida lost her balance and released him.

"If your papa were here young man, you wouldn't be acting this way." Fannie said, her remarks sounding more like a plea than a warning.

The lawyer wished aloud to Mr. Crusade how he would enjoy having a case against the kid in juvenile court.

Lee's fight with his mama didn't cease once she pulled him to the porch. A childish argument continued with Lee yelling. His mama's voice was almost inaudible.

Ida, out of breath, closed the door leading to the porch to shut out most of the noise. She staggered over to the what-not and with her foot, pushed the broken items against the wall. "I'll clean it up tomorrow," she mumbled to herself. She heard car doors slam and she rushed to the porch. The lawyer and the banker followed her. She saw Doctor Grady and Jasper driving their cars to the back entrance.

The doctor, surprised to see Ida, threw his

medical satchel back into the car and looked quizzically at Jasper.

"We think it's her mind, doctor. She's been acting sorta strange for the past few hours. She really needs help," Jasper said.

"Who did you say you were?" the doctor asked him.

"I'm her nephew, by marriage," he replied.

Ida overheard the statement and said, "He's absolutely no kin to me at all. I never saw him before today and I can't understand why he's here in the first place."

Fannie, still holding Lee's arm, led him toward his papa. Jasper saw immediately the embarrassment on Fannie's face and how terrified Lee looked. It was nothing new to see such expressions on their faces; it happened at the slightest disturbance and he had experienced the incident many times before. Jasper grasped the boy's arm with enough force that Lee's knees buckled beneath him. He knew what was in store for him when he and his papa were alone. He saw the big vein pop up on the right side of his papa's neck and knew he was in big trouble. Fannie too, was watching the vein grow larger and stared at it until it disappeared. She tucked her streaming hair back under her hat and smiled at the doctor.

Lee's papa led him to the short bench near the kitchen door as Fannie chattered away with Doctor Grady.

"I'm Fannie, Jasper's wife. I'm so glad to meet you. I would like so much to talk to you about poor Seth. I heard he had suffered so much these last couple of years. I want to know everything about him," she rattled on, all the time her hands busy rubbing the wrinkles from her dress.

Ida interrupted, "Doctor Grady. I gotta have something for my nerves. I'm all-to-pieces." She held her hand out. "Look. I can't hold myself still." Her voice was quivering. "Please give me something to settle my nerves."

The doctor reached in the back of his car and withdrew the tattered brown satchel, opened it and removed a bottle and a enormous needle and syringe. Ida's eyes grew big. "You ain't gonna stick me with that, are you?"

"It's the only one I have at the present."

"What are you doing, practicing to be a horse doctor?" she shrieked, backing against the wall. "You're not going to stick me with that!" she said, before turning to enter the parlor.

Lee left the bench to get a better look at the needle. His papa pointed to the bench and he returned to his seat. "I'll never be able to see anything," Lee grumbled to himself.

Jeffrey stood near the parlor door with his arms around Mary when Ida tried to enter. She snatched his arm from around Mary, entered and slammed the door behind her. She sat by the window to keep an eye on the folks standing on the porch. She couldn't hear what they were saying so she walked quietly over the creaky floor to the door and slowly opened it a tiny bit. Before she returned to the window, she heard a familiar car door slam. Hurrying to the other window she saw Horace standing alone by the hearse and thought how nice it was that he should return to check on her. She rushed to the mirror, slapped her face slightly to give her cheeks some color. She fluffed her hair, using her fingers as a comb. Her mouth was sagging, just like she remembered her mama's. She pushed the corners upward with her index fingers, looked at herself and tried to hold a smile until she got to the porch.

In the excitement of Horace's arrival and the sudden change in Ida's attitude, no one noticed Lee as he left the porch and went behind the hearse. When he climbed inside, he was too busy watching to see if anyone saw him enter the hearse. He quietly pulled the door shut. He saw a coffin and quickly slipped out on the other side of the hearse and went back to the bench.

Ida, all aglow at seeing Horace, chattered pleasantly for awhile and invited him in. He thanked her and held the door open. It had been years since anyone had opened a door for her. She liked it and smiled. "Thank you," she said. She knew all eyes were on them and she was pleased.

"Ida, my dear," he said in his pleasant undertaker voice and taking a chance that her temperament had mellowed, "I have something to discuss with you."

Ida moved to the settee and sat very close to him.

"We have done something terrible," he stammered

"What do you mean, we?"

"My brother and I. Please don't get excited. We can straighten it all out."

"What on earth?"

"It's just a small problem. When we had the grave dug, my brother went to the graveyard to show the negro man where to dig Seth's grave. He dug it beside another woman's burial spot exactly where Dudley had shown him, thinking it was Seth's first wife. My brother admits the mistake. I know I should have gone out there myself, but I thought they knew the site. But, then too, if Seth had put up a stone like we suggested earlier, we wouldn't have had this problem."

"Don't blame Seth," Ida said in disgust. "Are you going to move him? I certainly hope so!"

"We never put him in the grave. Once everybody left, we put his body back in the hearse. I have him outside. We didn't bother to unload him."

"Well, what am I gonna do with him?" Furious, Ida left the settee and walked to the window.

"We want to bury him quietly without anyone knowing about this. His new grave is only a couple plots away and we are having the grave dug at this very moment."

Ida whirled around and said, "We can't seem to put confidence in anybody these days!" For a moment she realized that no one seemed to have confidence in her, either, not anymore except Viola, and sometimes she doubted her. "I'm sorry I said that, Horace. I didn't mean that I had no confidence in you." She went to him and placed her hand on his shoulder. He stood, took her by the hand and before he could speak, she said, "It was just that negro man I was thinking 'bout. Please don't be offended. I would never offend you. Don't you know that?" They both smiled. "I'm sure things will be all right. Just bury him and let me know when everything is finished."

As he reached to put his arm around her, she sucked in her stomach to make it appear smaller.

"You're a nice lady," Horace said and smiled. "I will talk to you later and I promise I will see you very, very soon."

Ida saw him off, then turned to the crowd standing on the porch and asked, "Wouldn't you all like to come in the kitchen and let me fix everyone some cake and give you something to drink?" Everyone looked astounded to see Ida smiling. One by one they followed her into the kitchen.

Chapter 12

Lee, after sizing up the piece of cake Ida had cut for him, waited until the others were served before he announced that his piece seemed smaller than the others. He put his cake back on the kitchen table and stepped back.

"What's wrong, honey?" Ida asked. "Is it the wrong kind?"

"It's the littlest piece you cut and I wanted a big piece."

Every time Lee was so outspoken it stung his mama to the quick. Trying to act pleasant, Fannie leaned toward him and whispered, "Why can't you ever be satisfied with what you have?"

"Because I want a bigger piece," he yelled. "If I don't get a bigger piece, I'm not going to eat any."

"Don't give him anymore, Ida," Fannie said.

"Just eat it, sweetie," Ida said, pointing to what was left of the cake with the knife. "We'll have more for you later."

"If I can't have a bigger piece right now, I'm not going to eat any at all." Lee clasped his hands behind his back and tightened his lips.

"I'm not having you act this way," Fannie warned with squinched eyes. She waved him off by pointing to the porch.

Lee left and slammed the door behind him.

When the men had finished eating, they commented on the goodness of the cake and thanked Ida. Before they left for the back porch, Ida smiled and said, "Horace has told me so many times that I do make a good cake," knowing full well that someone else made this particular one and had brought it to the house.

Fannie, realizing how friendly and calm Ida had become since Horace's visit, pulled a chair up to the table and sat down. Ida began collecting the cake plates and Fannie insisted that she help.

"Oh, you just sit there, I'll get them." Ida placed them on the counter near the sink.

Fannie thought she was beginning to win Ida over. Since Horace left, the stern woman whom she hardly knew, had laughed and even talked to her cheerfully. Fannie was beginning to like her friendliness and didn't want her to stop chattering.

"I do declare Ida, that undertaker is certainly a amiable person and he's such a gentleman. How long have you known him?" she asked.

"Oh, my goodness! I've known Horace for years. We use to date a little years ago, that was before he and his brother got so tied up in the funeral business. He seldom had free time to do anything or go any place.

When we started courting, it was always a trip to pick up a body, or supplies, and we always had to go in the hearse. Can you imagine courting in a hearse?"

Fannie was taken back. "I bet it was exciting riding in the hearse."

"Exciting? Huh, I was totally mortified" She moved a chair to the other side of the table opposite Fannie. "I remember once we drove for miles, way out in the country, just to embalm an old man. Back in the early days all the embalming was done at home of the dead person when it was a bother to haul them all the way to the funeral home and back. Horace carried special linens to use on the bed during the preparation."

Ida thought about Lee and became fidgety, knowing he was always going through the house exploring. She left her chair and looked out the window. While near the counter she leaned against the sink and picked up a jar and poured water to prime the pump, then pumped water into the dish pan. With a slight grunt she lifted the full pan and set it on the counter. "I went with him one evening, and oh, the experience was gruesome. Horace wanted me to stay in the room with him and watch as he embalmed the old man."

"You stayed in the room with him while he worked on a dead person?"

"My goodness, yes. Nothing to it. I sat in a chair with my back to him while he strained to flip the stiff body over. I didn't dare turn around."

"You were brave, Ida. I could never have done that," Fannie said as she shivered. "How in the world could you stand it? I could never do such a thing."

"I thought it was a way I could impress him."

Fannie was about to ask another question, but Ida continued, "But wait. That's only the beginning of things to happen that evening. When Horace had finished and the man was lying on the bed in full dress, he asked me to go for the wife. When she came in and took one look at her husband, she yelled to Horace, `Put it back. Put it back, I tell you!'. Horace couldn't imagine what on earth she was talking about and asked what was wrong. `His moustache. I've never seen him without a moustache. The woman began to cry. `I'll fix it', Horace told her, then he asked me to take her from the room and try to calm her."

"What in the world could he do about the mustache after he'd shaved it?"

"Well, I led the woman out of the bedroom and into the parlor. We sat down and she began showing me pictures of her husband. Some dated way back, 'cause some of the photographs had nearly faded out. Let me tell you, that man, at one time, had the longest moustache in the county. She told me he had won several awards, too, and she seemed so proud of him. In the pictures, the moustache was curled up at the ends and I bet the handlebars were five inches long on each side of his face. It looked like he should have been in the circus."

"Was it still that long when Horace shaved him?" Fannie asked.

"I never even looked at the man until Horace was through with him and I brought the wife back into the bedroom. Horace told me later he thought the old man just hadn't shaved in a couple weeks." Ida began to laugh.

"You know what Horace wanted me to do?" Ida asked. "Let him remove a portion of my hair to glue under the old man's nose. I finally consented."

"How did it look?"

"I thought he did a good job, but when the wife saw it, she said it wasn't the right color so he had to do it over."

"What did he do then?"

Ida's eyes began to widen. "Horace asked me to leave so he could removed some of the man's body hair. Can you imagine what I was thinking?" Ida began to laugh aloud. "I stood just outside the bedroom door so the wife couldn't re-enter. I heard Horace struggling to remove the poor man's clothes."

The men were still on the porch talking to Mary and Jeffrey when Ida looked out the window. She didn't see Lee and wondered where he was and what he was doing. She turned to Fannie. "The hair he glued to the man's upper lip was the same color as the hair on his head, but with a slight curl in it."

Fannie stood, leaned closer to Ida. "My goodness, you don't mean..."

Ida cupped her hands around her mouth. "Oh, yes, that's where he got the hair from. Ida's stomach began bouncing as she laughed.

Fannie threw her head back, and again they laughed together. They were beginning to enjoy one another's company now and Fannie was appreciating the confidence Ida seemed to have in her. "Don't make me laugh anymore, Ida," Fannie said, laughing uncontrollable. "I'm about to wet my bloomers." She put both hands between her legs and bent forward.

"You've got to stop, Ida. You've just gotta stop. I can't stand much more of this laughing."

When Ida looked out on the porch she saw that Mr. Crusade and Mr. Pepperell weren't interested in the laughter coming from the kitchen. As suddenly as the laughter began, it ended when Lee entered holding two pieces of what his mama thought was broken furniture.

"Where did you get that?" Fannie asked.

Ida, with a half-sick smile on her face, gasped for breath when the boy held out two parts of a broken cradle. Shocked, Ida fell back in her kitchen chair.

Lee held firmly to the cradle parts as his mama dragged him to the porch. She asked Mary and Jeffrey to go in the kitchen to check Ida's condition.

Chapter 13

Mary was careful when she slapped Ida's face to bring her back to consciousness. She had done this many times before, but once she had overdone it only to learn Ida was pretending. She received such a harsh tongue lashing from Ida that she wanted to make sure the slaps, this time, were not too hard. During the time Ida really passed out was the only time Mary could do what she had always wanted to do.

Ida rallied. The first words she uttered were "Where's Lee? Get that boy out of my house right now before he tears up everything I've got left in this world." She heard Lee and Fannie quarreling about the cradle. Ida struggled to her feet. She staggered, put one hand to her head and grabbed the table to steady herself. "Where's that young'un?"

Mary led her out. When Ida went through the hall, she saw the open door under the stairs. Her best bed quilts were piled over in the corner and the broken cradle lay scattered about the floor.

Lee and his mama were still arguing.

"I didn't do nothing, mama. I swear I didn't!"

"Don't you swear to me. Show me where you got it from." Lee pointed to the open closet door. "If that door was closed, you had no business opening it," Fannie told him. Ida just gritted her teeth and listening. Fannie was scolding him so harshly, Ida could hardly keep her mouth closed, but she didn't interfere. After all, he had no business in that closet. Not even Mary had ever been in there, as far as she knew. It was her personal storage place.

The screws that held the hasp and lock on the door casing and the kitchen knife the boy had used as a screwdriver lay on the floor. The lock swung on the door knob. She instantly saw the stuffed homemade cradle mattress among the broken parts and grabbed it from the floor. Fannie snatched it from her and shook it at Lee.

"Did you break that cradle, Lee?"

"I just pulled it out of the closet a bit and got in it to see if it would rock."

Ida grabbed the little mattress from Fannie and stuck it under her arm. Lee fumbled with the cradle parts and tried to fit the pieces back together. Fannie pulled again at the pad, but Ida clutched it even tighter. Fannie let go and picked up one of the narrow slats from the cradle. Inscribed in pencil was February 3, 1922.

Just as Ida snatched the slat from Fannie, Mary entered and announced that the banker and her lawyer were leaving. She held the door open as Ida pushed Lee out of her way and kicked the cradle parts back into the closet. Ida closed the closet door and piled the bed quilts in front to block it.

Ida rushed to the porch just as Mr. Crusade was entering his car. "I want to see you at the bank first thing in the morning, Mr. Crusade," she called. "I have something rather important to discuss with you."

"You know we are closed on Saturdays."

"Well, I'll see you first thing Monday morning," she yelled. Her voice carried above the car motor.

He nodded, tipped his hat, and drove off, leaving Ida holding the lumpy little mattress under her arm. She waved the slat toward Mr. Pepperell and said goodbye to him. He cranked his car and drove off behind the banker.

While the rest went to the kitchen, Ida went back to the hall and picked up the armful of quilts. When she opened the closet, she continued to hold the little mattress but threw the quilts back on the floor.

There, in front of her, lay the reminder of her earlier life. As she gazed at the broken cradle she recalled the intimidations, her frustrations, her fears, and even the desire she once had to run away. She walked into the closet and pulled the door shut behind her. Kneeling, she switched the mattress pad under her other arm.

Darkness shrouded her and she began to sob. "Lord, I'm not ready to have my sins revealed. It's not a good time in my life right now. I gotta make restitution of things I've done wrong. I've caused people to hurt. I'm rude, Lord. I treat folks mean. I know that Lord. I gotta repent. I promised... I promise to begin a new life and be better. I'll try to do only the things that you approve of. Just bear with me a little while longer, Lord, and -- and -- and I will prove my sincerity to you."

Ida softened her sniffing and listened. There were no sounds nearby so she opened the closet door, reached for one of the quilts and pulled it inside. She closed the door and added it to the mattress to relieve the pressure on her arthritic knees.

"What can I say to you, Lord? Tell me what to say. You know me better than anyone else, except Viola. You know my weaknesses. You know that I have tried to grow stronger in my faith. But, you have also got to bear in mind, Lord, that I've... I've... I've had more than my share of troubles. All I'm asking right now is for you to be patient with me for the next few days. By then, maybe I will have gotten over Seth's death and Mary will be out of my hair and... and I can start on a new path in my life." She paused, then whispered, "Now don't let me down, Lord." She took a deep breath, relieved.

She heard voices in the hall. She wondered if she should stay there or come out? She didn't want to come out in front of everyone. She didn't want them to know she had been praying in secret, either. This was strictly between her and her Lord. After all, the scriptures said you should pray in the closet.

She waited until there was total silence, then slowly cracked the door. She waited until her eyes had adjusted to the light before she separated the rack of clothes above her head so she could grasp the bar and pull herself up. Under the strain, the bar pulled loose and her winter garments fell and covered her. Before she yelled for help, she searched for the cradle mattress and the slat.

Chapter 14

Seth's old fantail rooster mantle clock ticked away as Ida lay on the settee hugging the little mattress pad and gazing into space. Everyone had finally left and she had stretched out to rest for a spell. A few minutes alone were rare for her. The last three days had been taxing, not to mention the confusion caused by the strangers who came and tried to make themselves at home.

Home? What in the world was she going to do? She had to think and do a lot of planning. Where would she live? Maybe Viola would take her in. No, that wouldn't work, she thought, they were not on the best of terms right now and it wasn't a good time to mention it to her. The little prayer she said earlier made her to relax and she was beginning to feel a little closer to the Lord. She questioned, however, if she really meant all the things she had whispered in the dark closet. Anyway, Viola knew more about her problems than the Lord, and could help her right now and she wanted to see her friend.

The clock began striking. She lay still and counted the strikes... six, seven, and the gongs stopped. Usually, an hour of napping rested Ida, but she didn't feel any better than when she lay down. She got up, rubbed her eyes, and went to her bedroom. She pulled her gown from under the pillow and wished for bedtime.

It was too early to go to bed, but she undressed, anyway, and pulled her gown over her head. It had just settled below her hips when she heard a car door slam. She heard it again and peeped through the bedroom window. Viola and Bertha Whitmore had gotten out of the car. Bertha hadn't been at the graveyard, and Ida wondered why. Oh, she reckoned it was because her hair had just been set. The wind was blowing too hard out there in the opening and it would get messed up. She watched Bertha press the fingerwaves in her hair and smooth her dress as she followed Viola to the front porch. Bertha was always primping. Either her hair was out of place, or her rouge was not fanned out enough. She often painted her eyebrows on crooked and too dark and they never matched her greying, crimson-colored hair.

They knocked and waited. Ida rushed to put her clothes back on, but couldn't hook her brassiere, so she let it hang loose. She stuffed the cradle mattress pad under the bed covers and went to the door. The ladies were already holding the screen door open, so Ida invited them in.

"My Lord, Ida, you've got your dress on backwards."

"I knew I shouldn't have undressed so early. Have either of you ever been tangled in a tent of material?

It happens every time. You get in a rush and never find yourself presentable." She removed her dress right in front of them and turned it around.

Bertha had only said hello when they arrived, but when Ida turned her back to them to straighten her clothes she whispered to Viola, "I never..."

Viola whispered back, "She's that way. Don't pay her any mind." She asked Ida, "How long has your company been gone?"

"Not long enough. I am so tired, I feel I can't stay up another minute," Ida said, while relaxing her shoulders and breathing.

"Come, Bertha. Maybe we should leave. Sorry we bothered you, Ida," Viola said sarcasticly.

Remembering her promise to the Lord, Ida pleasantly said, "Please don't leave. I've been wanting to talk to you. Here, have a seat, Bertha."

Bertha and Viola sat on the settee. Ida sat near the window. Dusk was beginning to turn into darkness and pale stars pricked the sky. Ida loved this time of day and often sat alone in the darkness awhile before she had to light the lamps.

Just before she got up to light the kerosene lamps, Viola asked, "Have you heard about Dudley?"

"No. What about him?"

"We could hardly wait to tell you. We heard an hour or so ago that he passed out while eating an early supper down at the cafe. We didn't want to tell you since you've been through so much. We thought we should wait until tomorrow, but Bertha insisted that you should know tonight."

"What about Horace? Is he all right?"

"Horace is fine. A little broken up, but he's fine..."

Bertha interrupted Viola. "Now you know, Viola, he's terribly upset. He told us himself that he wasn't sure what he was going to do, and..."

"I must go to him," Ida said, "and offer my help. Poor Horace. He was here when I needed him, so I must go to him. I must go right now. Will you drive me over there, Viola?"

"How will you get back?"

"I'll find a way."

Ida picked up one of the lamps and left the room. She soon returned with her hat and pocketbook. Stepping to the door, she held it open for her visitors. When they were on the steps, she blew out one of the lamps and turned the wick low in the other and went out the door, pulling it shut behind her. She dropped her purse to the floor and searched for the key to lock the house.

Viola and Bertha were in the car before she could get the door locked. When Ida stooped to pick up her purse her hat fell off and bounced down the steps to the ground. She snatched it up, plopped it on her head and got in the back seat of the car.

"You've gotta hook you brassiere, Ida. You can't go in the funeral home all loose and shaking like that."

"My goodness. What would I do without you, Viola?

Viola drove off as Ida tussled with her undergarment. Her weight shifting in the back seat caused the car to rock from side to side. Viola slowed the vehicle and told her, "Slip over so Bertha can get back there and help you with it."

They had traveled a mile before Ida got her weight shifted to the other side of the seat. Before Viola could stop the car, Bertha had straddled the seat and was crawling over. Viola picked up speed and tossed Bertha head first into the back seat.

"Gee, Bertha. You're a spry old thing. I've never seen you move so fast." Ida said, laughing and bouncing all over the back seat. She couldn't help Bertha get on the seat and she couldn't control her laughter, either. It turned into a rollicking hee-haw and Ida wet her bloomers.

Viola couldn't see the humor in Bertha falling over the seat. "You've gone crazy, Ida, laughing as you do, and just after your poor husband was put in the ground."

Viola watched Ida in the rear mirror. Sometimes she had difficulty understanding why her friend had such sudden changes in her attitude, and said to her, "I declare, Ida. First you want to cry, then you get mad as fire, then you get completely hysterical with laughter. Don't you have any respect for death?

"Why, Seth has been buried for..." she looked at her wrist watch, "for nearly nine hours and he's just as dead as he'll ever be."

"Yeah, buried for nine hours and here you are off to see another man."

"Well, darn it, if you don't want to take me, turn around and take me home."

That's all Viola needed to hear. She applied the brakes and turned the car around in the middle of the dirt road. Bertha was trying to fasten Ida's brassiere and fell off the seat. Ida started laughing again, but stopped suddenly when she realized that Viola had lost her temper.

When they arrived back at Ida's house and before Viola said anything, Ida asked, "Will you be a sweet friend, Viola, and let me go in and straighten my clothes?" Ida paused and waited. "You will and take me back, wont you?"

Without answering, Viola turned the motor off and Ida squeezed through the car door. She was glad she wasn't in the front seat to have to listen to Viola complain about more stuffing being pulled out when she got out of her car. "Please hurry, Ida. I can't spend all night hauling you up and down the road," Viola said.

"I'll be right back, honey."

As Ida strolled toward her bedroom, she picked up the kerosene lamp from the hall table and turned up the wick. She stopped to look at herself in the mirror and decided her hair looked presentable. She spent more time hooking her brassiere and twisting it around and stuffing her large breasts in the cups than she spent changing her wet clothes. She pulled her dress down, powdered her face again and carried the lamp back to the hall table. Before she lowered the wick, she saw a note addressed to her from Mary, saying she was with Ellen Grace and would be back soon as she was going out later with Jeffrey.

Chapter 15

*J*effrey was to pick Mary up shortly after one o'clock, as planned. He opened the car door and his dog Spike jumped into the back seat. As Jeffrey drove towards Mary's house, the dog climbed over the front seat and settled his head on Jeffrey's leg.

Jeffrey knew that Mary was never comfortable with the dog around and he seldom let him ride when he picked her up for a drive. When his master gave commands Spike was gentle and very obedient, and that's the only thing Mary liked about him. His dirty-brick color repulsed her and despite Jeffrey's constant reminder that they were true markings of a prize winning dog, she didn't care for the animal.

Jeffrey stopped the car at Mary's front gate, snapped his fingers and pointed to the back seat. Spike hurtled over the seat and lay down. As Mary approached the car with an armful of broken cradle parts, Jeffrey didn't bother to help her. She balanced her load with a knee, opened the rear door with her left hand and saw the dog. She gave a disgusted sigh and placed the pieces of broken cradle on the back seat next to Spike.

"Why did you have to bring that ugly mutt with you?"

"Oh, come on, honey, he likes to ride, too. There's enough room for the three of us." Neither spoke of the dog again as they headed west into town.

Mary clutched the cradle mattress in her lap and kept feeling of the stuffing through the ticking. She heard the wooden parts of the cradle rattle on the seat behind them as the car bounced over the dirt road.

"Are you sure you picked up all the broken parts of the cradle?" Jeffrey asked.

"Yes. Everything I saw. I had to move the quilts in the closet, but I made sure I put everything back just as Ida left it. Unless she opens the closet to look for the parts, she'll never know I went in there."

Jeffrey took his eyes off the road and glanced at the little pad Mary was fumbling. The car hit a deep rut and parts of the cradle bounced off the back seat. "Gee, this darn road will cause every piece to splinter. That is, what's not broken already," he said.

Mary turned, raised herself and reached to place the parts back on the seat. The pad fell from her lap onto the floor. Jeffrey picked it up without taking his eyes off the road. "This is strange feeling stuffing" he said as he squeezed the pad.

"I think it's because the ticking is so thick on it. It's soiled anyway, so we'll ask someone at the repair shop if they can put a new cover on it." She took it from Jeffrey and tossed it over her shoulder to the back seat. Immediately he saw Spike through the rear view mirror scratching at it to use as a pillow.

"No, get it back and feel of it. It sorta feels like paper."

As she leaned toward Jeffrey and reached to retrieve the mattress pad from the back seat, she saw the dog was using it as a pillow and slapped his head away. Her hand filled with dog slobber. Her first impulse was to clean her hand on Jeffrey's shirt, but used the mattress instead. She turned the clean side down and held it in her lap. Before she settled on the seat, Jeffrey immediately grabbed her leg and slowly moved his hand higher. The little mattress fell to the foot of the car.

She giggled and said, "Oh, cut it out, Jeffrey. You do that all the time. We can't ride out anyplace that you don't start your messing around."

"You like it, don't you?"

"Oh, stop it," she teased. "You're greedy"

"What you mean, greedy?"

"All men are alike. Just have to mess around all the time. Do you always keep that on your mind?"

"Sure do. Don't you?"

"Certainly not!"

"I've never seem a woman yet who..." He abruptly stopped.

"You've never seem a woman, what?" Mary quizzed him. He didn't respond. She slapped his hand away. He remained silent, but she was determined to pursue the question further. She knew he was beginning to brag again of his conquests and felt a certain surge of jealousy of the other girls she'd heard rumors about. . "Go ahead and finish what you were going to say." She continued to stare at him, but he kept his eyes steady on the road. "So you're not going to say anything? Well, let me tell you something." She moved as far to her side of the car as she could and began to steam with anger. "I imagine you go as far as you can with any girl who gets in your presence. I've watched you so many times... like, like the night Papa died. I knew you went into that supply room with that red headed nurse. I saw you when you came out... bulging, but I pretended not to..."

"I was only helping her with those boxes..."

She didn't wait for him to finish. "I know what kind of box you were interested in." Her voice was quivering and got louder.

"But baby..."

"Don't `baby' me. Take me home. I'm not in the mood to go into town with you, anyway."

"But I didn't do anything with that nurse," he said. He stopped the car in the middle of the road.

"Don't suppose you ever did anything with Ellen Grace, either, did you?" Her voice was bitter.

Interest gripped his curiosity. "What do you know about her?"

"I know things. Don't play so innocent. Just take me... take me home."

Jeffrey turned the car around. She didn't look at him again until they arrived in front of her house. Before he turned the engine off, he placed his hand on her knee and started to apologize.

She pulled away. "You think touching me will cure everything, don't you?" She reached in the back seat and began removing the broken cradle parts and loading them in her arms, one piece at the time. Jeffrey didn't offer to help her. When her arms were full she asked him if he would mind opening the door. He reached over and his hand brushed against her cheek. The door opened and she got out, kicked the door shut, and walked toward the house without looking back.

He watched her put the broken cradle parts on the steps before he drove away.

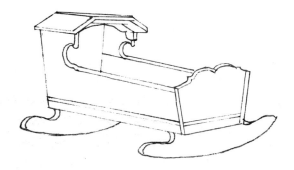

Chapter 16

Mary leaned against the porch post crying. She had no idea how long she had been standing there when she heard Ida speak, "What's wrong, Mary?" she asked in a soft, sweet voice. When Mary cried, Ida always became suddenly nice to her.

Mary straightened up, afraid of being questioned about the broken cradle parts. She shielded them with her full gathered skirt and didn't answer. She only stared at Ida. Her stepmother never seemed to have time to listen to her, anyway, so why try to explain?

Not getting an answer, Ida headed back into the house. Before slamming the screen door, she looked back and said, "Never mind. Handle it by yourself."

Mary let go the breath she held in a small sigh. She raised her head and suddenly moved to gather the cradle parts in her skirt. She didn't want Ida to return. If she did, she'd have to explain why she had taken the cradle parts out of the closet. It had been Jeffrey's suggestion to have the cradle reassembled as a surprise for Ida, hoping it would bring all of them closer together. Mary knew his motive and wanted to cooperate, so she didn't want Ida to find out.

She saw the barn door standing wide open as she rounded the corner of the house. Trying to keep Ida from seeing her, she headed straight to the opening. As she entered, a chicken flew over her head and into the yard. The cat sneaked out through the broken window. She hadn't been in the barn since Jeffrey's last visit. Breathing in the smell of last year's wheat straw brought back memories. Glancing at the corner where they had lain the last time they were there together, she saw the little patch of straw that served as their pillow and she wished he were there with her now. "How foolish I was to lose my temper," she whispered to herself.

When she had tucked the cradle parts away on a back shelf she went over to the make-believe bed and lay down. The mid-afternoon sun streamed in through the door opening so she got up to close it. The old rusty hinges squeaked and were stiff enough to leave the door partly open. Falling back on the hay, she tried to relax.

Hearing a tap on the door, she raised up and heard Jeffrey say, "Ida told me she saw you come out here. May I come in?"

For a moment she didn't speak. The old hinge squeaked as he slowly pulled the door wider. He saw her sitting on the straw and asked, "May I come in? I promise to behave myself."

He waited until she waved him in.

She looked away and fixed her eyes on the opposite wall. For some seconds she did not speak, and at last she spoke without looking at him. "I wish I understood, but I don't," she said. "I don't understand such things about men in general, or you in particular." She paused and lay on her back in the straw. "I can't bear looking at you or being near you or even being touched by you when I know you've been with another woman. Maybe I'm wrong, but this is the way that I am." She turned her head toward him. He was sitting so close she felt his body heat. "You say you love me. I don't know how it is possible. Maybe I don't know what the word love means to you, but I know what it means to me." She began to cry.

Jeffrey lay back and placed his arm under her neck and she rolled toward him. He enclosed her with his other arm and they clung together as she sobbed. His mind dwelt on Ellen Grace and he knew that Mary was more giving than Ellen Grace had ever been. Should he promise to give up all other women, or should he continue to make denials? She must know something, he thought.

She snuggled in his embrace. The longer he held her close, the more she felt his tenderness. Was it really love? she wondered. If not, she didn't care at the moment if she was becoming a physical slave to him. He was there beside her. From the moment he began rocking her body with his, she knew there was no false shame in her. He was convincing her it was love between them. Her blood was boiling. The words of advice her real mother gave her when she reached thirteen, about Men's insincerity, their deceit and illicit love affairs with loose women had suddenly lost their meaning. All she wanted at the moment was for him to tell her that he loved her dearly.

When their panting had eased, they lay back in the straw, relaxing. Neither said anything, just lay there holding hands after smoothing out their clothes.

Mary had learned a long time ago that Jeffrey was self-centered in his lovemaking and never talked very much afterwards. It caused her to question if their involvement was based on passion or good reasoning, yet she looked forward to these times together and for the moments she gave herself to him.

Respect came to her mind. She wanted more than anything else for them to get married, but was afraid to bring the subject up for fear he would not see her any more. She knew for certain that he had the advantage of winning other girls by the way he made love. She didn't want to risk losing him to someone else. She didn't turn her head to look at him when his hand relaxed in hers. It had happened too many times before. She knew he was sleeping.

Clouds were covering the sun and there were no shadows on the wall and no sunbeams filtering in through the cracks around the door or the broken window when she awakened. Jeffrey had turned from her and was breathing heavily. Lying there, she was trying to piece her life together when the barn door was snatched open. Mary sat up, rubbed her eyes and saw Ida standing in the doorway.

"Where's that mattress?" Ida yelled.

Chapter 17

Mary remained silent as she stood. Jeffrey got to his feet and brushed the straw from his clothes. Ida stared, first at Mary, then at Jeffrey.

"I asked, where's the mattress pad from the cradle? Just don't stand there like dumb asses. Somebody has my mattress," Ida yelled.

Jeffrey shrugged his shoulders as Mary stammered to speak. She looked at Jeffrey and demanded, "Where is it?"

"Didn't you take it out of the car with the cradle parts?"

"No, I did not. I only took out the cradle pieces."

"What in the world are you two talking about?" Ida inquired. "Where's the mattress?"

"Jeffrey and I were taking the broken cradle into town to have a repairman to put..."

"To heck with the cradle! Where's the mattress?" Ida demanded, wringing her hands. She grabbed the door facing and tried to pull herself inside the barn. There were no steps in front of the barn as it had been built low to the ground. The deteriorating door frame pulled loose and she lost her balance. Ida fell backwards and lay sprawled on her back, her full skirt up to her waist.

Mary rushed to her, but before she could pull Ida's skirt down over her knees, Jeffrey saw she was without bloomers. He put his hand over his mouth to stifle his laughter.

Ida cried out in pain when they tried to get her to her feet. "I've broken my hip! Get me some help," she begged.

"Run to the store and call the hospital for an ambulance," Mary told Jeffrey.

"Don't call for an ambulance from the hospital. Call Horace," Ida said, "He'll drive his hearse over here and take me to the hospital. I just know he will."

Mary flipped her hand toward Jeffrey for him to hurry. When he left, she went inside the barn and gathered an armful of wheat straw and returned and placed it under Ida's head. Ida began to shake. Mary went into the barn again and snatched several empty fertilizer bags from the rafters overhead, shook them out and placed them over Ida's body.

Ida rolled her head from side to side trying to avoid the fertilizer dust. "Can't you find something else other than these stinking guano bags?"

"You're having a chill, Ida. You need something to cover you right now," Mary said.

Ida's teeth chattered and her body shook. Mary became frightened. She sat on the ground and placed the woman's head in her lap and stroked her face. Ida's quivering increased and Mary pulled the sacks over her shoulders.

"Oh! The pain is more that I can stand," Ida cried

"Just hold on a few more minutes and Jeffrey will be back."

"The heck with Jeffrey! I want a doctor," she said, trying to lift her head from Mary's lap.

"You must lie still if you expect the pain to go away. Listen. I think I hear Jeffrey coming back. He'll have the ambulance here in no time."

Ida lay still and listened. "I don't hear nothing." She turned her head in the direction of the road. "He'd better have notified Horace, 'cause I ain't going to the hospital in no ambulance."

"Ida, you know the ambulance would be the best transportation. It has the equipment to treat you on your way to the hospital," Mary said. "Horace's old hearse has only a cot to haul the dead on. You certainly want to be more comfortable than riding in the hearse."

Ida whined, "But I want Horace to come for me," Ida cried.

Disgusted with her, Mary lifted Ida's head from her lap and bundled some straw for the pillow. She thought Ida's head looked a little too elevated, so she removed the straw. "Maybe you should lie flat for a while, or at least until you can get some blood running to your brain. You're not thinking clearly, Ida. Just be quiet 'til Jeffrey comes."

Ida whined and moaned. Mary saw her close her eyes, and thinking she saw the color drain from her face, gave her a little slap on the cheek.

"What are you doing? Can't you see I'm hurting enough?"

Mary stood and backed away. She stared at Ida and whispered, "You're not helping matters, Ida."

"What did you say?" Ida asked.

"I said... here comes Jeffrey."

Jeffrey's old Hudson automobile came to an abrupt stop in front of the barn. He jumped out and leaned over Ida. "Are you in much pain?" he asked. "The ambulance will be here in a few minutes."

"The ambulance? I told you to call Horace," Ida yelled out, still thrashing her head from side to side.

Jeffrey yelled back, "Horace isn't coming. He's over at the hospital visiting his brother."

"If he's at the hospital, I hope they aren't sending that little sawed off runt of an assistant they hired. He ain't worth a cuss. I don't want him driving me. I don't know if he can even drive a hearse or not. I wish they would hurry." Ida was digging her heel into the ground where she lay.

"They aren't sending the hearse. It's the ambulance," Jeffrey repeated, watching the guano bags and her skirt creeping up, inch by inch, exposing her naked rear. Mary wasn't aware that he was watching and didn't bother to cover Ida's exposed bottom until she saw him moving to get a better view.

The ambulance pulled up to the rear doors of the county hospital. The driver and attendant jumped from the front seat and rushed to take Ida into the emergency area.

Jeffrey parked too close to the ambulance and had

to back his vehicle up so the rear doors could be opened. He offered to help take Ida inside.

When Ida glimpsed Horace's hearse parked near the back entrance, she knew he must still be there. Before they carried her inside, she insisted that Jeffrey go tell him that she was entering the hospital and she wanted to see him right away.

As Ida was being wheeled down the hall, she saw Horace with his head leaning against the wall near one of the hospital rooms.

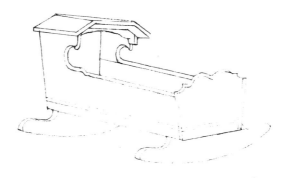

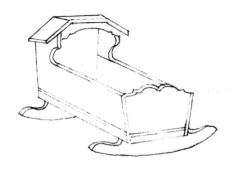

Chapter 18

The stretcher attendants rolled Ida past Horace and she groaned. She groaned a second time, making sure he heard her, but he paid no attention. Just before they turned her down the narrow hallway she said, "Hey, Horace."

Horace never looked up. Ida knew he probably didn't hear her anyway, being so deaf, but she would make her plans to see him again before either of them left the hospital.

The doctor's probing felt good to Ida. It had been such a long time since a man's hand had been on her body, and, in spite of the pain, she was enjoying every minute of it.

"Where does it hurt most?" the doctor asked, as he mashed her rib cage, thighs and stomach. "Does it hurt here?" He kept applying the pressure from place to place, "or here?" he asked.

"A little lower," she said, putting her hand on her left hip.

"Oh, it's in the back area. Well, let's see. We'll have to turn you over on you stomach."

Ida began unbuttoning her dress as she tried to turn on her right side.

"Don't you try to turn. When we're ready, we'll help you," the doctor told her. Her weight prevented her from moving with ease, anyway.

"Here, I'll show you how we will do it," the nurse said, grabbing her by the leg. As soon as Ida felt the nurse's touch, she let out a yell.

The nurse asked, "Why didn't you holler when the doctor touched you?"

"The doctor's got nicer hands than you've got, that's why." Ida was mad.

The nurse backed away.

Ida obeyed every move the doctor suggested and even though in pain, she smiled when he ask her to raise one leg at a time. Before he asked her to lift her arms, she placed one hand on his hip. He backed away and asked, "Is that necessary?"

She smiled and said, "Just for support," and removed her hand.

"Good. Now take several deep breaths for me." He listened to her chest. "I don't think anything is wrong except a possible pulled muscle. Let me give you a shot for pain." Ida turned her head, squeezed her eyes shut and grinned. The doctor plunged the needle into her upper left hip. "There. Now sit up for me."

She lay there awhile before grasping the sides of the examining table. She turned her legs around and pulled herself erect.

"Do you feel better sitting up?" the doctor asked while again examining her lower back.

"Yeah, I think I do."

"Then, it must be a pulled muscle."

"Very well then, I'll button my dress and be getting along. I have a friend in the hall I'd like to see before I leave, that is if he hasn't left yet."

Ida stood on the floor and twisted her hips from side to side. Not feeling much pain now, she thanked the doctor and gave the nurse a hard look and walked carefully out the door.

Turning the corner and entering the hall, she looked in both directions, but didn't see Horace. Slowly, she went from room to room, pausing briefly in front of each door and quietly called Horace's name.

Mary was just around the corner sitting at a table near the nurse's desk when she heard Ida calling for Horace. She rushed to her.

"Are you all right?" she asked.

"I've never felt better. It was only a pulled muscle, but the pain is gone now," and without further explanation, Ida straightened her shoulders and went to the next door. She called Horace again.

"He's in this one," Mary said, pointing to the door Ida had just passed. Mary stepped back, pushed the door open and held it for her.

Ida reached and pulled it shut without entering. "Where's that mattress? I'm not asking you another time. If you think that I won't call the law, just stand there and not tell me."

"Keep your voice down. I can assure you that Jeffrey will get the mattress back to you. If you'd only give us time to explain without biting our heads off, you could find things out a little quicker."

Ida paused and looked Mary squarely in the eyes. "Well, he'd better have it back at the house when I get there."

"Do you want him to go and leave you here to get home the best way you can?" Mary inquired.

"Well, I guess I could ask Horace if he could find time to take me.

"Would you expect him to leave his poor dying brother to take you home?"

"Well, he's not dead yet," Ida said, entering the room and closing the door behind her.

Mary found Jeffrey standing just outside the emergency doors, smoking a Bull Durham cigarette. "Is the mattress still in the back of your car?" she asked.

"I never thought to look. If you didn't take it, it's gotta be there. Come on, let's go see." She took Jeffrey by the hand and they walked toward the side entrance. Sunlight streamed through the glass panels. Jeffrey pushed the door open for Mary. They shielded their eyes from the brightness and walked hand in hand toward the car. Jeffrey opened the back and saw the torn mattress. Spike had chewed and ripped the mattress open and the contents were strewn on the seat and floor.

Paper money fluttered to the ground. Surprised, Mary picked up a couple of the bills, held them out to Jeffrey. "Look at this. I can't believe it! Hundred dollar bills. No wonder she was so concerned about the mattress."

Jeffrey searched through the other contents in the foot of the car and picked up a handful of other denominations of money. They began picking up the cash and stuffing it back into the badly torn mattress cover.

"What must we do?" Jeffrey asked.

"What can we do? There are no options. We'll just have to bring her out to see what old Spike did. There's no way we can pretend nothing has happened,"

"We'll never get the cover repaired enough for her not to notice."

"Certainly not. There's nothing to do but be honest with her. I'll go for her. You stay here and gather up as much as you can. I'll explain about the dog," Jeffrey said.

Mary had never in her whole life seen so much money. The way it looked, the money had not been folded when placed in the mattress, but wadded up and stuffed inside. She smoothed the bills out, one at the time, and began stacking them in a pile, then noticed a tattered envelope. It had been sealed and two cross marks had been made with a pencil across the flap. The glue that once held it closed had pulled loose and she saw a portion of a document that looked official. Suddenly she heard Ida and Jeffrey returning, so she stuck the discolored old envelope deep into her dress pocket.

Small pieces of the faded mattress pad were

scattered just outside the car. Ida noticed the shredded bits of the familiar material. "What in the Lord's name has happened?"

Mary held out the money for her to see. She looked at Jeffrey and said, "Explain to her."

Ida gasped and reached for the handful of money. Her hand froze in mid-air, then fell to her side.

Jeffrey began to tell how the dog came to chew up the mattress, and for the first time Ida did not interrupt. She kept her eyes glued on the handful of money. Before Jeffrey finished explaining, she snatched the money from Mary's hand.

"I know how much is supposed to be here and not one dollar better be missing." She didn't bother to count the money, but stuck most of it in her bosom and clutched the rest firmly in her hand. She quickly turned and got in the back seat. "Take me home. Take me home," she yelled.

On the way home, no one said a word. Jeffrey stopped the car in front of the house and Ida got out. As she turned and started walking away they heard her say, "You bastards." They watched as she made her way carefully and slowly to the porch, but when she reached for the corner post near the steps, she placed her hand on her hip, as if in pain. She hunkered down and waited a few moments before she sat on the steps and began counting the money.

"Should we go and help her?" Jeffrey asked.

"Not unless she calls us. You know how independent she is."

"Are we gonna just sit here until she counts her money and then watch her struggle to get in the house all by herself?"

"What would you suggest?"

Jeffrey sighed and scratched his head. "I suggest we go and snatch the money from her and you and I take off to some unknown parts."

Mary smiled at the idea. "Don't be foolish. Maybe if we play this right we can use the situation to our advantage."

"Yeaaaa-h!" Jeffrey said.

Chapter 19

When Saturday came, Ida hurriedly caught up on her household duties. She had slept well during the night without her back hurting. After her bath, she waited for Viola to take her into town to see Dudley.

On their way, they first stopped by the funeral home and learned from the little man sitting behind the front desk that Horace had been with his brother all night. "They called him to go and he left immediately," the little man said in a raspy voice. "Don't think he's gonna make it. Something went wrong with his heart, they told Horace." Before the man had finished talking, Ida was at the door beckoning Viola to hurry.

At the hospital, Viola waited in the hall while Ida entered Dudley's room. She found Horace standing by his brother's bed, staring into the grim pale face of a man she hardly recognized. Horace didn't bother to look at her until she slipped her arm around his waist. He felt thin. Her first impulse was to ask him home with her so she could fix him some supper, but Viola would have to go too. So she dismissed the thought. She wanted to be alone with Horace every chance she had and wondered if Viola would be offended if she asked her to go back home alone? She could have Horace to drop her off when he left his brother's bedside. Viola would certainly wonder what was going on, but Ida really didn't care what she thought as long as she was assured of Horace's attention. But maybe she shouldn't push. There were times when she grew restless and Viola always seemed to be there and it was nice to have her around. After all, she had volunteered to bring her to the hospital. No, she wouldn't cause her to get upset today.

She turned to Horace and said, "Have you had anything to eat?"

"No. I really haven't wanted anything."

"You've had nothing all today?"

"Only a cup of coffee, but that's all right."

"No, it isn't. I'll have one of them nurses fix you something right away. You've got to eat, Horace." She turned to leave, "I'll be back in a minute." She backed toward the door without looking and bumped into Dudley's hospital bed, moving it a few inches. Dudley stirred.

"Wait a minute. He's waking up!" Horace said.

Ida stepped back and took Horace's arm. Both lowered their heads as close as they could to Dudley's mouth and heard him mumble, "Don't spent much money... on my, on my funeral and my... my", his voice trailed off and his breathing stopped.

Everything went silent. Horace moved away,

wiping his eyes and watched Ida put her ear closer to his brother's mouth. "I think he's breathing, Horace," she said, pressing her ear closer.

Horace went back to the bed and put his hand on his brother's forehead. He laid his head on his chest. There was no movement. Ida moved to the other side of the narrow bed and also placed her head on Dudley's chest. She was face to face with Horace and just inches away. She could feel Horace's breath on her face and something spoke to her of his warmth and strength and she wanted to kiss him.

"He isn't breathing, Ida." Horace said, and stood. "I'm going for the nurse. Here, hold his hand while I'm gone."

Ida took Dudley's hand and put it to her face. She was surprised by the coolness of his limp hand and realized now that he was indeed dead. His face was losing its color and his lips were becoming an inkish purple. Ida placed his hand by his side, covered it with the bed sheet and slumped into the nearby chair. "Poor Horace", she thought. "I must make him realize that I'll be by his side at all times and be available for any help he needs," she murmured.

The nurse rushed into the room. Ida stood, looked at Dudley and began shaking her head. "I'm afraid he's gone," she told the nurse, looking around for Horace. He had not entered the room. Ida helped the nurse pull the sheet over the lifeless form on the bed, then went to look for Horace.

He was making his way slowly back to the room when Ida entered the hall. She rushed to him and threw both arms around his neck and pretended to cry. He, too, put his arms around her and sobbed.

"What will I do? He's all I had."

"We'll work things out", Ida said.

Viola was standing at the other end of the hall and saw the two embracing. As she approached them, she heard Ida whispering to Horace. She stopped to listen.

"You know I'll do all I can to lessen the hurt, Horace. Please lean on me." She paused. "I also need someone, too. We can be good for one another. Will you do that?"

He didn't answer.

Viola saw Ida arms tightened around Horace and his frail body seem to melt into Ida's oversize frame.

As the doctor rushed past Viola, she reached out and took him by the arm and said, "May I talk to you a moment, doctor?" He pulled away shaking his head and increased his pace. He went around the embracing couple and into the room with the nurse and soon returned, pulling the door shut behind him. Ida and Horace were still in an embrace when the doctor approached them. He put his arm around the two and asked, "Would you like for us to send him home or do you prefer that we call the Funeral home in Tuckersville?"

"No... no." Horace said as he released Ida. "He'll go with us. I want to take him back myself. That's the way he would want it."

Ida walked toward Viola and opened her arms. They embraced. "Why don't you drive us to the funeral home? Horace is in no condition to drive the hearse back across town. He's shaking like a leaf. I don't wanna drive either. He can have someone to come for it."

Viola agreed, but when they discussed the plans with Horace, he wouldn't hear of it.

"I'll take him home, myself. The hearse is already here." He wiped his eyes and strolled off to find the doctor.

"I hope he isn't expecting us to help load Dudley," Viola said when Horace was out of earshot. "I never want anything to do with loading bodies anymore. I haven't forgot when we tried to carry Seth up your back steps and into the parlor."

Ida became irritated. "Well, I'll stay and help him. You just run on along and see if I care. You don't seem to want to help anybody when they are in need." Her voice became bitter. "I know how you are. Just go on," Ida insisted, her hand motioning Viola to leave. She turned away to look for Horace without giving Viola a chance to reply. A few paces down the hall she looked back and Viola was gone.

Horace was sitting on the floor just outside Dudley's room, resting his forehead against his closed fist. Ida saw him and realized he had given way completely to his weariness. Now, she thought, was a good time to reassure him of her feelings and her willingness to help. She sat on the floor beside him. His long, thin face went white with anger. "Why did he have to die now?" he said, "just as I had arranged a big surprise for him? Why?"

She moved closer to him and put both arms around his frail body and pulled him next to her until his head reated on her shoulder.

"What kind of surprise, Horace?" Ida asked, not wanting to sound too inquisitive.

"His son, whom he hasn't seen in years, will be coming to see him in a couple of days."

"His son? What son?"

"He has a son no one knows about. He's grieved for so long and even prayed for him to come home. Now.. now that I finally persuaded him to come, his poor daddy is... is dead."

"I never knew he had a son."

"I'm the only one around who knows." Horace pulled a handkerchief from his pocket and blew his nose. "Dudley would have been fifty this coming Saturday and I had arranged for his son to come home. Now, I guess, he'll have to be buried on his birthday."

Viola came up the hall dragging two chairs. "For goodness sakes. Here. Take these chairs," she whispered, pushing them toward Ida. "You look so ridiculous sitting down there."

Putting one hand on Horace's shoulder and grabbing a chair with the other, Ida tried to push herself up. Horace bent under the strain, but she finally got to her feet. Viola grasped Horace's hand and helped him into the other chair.

Two young men quietly rolled a stretcher past them and into the room and closed the door. Horace buried his face in his hands.

Shortly, the stretcher was pushed into the hall, bumping the walls on each side as it was rolled toward the back entrance. One of the attendants looked back and asked, "Would you have us put him in the hearse?" Horace never looked up. Ida nodded "Yes" and looked away. She heard the back doors of the hospital swing shut. She put her arm around Horace's shoulder.

At the sound of the hearse doors closing, Ida and Viola walked with Horace outside. One of the orderlies held the passenger side door open for Horace and he got in. Ida stood there puzzled. "Surely, they don't expect me to drive?" Viola nodded and Ida got in on the driver's side.

"I'll ride with you," Viola said, "if the young man will open the rear door." The attendant opened and held the rear door and she crawled in the back with the body and the door was closed.

As soon as Ida started the engine, Viola called out, "Wait. Let me get my pocketbook out of my car." She fumbled for some time trying to get the back door open. When she was outside, the door slammed shut and automatically locked.

Thinking Viola had gotten back in the hearse, Ida drove off. She didn't see her running behind them, yelling "Stop! Stop!"

Chapter 20

Viola's rapid breathing caused her nostrils to fill with dust as she ran behind the hearse. She felt her lungs collapsing and tears flooding her eyes. Out of breath, she stopped in the middle of the road, bent over and lifted her frock to wipe her eyes and blew her nose on her petticoat. She couldn't see the hearse because of the dust, but heard the roaring of the motor. "Go ahead and kill yourself," she yelled, cursing Ida and shaking her fists in their direction. "You know Horace can't take care of two bodies all by himself, so maybe he'll send yours over to the funeral home in Tuckersville." She coughed and went back to the her car for her pocket book.

Ida, thinking Viola was in the back of the hearse, kept asking her questions. She never thought to look over her shoulder to see if she might be missing. Horace kept his head propped on the dash with his eyes closed and she wondered if he were still grieving or if he might be scared of her driving. After all, it had been a long time since she had sat under a wheel, particularly a vehicle as large as this hearse. She was amazed at her ability to drive and was proud that she remembered so well. She just knew Horace had to be proud of her too, and tried harder to display more confidence in what she was doing. Although he never raised his head from the dashboard, she occasionally called his attention to how well she was driving. If she continued to do her best, he would surely take more interest in her, she thought.

Without lifting his head, Horace said, "Ida, you've got to sorta slow down."

"I'm sorry. I won't aware we were going so fast." She slightly raised her foot from the accelerator, and called out, "Viola, can't you hear me back there? You haven't answered me yet." Again there was no answer. "Maybe the motor is making too much noise," she mumbled as she let her foot off the gas pedal.

The hearse almost came to a stop. Horace raised his head and asked, "Why are you stopping?"

"I'm talking to Viola and she can't hear a word I'm saying."

Just as Horace turned to looked in the back, a car passed so close to them, and at such speed, Ida jerked the hearse to the right and began to slide off the road. "Look out!" Horace shouted. Ida became excited, jerked the steering wheel again and applied the brakes. The rear of the hearse slid into the shallow roadside ditch. The two sat there looking at one another.

Horace said. "Turn the engine off. We don't want the thing to burst into flames."

The car that passed had stopped and was backing up. After the dust cleared, a surprised Ida said, "My Lord. It's Viola!" She didn't bother to get out of the hearse. Instead, she rolled the window down, stuck her head out and yelled, "What in tarnation are you doing? I thought you were in the back."

Viola bounced out of her car. "What ye mean, you thought I was in the back?" She was raving mad. "You know darn well you left me standing in the road when you drove off! I know why you did it, too!"

"Don't get so mad, Viola. You're sounding like a jackass."

"Don't you call me a jackass!" she shouted back.

"You are one, or you wouldn't be frothing at the bit, like you are!"

"If Horace wasn't my friend, too, I'd drive right off and leave you to get out of this mess the best way you can," Viola said.

As the women squabbled, Horace turned to check on his brother. Dudley had rolled from the stretcher and was face down on the floor. "My God, Ida. Look what we've done," Horace said. He began crying and wringing his hands.

Ida, too, began to cry. "What are we going to do?"

Viola stood just outside the hearse with her head stuck inside the window, surveying the damage. "I thought you all were bringing Dudley? What happened?"

"Whatcha mean, what happened? Can't you see what happened?" Ida leaned toward Horace and Viola saw the body sprawled on the floor of the hearse.

"Oh, Ida. Here, honey. Get out and let's get

Horace into town. I'll take him and I'll send someone to help you get out of the ditch."

"Here comes a truck. Flag it down," Ida told her.

Viola stepped to the center of the road and waved at the approaching truck. The driver slowed and tried to get around the hearse, but Viola stepped in its path and the truck stopped. "We need some help," she said. She saw chains in the back of the truck. She grabbed them and began dragging them off. They stirred up dust as they fell with a heavy thud.

The black man on the driver's side opened the truck door and came around to Viola and said, "Ma'am, we ain't much hep when it comes to gitting hearses out of a ditch. Now, we's can goes into town and send you some hep. My buddy up dere in the truck ain't very strong, and he ain't gonna be any hep, anyways." The black man backed away from the hearse and began to get back into the truck.

Viola walked around to the driver's side, put her hands on her hips and said,"Now, you just look here. We're in need here and we need help. All we gotta do is attach the ends of these chains to the bumper of this hearse and the other ends to your truck. We can tie one to my car and we can pull together until it's out. The ditch ain't that deep." She insisted. The man had no choice but to obey.

Viola didn't see Ida get out of the hearse and go to the back to survey the damage. Horace managed to get over the front seat and crawled to the back to unlock the rear doors. Ida crawled inside and she and Horace struggled to get Dudley back on the stretcher.

"You take his feet, Ida, and I'll lift his head."

They strained.

"He's not even bending in the middle," Ida said surprised.

"No. He won't bend. Just lift him straight up, and sorta toss him," Horace said, still sniffling.

Viola and the black man had finished attaching the chains to the front of the hearse and were in their vehicles. Viola gave him thumbs up, and they started their motors and stepped on the gas at the same time. The chains tightened. Ida and Horace had just placed Dudley on the stretcher and had pulled the sheet over him when the hearse lunged forward. Ida fell backwards through the rear doors and lay sprawled on her back with her dress over her head. Dudley's stiff body slid from beneath the sheet, out the back doors, and on top of Ida. The stretcher rolled out and tipped over on its side.

Ida yelled.

Horace slowly crawled to the back entrance of the hearse, swung his feet out, and stepped to the ground. Viola and the black man jumped from their vehicles and rushed behind the hearse to see what the commotion was all about.

The man, seeing the body lying on top of Ida, ran back to his truck. Viola held her nose to keep from laughing when she saw them and wanted to say, "There she is, at it again", but instead said, "Let me help you up."

Ida struggled to get from beneath the dead body, rolling it on its side. Viola and Horace took Ida's hands and tugged until she got to her feet. Horace was helping Ida to the hearse and as soon as their backs were turned,

Viola used her foot to roll Dudley over again on his back. Viola called out for the black man to come to help her lift Dudley back onto the stretcher. She waited, then called again. Still they did not come, so she decided to go for them.

The man on the passenger side of the truck sat with a bag over his head. "What in the world is wrong with him?" Viola asked the driver.

"Lordy, he's scared of hearses and dead folk and don't wanna see 'em. He wants me to drive off and leave dis place."

"You just can't drive off and leave these folks here. That's the man's brother back there on the ground. You gotta help us get him up."

"I ain't much help gitting up dead folks, either. We gotta go," the truck driver said.

"Well, get out of here, then. Some decent folks will come by in a few minutes and help us," Viola said angrily.

"I sho' hope so, missus," the driver said. He put his chains back into his truck and drove off.

In the distant, Viola saw a vehicle headed in her direction. She squinted as the dust from the truck stirred up a cloud of dust. She could make out a number of men riding on the back of a truck, however; and as the truck came nearer, she could see one of the men was holding a shotgun. The others wore striped suits. She placed herself in the middle of the road with her hands above her head and held her stance until the truck came to a halt.

"We need some help! You gotta help us. There's a man laying in the ditch behind this here hearse and we need to get him back inside."

All the prisoners looked from one to the other, waiting for a volunteer. No one moved. The guard lowered his gun and motioned for some to get out and help. Still, no one moved until he touched four of them with the barrel. The guard stood on the running board as Dudley was loaded, then ordered the men back on the truck.

"Thank you, thank you, thank you," Viola told them, patting the guard on the leg as she passed. She saw his stern stare and gazed back at him. He was of medium height and had short blonde hair. She watched the dust rise and settle as they sped off, wishing she could be on the truck with him.

When the truck was out of sight, Viola told Horace and Ida that she would follow them if Horace would do the driving. Ida was a little indignant, but switched seats, and they drove off.

Horace left the back dirt streets and drove through town to the funeral home. Upon arriving, they found a car there with Tennessee license plates. On the steps, around on the side entrance, sat a handsome young man.

Chapter 21

Viola drove up close behind the hearse in the back driveway of the funeral home and was out of her car before the hearse came to a complete stop. She saw a young man of medium height standing by the door with his suitcase. She walked over to introduced herself. "What a fine looking young man," she thought. "Just what Mary needs," she murmured to herself. She noticed a curl of his black hair resting on his forehead. It was wavy and as black as the color she recently had put on hers. He had good features on a square face, prominent jaw and a muscular neck. His shoulders and chest were athletic. His buttocks looked firm.

"I'm Viola Bentley," she said, "and who might you be?" Before the man had a chance to speak, she continued, "Looks like you've come to live here, with that big suitcase and that tied up box."

"Well, maybe I..."

"Well, you just might like it here, but there's

nothing to this little town. The only excitement we ever have is when someone dies," pointing toward the hearse, "and that's not too exciting unless someone one is killed in a fight or some tragedy happens. A natural ole death? Well, there's nothing much to them. We bury 'em and soon forget about them." She hardly paused long enough to take a breath. "Who'd you say you was and whatcha you doing in town?"

Without answering, the young man gave her a hard stare and went to meet Horace and Ida as they walked toward him. Ida stood aside and watched the two men embrace for a long time. Horace didn't seem to want to turn the young man loose until Ida placed her hands on his shoulders. They tightened their arm around one another, then separated.

"You must be Uncle Horace's wife?"

"Oh no, oh no. Not just yet. Not for awhile, anyway." Ida beamed. Her expression took on a glow of excitement as Horace took her by the hand.

"This is Ida Ridley. A very, very good friend," Horace said.

"I'm Wilbur Dunlock," he said, not giving Horace a chance to introduce them. For a moment they stood gazing at one another. Smiling, the young man turned to his uncle and said, "You look frail, Uncle Horace. Is anything wrong?"

"The last few days have been pretty bad. I've been at the hospital and haven't had much sleep for the last couple days and nights. It's your papa, Wilbur. I wish you had come earlier. He died a hour or so ago."

"Dead? But I came for his birthday. You wanted me to come." Tears filled his eyes.

Ida began to cry. Horace, too, started crying and put his arm around Wilbur. Ida strolled over and huddled with Viola and quietly asked her if she knew that Dudley had a son?

"My goodness! I'm shocked," Viola said in a loud voice. "I had no idea. It seems I've been knowing Dudley all my life and I've never heard a word about a son."

"For goodness sakes, Viola. Keep your voice down."

"How long have you been knowing it?" she whispered.

"I just found out today, myself. Horace was telling me that he had contacted his brother's son and wanted more than anything else for him to come and see his father on his birthday. They have been separated for so long."

"I didn't know Dudley ever got married," Viola said.

"My, Viola. You know you don't have to be married to have a young'un."

"Well, you should know."

"That was a mean thing to say. You won't ever forget that, will you?" They just stared at one another.

Ida placed her arm around Viola's waist and turned her around when she saw Horace taking his nephew to the back of the hearse. They watched them open the doors and crawl inside, pulling the doors shut behind them.

Viola, feeling sorry for offending Ida, started to apologize, but changed her mind and said instead, "I've always said you were the one with the big mouth, but

I've surely opened mine too wide this time."

"What in the world have you said?"

"I told Wilbur that death around these parts was never exciting unless someone was killed in a fight or in a wreck. Oh, Ida! When am I going to learn to keep my big mouth shut and my thoughts to my self?"

"Oh, you never have, Viola, and I doubt you ever will." She shrugged her shoulders as if to let the remark pass. "Don't worry about it. The truth is the truth and there's no way getting around that."

They walked to the back porch to wait. Viola dusted a spot on the steps to sit and Ida reached and pulled a chair to the edge of the porch and squeezed herself into it. Viola laughed when she saw Ida forcing her hips between the arms of the rocker. "It's kinda small, ain't it, Ida?"

"No. I'm just too darn large." They quietly laughed when she began to rock and the porch floor squeaked under her weight.

Moments later, Horace came out of the hearse alone and walked toward Ida. She saw in his expression that he wanted her help. She tried to get up, but was stuck in the chair. Her face reddened as she wiggled and twisted. Finally, in a half raised position, she pushed hard on the chair's arm rests and it dropped from her hips with a loud thump.

Wilbur came out of the hearse to investigate the noise. He wet his lips, but before he could speak, Ida said, "Its no fun being this large. I gotta get thinner." Viola laughed aloud. Wilbur joined in the laughter, not knowing what had happened. Ida saw his quizzical expression, but it soon turned into a broad smile and she noticed his gleaming white teeth and wondered if a man so young could have false ones. He was indeed handsome and did resemble Dudley.

"Let's all sit here for a few minutes," Horace said. We need to make plans for Dudley's funeral."

Ida started to sit again in the rocker, but shook her head and moved to the steps. Viola nudged her and whispered, "Try it again. Maybe you've stretched it a little."

"You're funny, Viola," she whispered sarcastically, slapping her slightly on the shoulder.

"Day after tomorrow is Dudley's birthday, you know," Horace said to everyone. "Wilbur has no objection to burying his father then, so don't you think we can go ahead with the funeral at eleven o'clock?" He raised his head, looked at Ida for her approval. "Will that suit you, Ida?"

Ida was pleased that he should ask her and said, "Yes, dear."

Viola turned slowly, looked at Ida and raised her eyebrows. Ida responded by smiling broadly at her and shrugged her shoulders as if to ask, "Well?" Viola's expression didn't change. Ida looked back at Horace.

"He wasn't a church member, you know," Horace said, "but we'll ask the retired preacher at the Methodist Church over at Lumber Bridge if we can hold the funeral there. Dudley liked him." He paused, wiped his eyes and placed his arm around Wilbur. "Brother has been in that church more than any other and I think he'd like it held there."

"You're not planning to do the preparation yourself, are you?" Ida asked.

"No. I'll ask my friend over in Tuckersville if he'll come over here. I'm sure he'll come."

It was Saturday and far from a perfect day for a funeral. The smell of rain hung heavily in the air and the weather clouds swept low over Lumber Bridge as if they had decided to wash the town away at any time.

Ida and Viola were wiping their feet on the worn mat just inside the door of the church when they noticed a wall of brown and black umbrellas hugging the natural wood walls in the vestibule.

Ida peeped through the crack of the doors that separated the sanctuary from the vestibule and whispered to Viola, "Them pews are nearly filled already."

"Guess they were afraid of the storm that's about to come up," Viola replied.

Just inside the sanctuary doors, Viola paused and looked around. She was looking for a place to sit, but Ida was studying the back of everybody's head, trying to recognize those attending the funeral. Viola saw a place beside Dora Skinner and squeezed pasted three others on the pew and sat by her.

Ida fumbled for so long through the fans on the vestibule table for just the right one, that Viola was seated when she entered. She slowly walked down the inside aisle looking for Viola.

Alberta Joyner had forgotten to pick up a fan as she entered, but noticing Ida was waving one furiously, she asked those on the pew beside her to tighten up a little. Eager to benefit from Ida's fanning, she pulled her down on the pew beside her.

The doors squeaked. Ida looked back and saw the preacher enter, followed by the coffin, Horace, Wilbur and six pallbearers. The mourners stood, but before Ida could pull herself up, the coffin bumped her pew and the flowers slid from the top of the coffin and landed in her lap. Alberta tried to help remove them, but Ida slapped her hands away. "I'll handle this," she said. She first pulled a flower from the pall, stuck it in her purse, then placed the flowers back on top of the coffin. The undertaker from Tuckersville quietly said he was sorry, thanked her and rolled the coffin to the front of the church.

Chapter 22

*U*pon arriving at the church, Mary had been asked to sing in the choir by some of the young ladies in the Lumber Bridge Methodist Church. She agreed when told the storm had kept a few of the choir members from getting there on time.

"I'm not in my best voice today, but if you really need me, I'd like to sing alto; that is, if I know the song," she said.

"We haven't had a chance to practice, but we all know the hymn. We sing it all the time at funerals. It's one of our best songs," they had said.

A brilliant flash of lightning suddenly filled the church and thunder rolled across the sky. It shook the wood building and Ida swore she saw the coffin rocking and the flowers on top of it shaking. Children clung to their mothers and some of the older ladies grasped their purses. Half the congregation jumped to their feet while others, unafraid, sat gazing through the tall windows. The thunder slowly roared off into the distance.

Ida had never been afraid of thunderstorms and sat there wondering what poor Horace was going to do now that he was alone. The lady in front of her said, "I've never in my life seen such a storm." Another crack of lightning caused the lights to go out. The preacher rushed to the pulpit, raised his arms and said, "Settle down, my friends. It's only our good Lord ushering our beloved brother into heaven. Although our lights are now out in this place, rest assured they are burning brightly for Dudley as he steps into that heavenly city of gold." A few of the people began to sit down. "Nowhere is there brightness as pure as that surrounding our Lord."

The preacher waved his arms up and down, signaling those milling around to be seated. With everyone settled, he nodded to the choir. They stood and a skinny lady in the choir loft bowed to the organist. The organ player began rocking from side to side, trying to pump enough air in the bellows to begin the music. One man on the back row of the choir started singing the moment the organ began, but he stopped and looked embarrassed. The lady in front turned and stared in disgust at him.

The organ squeaked through the last bar of "In A Land Where We'll Never Grow Old" and the organist started singing the first line of the hymn as a signal for the other members of the choir to join in.

Ida saw the preacher give a signal to the choir members to end the song after they sang the third stanza, but the organist failed to see him. Though she was out of breath from pumping the organ, she tossed her head back, adjusted her round gold-rimmed glasses with one hand, never missing a note, and continued playing. The choir did not sing and she gazed at them over the top of her glasses. Lifting one hand, she directed them to begin again and as they started the fourth verse, the preacher strolled to the pulpit. She stopped playing right in the middle of the song and the choir's singing came to a mournful abrupt end.

The preacher cleared his throat, mopped his face and eyes with a wadded up handkerchief. He shook the wrinkles from it and stuffed it in one of his inside coat pockets. He dug deep into his other one and pulled out some folded papers while telling the congregation, "Today is not a very good day for a funeral, but it is one the Lord has given us, so we'll make the best we can of it."

He unfolded the papers, held one of them out at arm's length and moved his head from one side to the other, trying to focus his eyes in the dimly lighted church. "Brothers and sisters," he said, "I must move over to the window since the lights are out. It's difficult to read my notes." He squeezed between the choir and the coffin and brushed against a tall homemade flower arrangement. The large vase of zinnias, larkspur and bachelor buttons rocked and finally turned over, splashing water on the feet of the pallbearers sitting on the front pew.

Ida immediately went to the front of the church, picked up the flowers and stuffed them back in the vase. She carried them to the other side of the altar and placed them on top of the organ.

"Don't put them there," the organist whispered. "I can't see the family with 'em up there. Take them to the foot of the coffin where they were."

Ida passed in front of the altar again and placed them on the floor at the foot of the coffin. Turning, she saw a vacant seat beside Horace.

Mary watched suspiciously as Ida went over and squeezed in next to Horace. Just as the lightning flashed again she saw the young man sitting with them. Another burst, and the light filled the church. Mary saw clearly his well-sculptured face and his white teeth as he smiled at Ida. Her concentration on the young stranger became so intent, the only words she heard the preacher say were, "heart be troubled, neither let it be afraid." She couldn't take her eyes off the handsome young man and when Geraldine shifted on the pew, blocking her view, Mary slipped closer to the lady next to her and continued to gaze at the young man. She was eager to meet him and would go to Ida as soon as they were out of the church. Maybe she could ride to the cemetery in the same vehicle with Horace if Ida was planning to ride with him. She could think of an excuse to tell Jeffrey why she must ride with Ida. She knew that he hadn't wanted to bring her to the church anyway.

Sheets of hard pounding rain beat against the windows and on the tin roof. She was glad the sun had been shining last week when her papa was buried. As the preacher read the scripture, Mary closed her eyes and said a little prayer that there would be room for her in the undertaker's car. She knew Ida would be taking up more than half the back seat, but she could wedge herself in beside her. After all, there would only be Horace, the young man and Ida, along with the driver. Surely the car could hold all of them.

"This dear brother, lying here in front of us today, has shrouded so many folks to be ushered into heaven, that I am sure he is anxious to see all of them again. Yes, this would be his time to rejoice. As all of us know, he has wrapped many people in swaddling clothes, dressed them to perfection for their journey to meet their Lord at the pearly gates of heaven. And, oh yes" the preacher continued in a sing-song voice, "I am also certain that he has dressed some who bypassed the pearly gates and went right on down to meet their eternal doom within the raging fires of hell. But," he paused and took a deep breath, "as I stand before you today, my good friends, I can assure you that this lifeless creature here before us now is being escorted right through this storm and them clouds above us right to the feet of Jesus and will live there for eternity."

Will it be eternity before he gets through preaching this funeral? Mary wondered. She glanced at the back of the church and saw Jeffrey.

"Sin in this world..." Mary heard the preacher say, as she watched Jeffrey stretching his neck as if searching for someone, "will find us all reckoning with ourselves when sin creeps inside us..."

Mary suddenly felt her interest in Jeffrey drain from her. She looked back at the young man on the front pew and knew nothing could be sinful about this man, as handsome as he was. He looked so pure with his blue eyes, accented with black eyelashes, which curled slightly upward. Blue eyes had always been common in her childhood dreams of lovers. She didn't want to stare at him, but sitting so close, she studied every inch of his face.

A loud "Amen" from the back of the church jolted her back into awareness. The preacher raised his arms and the congregation stood as the pallbearers marched out of the church behind the coffin. The ushers came down to the front to lead the mourners out. Ida got up and followed directly behind Horace.

Mary watched as the three filed down the aisle toward the entrance. She noticed how erect and tall the young man was and she became anxious for the choir to leave, but no one moved until the last of the congregation went through the front door.

Mary scrambled past the other choir members, not waiting to respond to Geraldine's `Thank you for helping us'.

Once she stepped out of the choir loft, she left through the rear door of the choir room and rushed around the church to the waiting car in front of the hearse. "Will there be room for me to ride with you all?" she asked Ida.

"Didn't Jeffrey bring you?" Ida asked as she opened the door for Mary. "Here, get in out of the dampness, dear, before you catch your death of cold." Mary knew she was being polite just to impress Horace and Wilbur.

"Yes, Jeffrey brought me,but he has somewhere else to go. I told him that I would find a way back if he would bring me."

Ida touched Horace on the shoulder and asked, "Don't you think it will be all right for her to ride with us?"

Before he could answer, Wilbur said, "Of course. There's plenty of room."

The rain had turned to a light drizzle. The driver had not yet come to the car, so Mary quickly got out and rushed over to Jeffrey who was talking to Geraldine on the church steps. "I'm going to ride with Ida to the cemetery. I'll see you later this afternoon," she said.

Jeffrey acknowledged with a mere wave of his hand. Mary strolled back to the waiting car. Wilbur jumped out and opened the back door. "Thank you so much," Mary said. They smiled at one another.

Before Mary entered the car, Ida said, "Wilbur, this is my stepdaughter, Mary."

They stared into each other's eyes and said "Hello" at the same time. They both laughed. Mary caught a whiff of his aftershave lotion. It overpowered her Evening in Paris perfume.

As the car headed toward the cemetery, Mary leaned her head on the back of the seat, closed her eyes and dreamed of acres of lilacs in full bloom. Her heart began beating faster and she wanted to touch Wilbur to assure herself he was real.

Chapter 23

When the funeral director drove through the cemetery gates, Mary saw the wreaths of flowers that had already been placed at the graveside. Only a few arrangements had been in the church during the funeral service and she had wondered why there had not been more. Dudley was one of the most popular men in the surrounding communities. Maybe they handle things a little differently in Tuckersville, she thought. Anyway, she was glad for Wilbur's sake that more flowers were at the graveside.

The blackened storm clouds had vanished when they arrived. The sun felt warm on Mary's back as she walked behind Ida, Horace and Wilbur to the chairs beside the grave.

Ida sat very erect, tightly clutching her overstuffed pocket book. She wanted to make sure Viola saw her sitting with the family so she shifted several times in her chair to get her attention. Mary held her breath and wondered if the chair was going to collapse under the strain. When Ida caught Viola's eye, Ida winked at her and Viola winked back. Ida straightened her shoulders again and felt important sitting next to Horace.

    Mary sat in the chair next to Wilbur. The undertaker had placed the chairs close together and when Ida was seated, her left hip overflowed and partly rested on Mary's chair, forcing Mary to rest her thigh against Wilbur's.

    There were people sitting on the row behind them, all unknown to Mary. They had to be family. She heard Horace ask one of the women how his cousin Mable was and why she hadn't come to the funeral.

    Horace motioned to Wilbur. When he stood to be introduced, his elbow brushed against Mary's breast. He blushed and immediately apologized to her.

    "Oh, that's all right," she said and smiled.

    After turning back around, he patted her hand and whispered again, "I am really sorry." She only smiled and he continued to gaze at her.

    Sunlight streamed under the rim of the canopy covering the grave as Mary sat staring straight ahead. She knew Wilbur was watching her and that he would notice the hint of reddish sheen on her hair.

    She wanted to turn to him, but didn't because so many of her friends were watching. She wondered what they were thinking as she sat there with a man she didn't yet know. At the moment, she really didn't care. She was only concerned about Wilbur's smile when he had jumped out of the car at the church and opened the door for her.

Mary was more embarrassed by being stared at constantly than by sitting with a man she didn't know. Some of her friends were envious. Yes, nothing but puretee envy, and she was going to enjoy the moment. She glanced at the young women gazing at her, tossed her long hair back with a jerk of her head and gave them a slight smile. She didn't want to waste her time thinking about trivial things such as their envy, or even what the preacher was saying.

She glanced over at her Papa's grave, only a few yards away. The rain had freshened some of the flowers, but some had died and should be removed. She would ask Jeffrey to drive her over tomorrow so she could pull them out. Tomorrow? Maybe she shouldn't ask Jeffrey. He might think it was an opportunity to make love to her and she didn't want that now, not after meeting Wilbur.

Thoughts came to her mind how her Papa's death would bring changes in their lives. She had already noticed how Ida's disposition was changing. If only Ida had been a little kinder to him the last few years of his life, maybe her papa wouldn't be under that mound of sod right now. But, as always, Ida had neglected him and thought only of herself. Maybe it was best that his estate turned out the way it did. She and Jeffrey had made plans, but she couldn't think about that at a time like this. Wilbur was on the scene now, so she must wait. Her mind raced from one thought to another.

Tomorrow? Maybe Wilbur would want to come back and visit his papa's grave. If so, wouldn't it be nice to come with him? But, how would they get back out here? He'd have to drive his Uncle Horace's hearse.

Well, that wouldn't be so bad. Yes, that's what she would do, she'd talk to him about it on the way back to the church. Maybe Ida would ride on the front seat with the driver and Horace and she could sit on the back with Wilbur. She sat there, not listening to the preacher's graveside sermon. The only thing she knew was that it seemed long. Wilbur looked at her again. She lowered her head and glanced toward Ida. There she sat, her legs crossed at the ankles and wearing a dark brown shoe and a black one. Mary looked up in time to see the preacher close his Bible. He pulled a few petals from a flower and sprinkled them over the coffin and after saying, "Ashes to ashes, dust to dust," he nodded to the gathered crowd and walked toward the family.

Ellen Grace, Geraldine and Ruby began rushing over to Mary as soon as the preacher finished shaking hands with the family. She saw them coming and went to meet them. "Oh, how nice you look, Mary," Ellen Grace said, looking past her, trying to see Wilbur. "Isn't that a new frock you're wearing?"

"This old thing? Oh, no."

"It's very pretty. I bet your friend likes it," Ruby said.

"Well," Mary said shyly, "he hasn't told me so, but then, we haven't had much of a chance to talk. He just arrived in town a couple days ago."

"Gee. Tell us where he's from. I've never seen such a gorgeous fellow. Tell us Mary. Tell us," Geraldine said excitedly.

"Oh, I'll never tell you vultures," she teasingly said, swatting the air with her hand.

"He's so good looking! You've got to tell us

everything about him," Ellen Grace said. "If you don't we'll march right up to him and ask. Now, you wouldn't want us to do that, would you?"

"If you've got the nerve, just go right ahead," Mary said. "But you wouldn't dare, would you? Furthermore, I saw him first and you haven't got a chance." The four giggled like school girls.

"Here he comes," Ruby said.

Mary turned to face Wilbur. His fingers hooked leisurely into his belt, he pushed himself through the crowd and headed straight toward them.

Chapter 24

Mary returned Wilbur's smile as he approached.

Geraldine smoothed out the wrinkles of her dress and patted the disheveled fingerwaves in her hair the wind had disturbed. She smiled too, and was the first to speak to Wilbur.

"It turned out to be a nice day for a funeral, didn't it?" Geraldine asked.

Mary was quick to reply to the question, knowing full well it had been directed at Wilbur. "Yes, it did, despite what the preacher said when he began the service at church."

Mary thought she saw daggers coming from her Geraldine's eyes.

"Gorgeous day, absolutely gorgeous." Geraldine said.

Wilbur slipped his hand into Mary's and softly said, "I think Uncle Horace is ready to go. Wouldn't you like to ride back with us?"

Mary's heart began to skip and she forgot to introduce everybody before they turned to leave.
Halfway to the car, she looked back and waved to the young women standing apart from the crowd. They were still gazing at her.

Mary removed her hand from Wilbur's, but followed him as he maneuvered his way through the headstones of the older section of the town's only cemetery. He wanted to show her the graves of his grandparents that Horace had pointed out when they came to the cemetery with the grave diggers. He paused, smiled and waited for her to catch up. He extended his hand as she came nearer. As he stepped behind a large headstone, his weight caused the grave to collapse. He tried to release her hand but she held firmly, trying to pull him back. Unbalanced, he almost pulled Mary in on top of him as he fell into the hole. She pulled harder, looking around to see how many people were watching.

Bracing herself against the tilting headstone, she continued to pull and yelled for help. Several men rushed over and pushed her away from the cave-in just before the grave marker toppled toward Wilbur. She watched the men struggling with the headstone. They finally reached in for Wilbur. "I think my leg is broken!" Wilbur said.

Mary gasped, "Oh, my Lord!", putting her hand to her face. She backed away and leaned against a tall headstone but never took her eyes off him. Somehow, she felt the pain he was experiencing as she watched his contorted face. His right leg dangled as the men raised him from the hole. It's broken for sure, she thought.

They laid him flat on the rain-soaked grass. Mary

was concerned about his fine looking double breasted suit and wished she had brought her raincoat to put under him. She rushed to him and wiped his face with her handkerchief. He took her hand again.

"Someone bring the hearse over here," one of the men yelled, looking over the small crowd still milling around the grave. "We've got to get this fellow to the hospital, right away."

Wilbur tightened his grip around Mary's hand and she began to cry. "Oh, don't cry. I'll be fine. It isn't fatal, you know," he said, trying to smile through his pain. He released her. She brushed her hands across both her cheeks to remove the evidence of her crying. She stared directly into his face and he looked into hers. Her heart pounded and she could feel the blood in her face and wondered if others could see her blushing. She wanted to speak to him but, with so many folks having gathered near, she had to phrase her words carefully. "I know you're alone with no one to care for you," she whispered, "and I want you to know I'll help you as much as I can."

The hearse had been driven as near as it could to where Wilbur lay without getting out of the narrow path that encircled the old section of the graveyard. Mary backed away as the men began discussing how he should be moved.

Most of the crowd had left the gravesite and assembled near the cave-in to watch Wilbur's rescue. Ida and Viola elbowed their way through the horde of people and stood in front of everyone, not wanting to miss the excitement.

"I've got some wide boards in the back of my pick-up truck we can lay him on," Ida heard a man say,

"Let's use them and see if we can get him in the back of the hearse."

Wilbur's clothes were becoming saturated. The ground was soggy and Mary was also concerned about her shoes until she saw Wilbur searching for someone in the crowd. She went to him. Stooping, she wiped his face again with her lace handkerchief and smiled. "They'll have you in the hospital soon and they'll give you something for pain," she said. His forehead was wet with sweat and she continued to dab it while leaning close to him.

The truck arrived. The preacher motioned to the driver to park behind the hearse and before it stopped, two men jumped on the flatbed, picked up the boards and dropped them flat on the wet ground. A spray of water splashed from the grass and the spray covered those standing near. Geraldine's flowered voile dress caught most of the splash and she whispered "Damn".

The Preacher, standing next to her, overheard the remark and said, "Why, Geraldine, I can't believe you said that." He began brushing her clothes to remove the tiny pieces of wet grass that had stuck to her when the water splashed up.

"Look at my shoes," she cried.

"Here. Let me wipe them for you," the preacher said.

Geraldine stuck out one foot. The preacher stooped and brushed it clean with his hand. She put the other one forward and he also cleaned it. Just as he finished and was about to raise up, a puff of wind filled Geraldine's heavily pleated skirt and the preacher's bald head was caught underneath.

Ida saw and grabbed Viola's arm, turned her around and pointed toward them. The preacher struggled to get his head free, pushing Geraldine's skirt high above her knees. There were a few quiet snickers from those who were watching, but neither Ida nor Viola could control their laughter. They even heard Wilbur laugh through his pain.

After the red left the preacher's face, Ida whispered to Viola, "I've laughed so much, I've wet my bloomers!"

Viola became hysterical with laughter and started walking away from the crowd. Ida followed her.

"Now," Ida said. "I bet I can tell you what his sermon will be next Sunday!"

"It'll have to be,`From Darkness Into Light' Viola said laughing.

"Oh, I don't think it will be that. There was no darkness. You could see right through that voile dress." Ida was laughing so hard she was gasping for breath. "It'll be more like," she gasped again, "like, like, `Putting your talents under a bushel'".

"Stop it, Ida Ridley. I can't take it. I've also wet my britches too. You gotta stop making me laugh!"

Ida noticed the big wet spot on the tail of Viola's dress. She looked around to see if they were being watched. The crowd seemed to be more interested in watching Wilbur being loaded into the hearse than noticing them. She turned around. "Does the wetness show on my dress?" she asked Viola.

"You wouldn't believe how wet your hem and stockings are. Can't you feel the water in your shoes? And the size of your bottom. Wow!"

"Whatcha you mean, the size of my bottom? I'll tell you what we can do. Let's sit on the ground and when them folks see us, we'll git up and they'll think it was the wet ground," Ida suggested.

"Now wouldn't that be silly? What would we be sitting on the ground for? Why, there wouldn't be enough space for you to sit with that big bucket of yours." Viola continued to laugh.

"Now, that ain't funny, Viola," Ida said, slapping her hard on the shoulder.

In a playful mood, Viola gave Ida a slight push and Ida lost her footing and fell backwards. She hit the wet ground and Viola thought she saw her bounce. Ida landed on her left shoulder and let out a loud scream.

"You've caused me to break my back." She began to cry. Viola sat on the ground beside her.

A long narrow shadow fell over them. Viola looked up and saw Horace wringing his hands. "What happened?" he asked.

"Ida fell and we think she's broken her back."

Before Horace could speak, Ida said,"Fell, hell. You pushed me!"

"Let me stop the hearse before it leaves. Maybe we can take Wilbur and you to the hospital together." Horace rushed over to the crowd, waving his arms.

Ida stayed sprawled on her back. "We gotta get you up," Viola said. She placed her hand under Ida's head. Finally, she was able to pull her in an upright position.

"Look at my arm. I can't move it. It's broken too." With her good arm, Ida lifted it and placed it in her lap. "Don't you ever touch me again, Viola Bentley. Not ever!"

"Now Ida, you know I didn't do it on purpose. I wouldn't ever hurt you. You know that." Ida gritted her teeth and looked in the other direction. "Don't do that, Ida. Look at me. Do I look like somebody that would go around hurting people?" She squatted and placed her arm around Ida. Neither said anything until a couple of men arrived with the boards they had used to lift Wilbur into the hearse.

One of the men walked around surveying Ida. "How we gonna do this?" he asked the other man.

"We'll get the other boards, double them and ask some of the stronger men to assist us."

"Is there room in the hearse?"

"Oh yes, but our problem is getting her over there."

Wilbur had been placed inside the hearse and the crowd had moved over to where Ida sat.

"Wouldn't it be easier to drive the pickup over here and put her on the flatbed?" someone asked.

"Don't you think it's too muddy?"

"Well, it would be easier to get the truck unstuck than take a chance of getting our feet bogged down in this wet ground to where we couldn't move. At least, maybe we could push the truck out if it did get stuck." The man removed his hat and scratched his head. "Then too, what if the boards broke on the way to the hearse?"

"Maybe we should first try it your way.

Hey!" he yelled to a man standing next to the truck. "Drive that pickup truck over here!"

The truck sped over, the tires spinning through mud, tearing up the grass and spewing mud in all directions. It came to a stop just a few feet from Ida.

"Your clothes are wet already, Ida, so why don't you try to lie down and we'll try to slide you on these wide boards and lift you on the truck," one of the men suggested.

Ida groaned and cried out as she tried to move, but with help, she managed to stretch out on the double thick, wide boards. The tailgate to the pickup was lowered and six men heaved and finally lifted her to the flatbed just as the boards began to bend and crack.

"Oh Lord, don't let them drop me!" she prayed.

Chapter 25

𝒟r. Grady was leaving for lunch when the hearse and the pickup truck pulled up at the emergency doors of the hospital. He heard Ida yell.

"Don't leave now, Doctor, you've got two hurt people here!"

Dr. Grady rushed to the pickup and saw Ida grasping its sides and lying all balled up on the flatbed. "What on earth happened to you?" he asked.

"Don't bother with me right now. Go over to the hearse and check on Wilbur," Ida grunted. "He's hurt worse than I am. My pain has sorta eased off." She rolled over. "See?" She moved her arm and wiggled her fingers. "You can look at my back and hip after you check Wilbur out. I'll just stay here on the truck 'til you're finished with him."

"You must be still until I get back to you," the doctor said, and rushed over to the hearse.

Viola had driven up and parked her car next to the truck. Ida was alone. One of the men from the graveside who had agreed to ride in the back of the hearse to the hospital had taken a sheet from the storage box in the vehicle and spread it over Wilbur.

Just before the rear doors of the hearse were opened and the stretcher was pulled out, Wilbur, hearing all the voices outside, managed to pull the sheet over his head.

Mary and Horace arrived and started toward the pickup truck, but Ida waved them on, saying, "I'm fine. Go on over and check on that nephew of yours."

Horace was hurrying to get to the hearse, but Mary lingered, trying to think what she would say to Wilbur.

"Oh, my gosh! He's dead!" She heard a lady say. Mary ran immediately around to the back of the hearse. The stretcher had been pulled partially out. She reached for the sheet and slowly pulled it back. Wilbur's eyes were closed.

"You can't be. You just can't be! I just met you," she whispered and began crying.

Wilbur opened one eye and saw the horrified expression on her face and reached for her hand. Mary screamed, jumped back and covered her mouth. She hesitated for a moment, wiped her eyes with the back of her hand, then took his hand in hers and squeezed it. She wondered why he would display this kind of humor if he were in pain? I'll get to know him, she promised herself.

Dr. Grady held the hospital doors open for the stretcher to enter. "Take him to the room on the right," he ordered.

Mary followed, but was asked to remain in the hall. A nurse closed the door. Mary paused briefly before leaving.

Ida was sitting on the back of the pickup with her feet dangling off the tailgate. A few folks had gathered and were standing close, but backed away when Mary approached.

"Gee, you must be well, sitting up like that," Mary said, helping Ida pull down her dress to cover her knees. "I sure hope I'm sick," Ida said. "I'd hate to feel this way if I'm well."

"Has Dr. Grady seen you?" Mary inquired.

"He stopped by, but and I told him he should go to see about Wilbur. Did you see him? How is he?"

Mary did not respond but kept glancing toward the hospital and wringing her hands. Viola noticed how fidgety she was and said, "Why don't you go back and stay with him? I won't leave your mama until the doctor sees her. He doesn't want her to move until he examines her. Run along, now."

At the hospital doors, Mary looked back and saw Ida trying to get off the truck. "Don't let her do that, Viola," she yelled. Viola waved her on and watched as she went in the hospital's emergency entrance.

"There's no sense in you trying to get off that truck, Ida. Do you wanna hurt yourself worse? Stay up there, or I'll just go and leave you alone," Viola told her.

Ida slowly leaned back, hugging her pocketbook.

"You don't have to clutch that pocketbook like someone's gonna snatch it from you, either," Viola reached for it. "Here. Give it to me. I'll lock it in my car." She took it from Ida.

Ida snatched it back. "How many times do I have

to tell you that no one touches my pocketbook?" Ida asked, raising herself in an upright position.

"Well, you're always complaining that you ain't got no money. Whatcha you got in there? Love letters from Horace?"

"Just tend to your own business."

"Don't fool me. I know enough about you to know that you're sweet on him."

"Me? Sweet on him? I'll swear that I've *never* even been kissed by him."

"Well! Now, ain't that enough to swear about?" Viola said, placing her hands on her hips.

Ida swung her foot to kick her, but missed. She cried out in pain.

"See. If you'd behave, you wouldn't be hurting."

Ida stretched her legs, twisted her body from side to side and raised her arms above her head several times.

"Taking your yearly exercise, I suppose?" Viola asked, stepping back and folding her arms.

Ida lowered herself to the ground and stood straight up. "Look at me. I feel so much better. What about taking me home."

"Don't you want to wait and get Horace to drive you? You might enjoy a ride in the hearse."

"He's too busy with his nephew. Come on," Ida said and started walking toward Viola's car. "I gotta pee, anyway."

"I really think you should wait until after the doctor's seen you."

"To pee?"

"No. For the doctor to examine you before you leave," Viola paused. "Maybe he should check your bladder, also."

"There's nothing wrong with my bladder. I just have to pee."

"As often as you have to go, sometimes I think it's shrunk to the size of your brain."

"Bladder or no bladder, I told you I feel fine. Why pay him all that money for him to just tell me there's nothing wrong with me?"

"I know you've got money, Ida. Everybody knows it. The ...the way you hug that pocketbook of yours all the time, why it's a dead giveaway."

Ida opened her pocketbook. She fumbled around inside. Stretching it wider, she searched frantically. She went back to the truck and dumped everything out on the flatbed and scrambled around in the contents. "Where is it? Where is it?" she kept asking herself.

Viola was curious and asked, "What you looking for Ida?"

"I know I put it in here. I just know I did."

"What, Ida?"

"I had a little white cloth bag stuffed deep down inside this here pocketbook and now I can't find it. You gotta take me home right now, Viola. I must have left it there." She started raking the contents back into her over-stuffed pocketbook. "My Lord! I left the house unlocked, too. We gotta go, Viola. We gotta go right now."

As they drove from the emergency parking grounds, Ida looked through the back window and saw Mary, Horace and the doctor as they stepped outside the building. She watched them until the trees blocked her view.

Chapter 26

Ida had no particular reason to think someone had been in the house when she asked Viola to bring her home from the hospital. As they approached the house she saw all doors were closed. She remembered leaving through the kitchen door after hooking the front screen and pulling the windows down, because of the threaten thunderstorm approaching. She didn't notice the small thin piece of a wood slat on the back porch as she entered. The back screen was ragged. Jeffrey had promised several times to replace it but never seem to find time to do so.

Ida was still in the bedroom searching for the small cloth bag when she heard Viola call out, "Ida, did you see this here little slat that looks like it might have been torn from the kitchen door?" While waiting for a reply, Viola noticed a date written on the dark side of it when she turned it over.

"I'm not interested in that right now. I'm still looking for the cloth bag. I'll be there in a minute."

Viola tossed the strip of wood on the pump shelf

and entered the kitchen. Standing in the doorway, she watched Ida searching for the bag. "Could I help you look for it, Ida?" she asked.

"No. I doubt that you could find it any better than I can."

"Did you look in the chiffarobe?"

"I wouldn't have put it in there. Why would I put it there?"

"Well, if you know where you didn't put it, why can't you find it, then?"

"I know what I'm doing, Viola," Ida snapped.

"Well. You just look for it all by yourself." Viola went to the back porch, slamming the screen door behind her. She waited several minutes for Ida, but when she didn't come, she stuck her head inside and yelled, "I'm going home since you don't need me. I'll see you later this week."

"Wait a minute. Wait a minute," Ida said as she hobbled to the porch, holding her hand on her back. She eased herself down on the bench. "I can't imagine what I did with it. I'm getting so forgetful, Viola."

"It happens to all of us. If it's all that important, just give it a day or two and you'll remember."

Ida leaned toward Viola and whispered as if someone else was around. "It's the money, Viola. It's the money. Now, can't you see how anxious I am to find it?" She pulled her lace handkerchief from her wet, muddy Sunday dress pocket and mopped her brow. "It's the money I had hidden away in the cradle mattress. And they were big bills, too. What could I have done with that bag?"

The sound of the hearse door slamming perked

Ida up a bit. She struggled to get up. Holding her hand to her hip, she rushed to the front of the house and got there just in time to hear Mary thank Horace for bringing her home. Before she could get the front door unlocked and holler to Horace, he was driving off.

Viola saw Mary wave at Horace as she rounded the house. She walked over to Viola's car. "You aren't leaving, are you?"

"Now that you are here to be with Ida, I'll just go on. I've gotta get out of these wet cloths and do a few chores when I get home. Ida seems to be upset. See if you can help her find something she's looking for." She suggested to Mary, "See you, maybe tomorrow."

"Why did you and Ida leave the hospital? Dr. Grady was concerned."

"Oh. You know how Ida is. Sometimes I think she only craves attention. She's all right. Doesn't seem to be in any pain." Viola cranked her car, waved, and drove off.

As Mary was about to enter the kitchen, Ida returned to the porch. "Did you by chance see a small cloth bag anywhere before you left for the church?" she asked Mary.

"I noticed something on the hall table when Jeffrey and I went to the porch to wait for you. I didn't pay much attention, though. Jeffrey picked it up and asked what it could be and I told him something like, maybe it's recipes you had collected or something of that sort, since you're always clipping things out of the paper." Mary didn't seem too interested. "Did you see all those strangers at the funeral? Who in the world could they have been?" she asked.

"I'm not concerned about the strangers at the funeral. I'm only interested in the money I had in the cloth bag."

"You had money in that bag and left it on the table? Why did you do that, Ida? You never lock the house, you know."

"Since Jeffrey didn't stay for the funeral, you don't suppose..."

"Jeffrey wouldn't do anything like that. You know that."

"I've told you all along that I didn't trust that boy."

"Now, just don't start jumping to conclusions until we've made a complete search of this house. You know how you misplace things."

Mary held the door open and the planks in the porch squeaked as Ida stepped on the threshold and into the kitchen.

"Isn't this one of the slats from the cradle, Ida? I thought you put all that away." She turned the slat over and read the date. "What's the date written on it? Does it mean anything?"

Ida stepped to the back porch from the kitchen, took the slat from Mary and went back to the kitchen without giving her an answer.

Mary followed and they sat down at the table. Ida said, "You know, folks in this community have more curiosity than they have sense. I've never heard Viola say a word that she didn't have a question somewhere in her talking." Ida heard a door slam and looked out the window. A man got out of the car.

Mary knew that she must have recognized the man when the color left Ida's face and her hand went to her mouth and she gasped for breath. Mary rushed around the table to her. "Are you all right, Ida?"

Ida rose, staggered, and balanced herself by holding to the table. Mary helped her to a cane bottomed chair and heard the cane crack as she dropped into it. They heard someone step heavily on the front porch as Mary reached for a cloth to wipe Ida's face. "Someone's at the front door. Are you all right?" Before Ida could answer, Mary wadded the cloth and dropped it in her lap and started to the door.

"Wait a minute," Ida whispered. "Let me gain my composure and I'll go to the door." Mary hesitated.
"I'm sure it's somebody who wants to see me. I'll be all right in a minute. Don't bother to go, I'll go. Here. Give me your hand."

Ida strained and pulled on Mary until she get got on her feet. She steadied herself and walked slowly to the front door without looking back to see if Mary was following. She didn't bother to unlatch the screen door, only gazed at a man whose name she couldn't recall.

CHAPTER 27

He was no ordinary-looking man. Ida had liked his appearance and made no bones about it when she had first met him. She had often bragged of his good looks to others when they asked about her new friend. But that had been years ago. Looking through the screen, he seemed larger than she remembered. The hair on his robust chest didn't show through his shirt as it once had. She remembered it being blacker than the hood of hair that once covered his now receded hairline.

She thought his face had changed, but Ida caught a glimpse of that youthful smile that once captivated her. There was no shadow of his black beard. Maybe it is now gray. She thought with a fresh shave there wouldn't be a trace of it, anyway. His face had changed from that manly look to one of wrinkled baby skin.

Ida couldn't keep her eyes off his large belly. Once a giant of a man, he didn't look as tall. How could he have gotten so large, she wondered. But then, how could she have gotten so large?

She unlatched the screen, pushed Mary slightly away with her arm and asked,"Would you like to come in?"

Neither said anything until Ida led them into the parlor. She motioned Rufus toward a chair and when he started to sit in the one with the sagging bottom, she said, "No, sit over there. That's the one I sit in."
Ida liked that chair. It gave her a good view of anyone who might be visiting.

She watched him fumble with his hat before he eased himself down on one end of the mohair settee. He glanced shyly at her, "I'd like to talk to you in private," he said, not looking at Mary. Mary didn't wait to be asked, but turned and left the room.

Rufus stood and said, "Come sit by me on the settee, Ida."

Ida placed her hands on the arms of her chair and struggled to pull herself up. Rufus went to assist her. "Oh, I'm all right", she said. "It's just that this chair is built a little too close to the floor."

Rufus lowered himself back on the settee and Ida sat down next to him. He reached for her hand. She withdrew it.

"Ida, remember 1922--?" he began.

"That's a strange question. Of course I remember." She stared straight ahead.

"That year has haunted me for a dozen years now."

Ida turned away from him and rubbed her forehead.

"Ida. Look at me." He took her hand and again

she pulled away. "Don't turn away."

She heard a noise and glanced toward the door. Mary's shadow fell across the hall floor. Ida got up and the shadow disappeared as she neared the door to close it. When she sat again in her chair, Rufus came and knelt beside her. He took her hand in his once more. This time she let it stay. She gazed into his eyes and saw a tear trickle down the side of his nose. "Are you not well, Rufus?"

"Oh, yes. I'm fine. I'm not physically sick. I guess it's-- it's a broken heart that has a hold on me."

Ida tried to laugh, but read instead the serious look on his face. Is he trying to tell me something that he has denied for so many years? she wondered. Did she want him to admit he was a rascal to have left her so abruptly, alone, with no one to whom she could turn when she so desperately needed someone to help straighten things out in her life?

"Rufus. Before we get into a serious discussion, I want you to know that I do not want to begin things all over again." She stared out the side window, overlooking the barn. She saw a rooster chasing her prize laying hen. She didn't look at Rufus. "Oh yes, I suddenly feel an awakening within my soul about you, but that's over." Ida swallowed hard. Her breath came short and her heart beat rapidly.

On his knees in front of her, holding her hand, Rufus felt her trembling. "I didn't come to begin our relationship again, I only came to tell you--."

Ida heard a crash in the hall and saw slivers of broken glass slide under the closed door. She knew that Mary, so eager to hear what was going on, must have stumbled and knocked from the hall rack the porcelain vase Ida's mother had left her in her will.

Rufus struggled to get to his feet. Grabbing Ida's chair, he pulled her forward. Ida pushed against him and saw him grasp his chest as he fell over backwards. All the color left his face. Her scream brought Mary suddenly rushing into the room. "What in the world has happened? Is he all right? Do I need to call a doctor?" In a panic she stooped beside Ida who was trying to take his pulse.

"I don't think it's necessary. I think the man's too far gone, already. Here. You feel for his pulse."

Mary put her ear to his chest. Unable to hear a heart beat, she felt for his pulse. His lips had turned purple and she felt the dampness on his face. "This man is dying. Who is he?"

"Never mind who he is. Run down to the store and call the doctor. No! Wait. Go call the funeral home. Ask Horace to come."

"What am I going to tell him? That some strange man has died in your parlor?" Mary backed toward the door.

"Don't tell him nothing. Just ask him to git out here."

"Shouldn't I ask that he bring the hearse?"

"You know he'll drive the hearse. He don't have nothing else to drive. Hurry. Run along." Ida shoved her away.

Assured that Mary was out of the yard, she struggled to roll Rufus over on his side. Ida pulled his wallet from his pocket, whispering to herself, "Maybe I can find out something about him." She opened his wallet and a picture fell out. She couldn't tell much about the woman's appearance, other than she was a buxom woman dressed in a wedding gown that must have taken a hundred yards of cloth to make. Most of it billowed from below her waist. It was skimpy at the top with half of her breasts exposed.

She stuck back a few notes of scrap paper in his wallet after looking at them. On a piece torn from a brown paper bag, she read her name and address. In a different handwriting, the words "One day I'll look her up" were written on the back. There was a Tennessee driver's license and a receipt from a funeral home for six hundred fifty dollars.

Ida glanced at Rufus' face. Both eyes stared at her. Quickly she stuffed the rest of the contents back in the wallet, rolled him over on his back and felt his neck, cheeks and forehead, then laid her head on his chest. Again, no heart beat. With her index finger she closed his eyes.

From his shirt pocket she pulled out a letter, unfolded it and began to read.

Mary quickly entered the room. "What's that?" she asked.

"Oh, just a scrap of paper. I've tried to find something that would have some kind of identification on it. He's dead, Mary. Is Horace coming?"

"No. He can't. He's sending Carless."

"That hateful man? I told you to have Horace come out."

"Horace is tied up with a family making funeral arrangements."

"Did you tell him we have a dead man out here in

our parlor?"

"No, because I didn't know he was really dead." She offered her hand to help Ida get to her feet. In secret, Ida stuck the letter next to her bosom and rushed off to the kitchen, slamming the parlor door.

"You don't think I'm gonna stay in here with a dead stranger all by myself, do you?" Mary yelled as she jerked the door open.

So determined to read the letter alone, Ida rushed into the kitchen and closed the door behind her and bolted it.

"Why are you doing that?" Mary called as she knocked on the kitchen door.

"I want to be alone," Ida yelled from behind the closed door. She pulled the letter from inside her dress and slowly unfolded it, careful not to make a sound. She heard Mary walk away and she peeped through the window when she heard the back screen door slam. Ida sat at the table and began to read.

April 3, 1939

Dear Sir:

I do not know how to greet you as I write this. For weeks I have tried to get my thoughts in a letter to you but find myself struggling with the right approach. I know of no other way than just being straightforward.

A few months ago I ran across some papers in my father's law office and discovered adoption papers which bore your name and address. I questioned my parents and they admitted that I was adopted. They tried to talk me out of writing you, but finally gave me permission. There are a few questions I want to ask you. Will you meet with me?

Being the only child, I feel a need to search out my real parents before going out in this world on my own. Please arrange a convenient time for us to meet and write me.

Sincerely,
Adam Millbrook

On tiptoe, Ida returned to the parlor and cautiously slipped the letter back into Rufus' shirt pocket. She wanted to search further, but heard the hearse pull up in the yard. She wondered why the driver didn't pull around to the back. Quickly she brushed the wrinkles from Rufus' clothes and folded his arms across his chest. She grunted as she rose from her squatting position.

She heard the engine stop. She decided she wanted to keep the letter, so she removed it and stuck it in her bosom then rushed down the hall to the front door.

Passing the hall table, she bumped her thigh on its corner and saw the cloth money bag dislodge from its hiding place and drop to the floor. She was hurting, but managed to pick up the bag and held it with her teeth while she lifted her skirt to check for bruises.

Chapter 28

*I*da heard the engine start up and saw the hearse moving to the rear of the house. She hobbled through the parlor toward the back, stopping again to look at her thigh before she greeted Carless. She saw him carefully stepping around the rotten planks in the floor as he crossed to the door. Although Carless could see Ida through the screen, he knocked on the door facing and waited to be invited in. Ida lowered her skirt and tossed the cloth bag behind the settee.

Smoothing out the wrinkles in her skirt, she stepped outside the door. She leaned against a support post after greeting Carless. She peeped around. She abruptly asked, "Why didn't Horace come?"

"It's good to see you again, Mrs. Ridley."

"Huh!" she snarled."Why didn't Horace come, I asked?"

"He'll be out shortly. He's busy with some folks right now. He told me to come ahead. He'll come later".

"Later? We need him now!" Ida said in her usual

domineering voice. She limped over to the pump shelf, and in disgust, slapped it with the palm of her hand. Pausing for a moment, she gazed out across the garden. She remembered how long she had to wait for someone to come when Seth lay unconscious across the bean row. No one ever seemed available when she needed them. The last words Seth had said to her were muddled, but those she understood were still ringing in her ear. She mumbled quietly while cursing Mary and Jeffrey under her breath.

"Are you all right, Mrs. Ridley?" Carless asked.

She swirled abruptly toward Carless and ripped out the hem of her dress on a nail protruding from the side of the pump shelf. "Why can't people be around when you need them?" She lifted her sagging skirt and Carless turned his head. "Mary! Mary! Where are you? We need Horace, right now!" she cried out.

The assistant undertaker asked, "The man ain't dead, is he?" almost shouting so he could be heard above Ida.

"You don't have to yell," Ida shouted.

Carless lowered his voice. "Well, anyway, Horace ain't coming right now. If the man's dead, I'll move him. If he ain't ..., we'll keep him comfortable until we can get a doctor out here."

Carless opened the parlor door and waited for Ida to enter.

"If you're not going inside, close the door so the flies won't go in," Ida ordered.

Her harsh demand caused Carless to soften his voice and said, "Please, Mrs. Ridley, you first." He waited and she proceeded to the parlor. He followed.

Rufus was lying on his back, stretched out in front of the settee, his eyes closed and his hands crossed over his chest. Carless nudged him with his foot. His body slightly shook.

"This man is dead. What happened to him?"

"What's the matter with you? Ain't you got any respect for the dead? Why did you kick him?" Ida asked, avoiding the man's question.

"Kick him? I didn't kick him. Just wanted to see if there was life in him."

"At least you could have leaned over and shook him. You're not so tall that it would have bothered you." Ida said.

"I bet you have more trouble bending over than I do." His tone was sarcastic. Ida sucked in her stomach.

Immediately, Mary entered the parlor through the front door.

"What took you so long? The hearse has been here..."

"He is dead?" Mary exclamed.

"I asked you what took you so long to get back? I bet you had to meet Jeffrey somewhere, didn't you? Or was he at the store? He's always hanging around there waiting for some gal to go in there."

Mary didn't bother to answer. She looked at the ash gray face of the man. "Who is he? What happened to him?"

"I have no idea who he is and no idea where he came from. All I know is ... he's dead."

"You'd better have a better answer than that when the coroner begins asking questions."

Ida thought Mary's warning was rather stern. "I'm

able to take care of myself," she snapped.

"Well, Jeffrey called the doctor and the sheriff. Dr. Grady is to call the coroner and all of them will be out right away. The doctor said if the man is dead, the coroner wouldn't want us to touch anything until they get out here."

Ida grabbed at her chest and heard paper crunch. She left the room.

Mary looked at Carless, then at the man lying on the floor. "He had to have a heart attack. He looked perfectly healthy when he arrived," Mary said.

"I heard you ask your mother who he was and she ignored you. Do you know who he is?"

"I have no idea," she said. "He just showed up here after we got home from the funeral."

Suddenly, Mary spotted the cloth money bag that Ida had dropped when she bumped her thigh. There it lay, right in plain view, on the floor at the end of the settee. "Thank goodness! Jeffrey didn't take it," she whispered to herself.

"What did you say?" Carless asked.

"Oh, nothing," she said nonchalantly while picking up the bag. "I'll be back in a moment." As she left to look for Ida, she thought it was strange that Carless should close the door behind her.

As Mary entered the kitchen, Ida was trying to smooth out the corner of the worn linoleum rug which protruded from behind the wood cook stove.

"Here's your money."

Surprised that Mary had been watching, Ida went over and snatched the bag from her. "I had already found it. I'm gonna count it to make sure all of it is here."

She untied the drawstrings and pulled out a fistful of large denomination bills. Mary blinked hard as her eyes grew big.

Ida sat down at the table, pressing out the money and began sorting it in individual piles.

Mary watched in amazement. "Can't you wait and do that later? There's a dead man up front in our parlor."

"There's not a thing we can do until they get ready to move him. Just go on back and stay with Carless. I'll be there in a minute," Ida said, her eyes following Mary to the door. "Go on, go on," she urged. Mary left, pulling the door shut behind her.

Ida was so engrossed in counting her money she didn't hear the sheriff and coroner arrive. She heard someone talking, but thought it was Mary and Carless and continued sorting the bills. Hearing someone clear their throat, Ida looked up and saw the two men standing just inside the kitchen. Mary was behind them, watching as Ida swooped up the cash, crumpled it in her hands and poked it deep inside her dress pocket.

The men looked at each other.

"Miz Ridley, we would like to talk to you a moment."

"Sure, gentlemen. Have a seat." Ida pointed to the chairs at the table opposite her. She didn't bother to get up.

"No. We'll just stand."

Ida stood, pushed the chair back with her hips and it toppled over. The coroner picked it up and set it against the wall. Ida pulled it back and placed it at the table and sat back down. "What's your problem, gentlemen?"

Chapter 29

"We need to ask you a few questions, Mrs. Ridley," the coroner said.

Ida got up and placed the chair back against the wall and walked over to the sink. She didn't look at the two men as she fumbled and rattled the leftover dirty dishes while shifting them. "I'll be glad to answer any questions you might have, Gentlemen"

"Can you tell us anything about the man lying on your floor in the parlor?" the coroner asked.

Without turning from the sink Ida said, "All I can say is, he showed up here right after me and Mary got back from the funeral." Glancing at Mary, she continued, "He just showed up on our porch, didn't he, Mary? And we invited him in. He said he wanted to talk to me in private about something."

"Ah-ha. In private, huh?" the coroner asked.

Ida didn't like the tone of his voice and became nervous. "There's no mystery about his being here. I've had unknown men to call on me before," her voice sounded boastful, "but believe me, I've never had one to die right here before my eyes."

"Then you were with him when he died?"

"Oh, yes. He was right there in front of me. He just keeled over. I didn't know what to do. I yelled for my daughter Mary, didn't I, Mary?" Ida was pleading, nodding her head for Mary to confirm her statement. "I had her to rush off to call Dr. Grady, here," waving her hand in the direction of the doctor, "'cause I didn't know what else to do."

Remembering she had searched the man before Mary returned and advised her that the victim should not be touched until the investigators arrived, she rushed to say, "I only took him by the shoulders after he fell and shook him real hard. I shook and shook, but I didn't get any kind of response." She kept chattering. "Now ain't that strange? There he lay, motionless and I couldn't get a word from him."

"He came to your house, and you have no idea why he came, but you invited him in, and he didn't mention the reason for coming?" the coroner asked.

"That's exactly right, isn't it, Mary?"

Mary didn't respond to her question and Ida figured she didn't want to support her story. "Well, ain't that right Mary?" she asked again, sounding agitated. Still, Mary didn't answer.

Dr. Grady backed up and leaned against the kitchen counter. The coroner stepped toward Mary.

"What's your version? Did you have a chance to talk to the man?" he asked her.

"No, sir, I did not. I was asked to leave the room

so I came to the kitchen and..."

Ida realized that Mary was not coming to her rescue, and harshly interrupted, "For once she did what she was asked to do." She stared at her until Mary turned her head.

The coroner, still looking at Mary asked, "How were you asked to leave them alone?"

"I didn't have to be asked. I could tell by their look that I shouldn't be in on the conversation, so I just left."

"Was there anything said to make you believe the two might have known one another?"

Ida interrupted the coroner. "Are you doubting me, sir?" Ida asked, angrily.

"No. This is just preliminary questioning."

Ida jerked a chair and placed it at the table and sat down again. Putting her hand in her dress pocket, she felt the money. She clutched it and heard it crunch. She needed support, even if she couldn't expect Mary to help her feel secure. She had the money and it felt good. She kept her eyes on her stepdaughter, waiting for her to answer the coroner's question.

Mary stammered, "My goodness, I... I can't remember what was actually said. I became so terribly upset when I went into the room and saw the poor old man stretched out on the floor. Why, I... I...I couldn't have told you my name at that time."

The door suddenly opened and Horace asked the coroner if he could move the corpse.

"Give us a few more minutes, if you don't mind waiting," he replied.

Ida pushed against the table as she pulled herself

up from her chair. "Oh, you did come," she said as she smiled and started toward Horace. He backed from the door and stepped out on the porch. Mary followed and closed the door behind her. Ida was left standing alone with the doctor and coroner.

"Miz Ridley, what do you think killed the man?"

"How would I know? You're the coroner. If... if you can't determine how he died, the undertaker is here so why don't you ask him? Horace! Come here," she yelled. "He knows more about dead folks than all of you put together."

The coroner stuck his head out the door and said, "Never mind. I'll talk to you later"

"I'll leave you two alone," the doctor said. "I'll be in the parlor."

Ida started to follow the doctor out. "Wait a moment, Miz Ridley," the coroner said. "There's a few more questions I would like to ask you."

"I've given you all the information I know. I think you're just here to stir up trouble. Furthermore, I have company here that I've gotta see." She abruptly left the coroner standing in the kitchen.

From the porch she saw Mary, Dr. Grady and Horace as they stood by the hearse under the shade tree, whispering quietly to one another. Wanting to hear their conversation, she smiled again at Horace and moved toward them. She glanced back and saw the coroner on the porch. He was waving the doctor toward him. Horace too, moved toward the coroner, leaving Ida and Mary alone. Ida placed her hands on her big hips and took a deep breath when Horace turned away.

"What were ya'll talking 'bout?" Ida asked Mary.

"They're really concerned about the identity of that man in there. If you know anything at all about him, Ida, anything, I think you'd better let them know."

"I've told them I don't know anything about him. When you don't know anything, what can you tell 'em?"

The screen door slammed. Ida saw Carless as he joined the men and said something to them. They followed the undertaker assistant toward the parlor.

Ida rushed to the porch in time to hear Carless tell them about some papers he had found in the man's clothing. Ida stepped back as Mary held the door open for her, but she refused to go in. Mary shrugged her shoulders and entered, pulling the door closed behind her.

Ida put her arm on her forehead and leaned against the dusty, paint-chipped wall.

Chapter 30

The coroner removed all the contents from the dead man's wallet. He counted the few dollars which were folded neatly and tucked separately away from the other items. Everything was examined and placed in an envelope. Sealing it, he put it inside his wrinkled suit coat pocket. "I'll take care of this, gentlemen," he said, and left the room.

He saw Ida leaning against the wall and he paused for a moment. "Are you worried, Mrs. Ridley?"

Not moving from her position, she asked, "Am I worried? Of course, I'm worried. What if some stranger died in your parlor, and suppose it was a woman? Wouldn't you be worried?

"Well, all I can say is, don't worry right now. If everything checks out with the sheriff and the doctor, there'll be nothing to fret over."

Ida straightened and pulled at her gathered skirt, looking at the torn hem. She didn't look at the coroner.

"On the other hand," he said, "if things are at all suspicious, according to their investigation, we'll have to take you in."

"What ye' mean,'take me in'?" she asked, glaring at him.

"Have you ever heard of jail, Mrs. Ridley?"

Her eyes grew big and her mouth begin to twitch. "Of course I've heard of a jail. But you don't think you're gonna take me there, do you? I don't think you will," her voice sounded like a threat. She shoved past the coroner.

She jerked the parlor door open just as the men began placing the body on the stretcher. She stepped inside and held the door open for them to pass. She was glad they had covered Rufus with a sheet because she never wanted to see his face again. Somehow, seeing him covered completely dispelled her fear of being jailed. She couldn't explain, but surprisingly she felt elated.

Ida watched Mary wringing her hands and moving about, straightening the crocheted small spread on the back of the chairs. Although Ida kept her distance, she saw Mary stoop and quickly pick up a small piece of paper after the three men lifted the stretcher. She saw her tuck it safely into her dress.

The men carefully maneuvered the stretcher through the door. Ida blocked Mary's exit by closing it after the others were outside on the back porch. "What's that piece of paper you picked up when the stretcher was moved?" she asked Mary.

"Oh, it's nothing."

"Then, may I see it?"

"Well, it doesn't belong to you." Mary said and left the room through the hall. She didn't see Ida watching as she removed the paper from inside her dress and began to read. Recognizing a date, she read aloud, "February 3, 1922". Suddenly, she turned to go back into the parlor, but there was Ida standing behind her. They stood facing one another, staring deeply into one another's eyes. Ida, for the first time in years, felt her stamina drain from her.

"It's the same date that's written on the slat from the cradle, isn't it?" Mary asked. She saw an expression on Ida's face she had never seen before, a look of hurt and bewilderment. Ida lowered her head and buried her face in her hands. Mary walked toward her with arms outstretched and wrapped them around her. She felt Ida's heart throbbing.

"Oh, Mary, Mary," Ida cried.

"Its alright, Ida. Its alright" Mary led her down the hall to the kitchen. They heard the men talking in the porch but ignored them and closed the door.

From beneath the linoleum rug, behind the wood cook stove, Ida removed the letter that she had taken from Rufus's pocket and handed it to Mary. "Let's go to the bedroom," Ida suggested.

Mary sat on the foot of the bed. "Are you sure you want me to read this?"

"Why not?" she said, "I can't go on holding this back any longer. I need release from all this, Mary. Please try to understand." She threw herself on the bed and began to cry. "What should I do, Mary?"

Mary's eyes passed quickly over the letter. Finishing it, she did not speak, but instead laid down beside Ida. Her washed-out honey blonde hair fell around her face. Finally, she raised her head and looked up. Ida's face was white and had taken on a look of calmness. There was no coldness, but a warm stare. "Let's call Horace," Mary suggested, "and tell him what has happened."

"I can't tell Horace. I just can't."

"Then, what about Dr. Grady?"

"Oh, how I wish Viola was here. She's the only one who would understand."

"Then you don't want to tell the doctor?" Mary waited for answer.

Ida got from the bed and walked to the window overlooking the porch and the field. Full sunlight was streaming in below the ash-gray scattered clouds overhead.

Mary heard her muttering something inaudible.

"What are you saying, Ida?"

Ida turned her back to the window and faced Mary. She continued to cry. "I've got to somehow. . . I've got to get this all straightened out. I can't keep shoving it deeper and deeper in the back of my mind." She dried her eyes with the hem of her torn dress. Not looking at Mary, she said, "I'm beginning to understand how Rufus must have been feeling to have driven from Tennessee to see me."

Mary walked over and again put her arms around her, this time resting her head against Ida's. "Do you want to tell me about him?"

"If I'm gonna confess, we might as well tell the others."

"Would you like for me to ask them in?" Mary

whispered softly.

Ida said only, "Yes." She lifted her head from Mary's shoulder and saw the full sunlight caressing her face. As they stood by the window, she took Mary's head in both hands and saw her long curling lashes were holding tears and reflecting light. They released one another and Mary turned to leave.

"Wait," Ida said. "Maybe, after all, you and I should discuss it before asking the others in."

Mary paused. "We'll do whatever you think is best," she said, "and I'll help in any way I can."

"Mrs. Ridley," a voice called out.

Ida and Mary went to the door. Just as Ida opened the door, they stood face to face with the coroner. "Dr. Grady thinks from the signs he saw, the man might have had a heart attack. Don't think there's any need for you to worry. The doctor had to leave, but said he would talk to you later should you have questions. We'll be going on now."

Ida sucked in a deep breath of air and her shoulders dropped as she let out a sigh. The coroner tipped his hat and went to his car.

Mary tightened her arm around Ida's waist. "Together, we'll work things out. I do love you, Ida, and I promise I will help you in any way that I can. Please know that."

Ida kissed her on the cheek.

They slowly descended the back steps and went to the driver's side of the hearse just as Horace turned the ignition on. A billow of raven-black smoke spread over the ground and spewed from beneath the vehicle. Ida held her breath until the smoke floated away then placed her arms in the rolled down window and stood gravely silent for a moment.

"Ida, you've been crying," Horace said as he touched her on the arm. She wanted to hug him, but instead, she placed her hand on his shoulder.

"I need to talk to you, Horace," she whispered.

"I can't, right now."

"Can we make it soon, sometime today? It's very important."

"Well, let me see. If there's no one at the funeral home to see me, maybe I can run back out here while Carless is trying to contact someone in the man's family. He was from Tennessee." Horace scratched his balding head and thought for a minute. "May have to put the final preparation of the body off for a few days, but there's things we must do right away to prepare it." He paused. Ida waited.

"If I can't get right back out here, I'll come as soon as I can."

"Please. As soon as you can, then," she said, happy that Horace was willing to see her. Smiling, she patted him on the shoulder.

Before backing away, she glanced at the covered form in the back of the hearse. Maybe I should let all our secrets be buried with him, she thought. Had she gone too far, having told Mary, and now on the verge of telling Horace? What would his reaction be? "If I had only waited a little longer," she said aloud as the hearse began to move away.

The engine of Dr. Grady's car started up and began following the hearse out of the yard. The doctor yelled at Ida and said, "If you need a sedative, just send

Mary for it."

Above the roaring motors, Ida yelled, "Wait. Wait. Will you do me a favor, doc?. Stop by Viola's house when passing and ask her to come out to see me. It's rather important," her voice getting louder. "Do you mind doing this for me?"

Dr. Grady drove away, nodding and waving as he entered the dusty road.

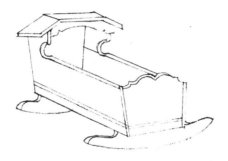

Chapter 31

Ida agonized about the letter she had removed from Rufus' pocket as she began to undress. She pulled her Sunday dress over her head and threw it on the heap of clothes already piling up on the bed. Seldom did she hang anything up. Pushing the pile aside, she sat on the edge of the bed to take off her shoes and stockings. She struggled to untie the knot in the elastic garters that were cording her legs. "I've got to make them larger one of these days," she said aloud. She picked up her dress.

The hemline was sagging more and more. Examining it, she began looking for a needle and matching thread to stitch it. Not finding either, she said, "I'll sew it up tomorrow," and flung it on the bed.

Mary was standing in the doorway and asked, "What did you say, Ida?"

"Oh, nothing."

"Well, Horace is here to see you."

Surprised to hear that he was back so soon, Ida pulled another frock from the chiffrobe. Tossing it aside, she chose a more colorful one. She glanced at the door, but Mary had left. She pulled a dress from the hanger. "I bet he'd like this one," she said, holding it in front of her. She turned toward the wall mirror, sniffed under the sleeves, then pulled it over her head. Most of the wrinkles smoothed out when she tugged to get it down over her large hips. Forcing her feet in the shoes, she didn't bother to put on her stockings. She rushed from the bedroom, slamming the door behind her.

Mary and Horace were talking on the back porch as she approached. She smiled and said, "Glad you could come back, Horace. Come on into the parlor." Mary held the door open for them to enter, then left for the kitchen.

Without asking Horace to be seated, Ida just motioned to a chair, then took a seat opposite on the settee. The room was silent for sometime before Ida finally said, "Please don't let this come as a surprise to you, Horace, but there are a few things I would like to discuss with you." She fidgeted and her voice trembled, but she managed to say, "I know Seth hasn't been dead very long, and now that your brother is gone, I was wondering," Ida swallowed hard and continued, "I wonder if you might need some help at the funeral home?" She paused.

Horace shifted to a more comfortable position and picked up the pillow on the end of the settee and placed it in his lap. The muscles in his neck twitched and he cleared his throat. Before he had a chance to speak, Ida said, "I know it's rather sudden, my springing this on you, but I just thought there might be a possibility that you could use some part-time help over there. You'd be surprised how much I could help."

Horace was so long responding, she thought he must not be interested. She began to feel embarrassed and was about to change the subject when he said, "I have thought about asking if you might be willing to help out when things got really busy. There's lot of things you could do to improve our services. We've always needed a woman's touch in so many things. Brother was good at such things, but..."

Ida interrupted. "Good. I'll be glad to volunteer whenever you need me." She went quickly over and sat beside him. "I'd love to help you." The idea of being with him everyday excited her.

"Another thing," she said as she moved to the edge of her seat. "If you're interested in remodeling your building, I have some extra money I would like to put into the business."

"You have a little money you'd like to invest in the business?"

"Yes. I've been saving for some time. Seth's sickness wasn't a lengthy one, so we didn't have to spend it for medical bills. I've been able to hold on to it."

Horace walked over to the window. "I couldn't expect you to use your money that way."

"Well, you know money's no good unless you spend it, or invest it."

"You're very generous, Ida, but I couldn't use your money." He left the window and walked around the room. "Is that what you wanted me to come back out here for, to tell me you would like to invest in the funeral business?" He returned to the window. The golden light of sunset reflected on the metal roof of the barn. "If so, that's nice, but I couldn't let you do that. However, I would like to have you come work with me."

He sat down on the settee, again this time closer to her and reached for her hand. "You're a nice woman Ida, and I wouldn't do or say a thing that would hurt you. But, there is one matter, however, I consider rather serious and I want to ask you about it."

She thought he appeared nervous so she smiled at him to set him at ease. She jokingly said, "Oh, my goodness. As open as we've always been? I can't imagine what could be so serious. What in the world could it be, Horace?"

He began to stutter. "Car...Carless found a rather important letter in a pocket of Rufus Cortly. He's the man we carried from here to the funeral home."

"His last name was Cortly? I could not, for the life of me, remember his last name." She had grown accustomed to it and did not flinch when it was mentioned.

"Then, you did know him?"

Ida rose and moved over to the what-not and fumbled with the small figurines. "Yes. He introduced himself when he arrived, but I couldn't remember his last name."

She watched Horace and raised her eyebrows as he reached inside his coat pocket, pulled out a letter and unfolded it.

"It's addressed to an Adam Millbrook." Horace

separated the sheets, his eyes quickly scanning each page. "It mentions in here an Ida Stacy as being Adam's mother. We read the letter several times and decided that you might know something about this man. Carless and I thought it was strange that Mr. Cortly should die at your house."

"What did the letter say?" she asked, reaching out her hand. "May I read it?"

Horace said, while holding the letter in front of her, "Adam Millbrook's address was the only lead we had, so Carless and I got in touch with him by telephone and explained the letter. He wanted us to read it to him."

"Adam Millbrook?" Ida asked.

"Yes. From what we were able to piece together from the letter, it seems that he was a son of..."

Ida interrupted again. "What did his son say on the phone?" She stood quietly for a few moments, wondering if she should lie to him. And, if she did, and later he learned the truth, then what?

"After we explained the reason for our call, he was surprised, of course, that his father was dead and wanted to know what happened. He said he had just learned about his adoption and had written a letter to the man a couple weeks earlier, but hadn't heard anything." Horace observed Ida's uneasiness and moved toward her. "This letter, which looks like the original, apparently was never mailed to the boy. I say boy, because, when I talked to him, he sounded so young."

Ida laughed but couldn't keep back the blood that flushed her face and brow. "How can you tell by talking to someone on the phone that they're young?"

"There were other little clues that led me to

believe that he was quite young."

"How old would you say?"

"Oh, maybe in his mid-teens."

She pleasantly asked, "Are you gonna let me see the letter?"

"Sure." Horace said, and handed it to her.

Her hands were shaking as she reached for the letter. She sat down in her favorite chair and begin to read. She turned slightly and rested her hands on the arm of the chair to steady them and to cover up her nervousness.

The letter was long and in detail. It did indeed name Ida Stacey as the boy's mother. She slowly read it again, trying to absorb every word and memorize some of the lines. She tried to reason with herself that Rufus must have brought the letter for her to read before mailing it. For years she had tried not to think of herself as a mother.

Horace waited.

She read it over again. Horace saw tears in her eyes, and asked, "Are you all right, Ida?"

Chapter 32

Viola stepped from her car, rubbed the wrinkles from her dress before slamming the car door and heading for the back door of the parlor.

"Didn't expect you so soon," Ida yelled from the porch steps, "but I'm glad you're here. Horace just left. Come on in. It's a little warm in the parlor, but we'll be able to talk in secret."

"I declare, Ida, you have more secrets than Carter has liver pills."

Ida held the door open for her and before they sat down, Ida said, "Guess what?" as she reached out to hug Viola. "Horace has asked me to assist him at the funeral home. I'm so excited I just had to let you be the first to know. I gotta thank Doctor Grady for stopping by to tell you to come out to see me. Thank you for coming, my friend." She released Viola, holding her at arm's length. "When he told you, did he make it sound important that you should come out?"

Viola pushed back the loose graying strands of hair from her face and tucked them under a hair pin. "He only said that you wanted to talk to me and I should come out right away," she said, as she moved toward the settee and sat down. She kicked off her shoes, threw her feet across the cushions and pulled the pillow toward her with her toes.

"I'm so excited Viola. Why, I'm just beside myself."

"What brought all that about?"

"He needed a woman's touch in his business. Said his brother applied all the makeup on the bodies and he thought I could do that. My! Do you think I'll ever be able to do anything like that...touching all those dead folks?"

"Well, it depends," Viola said.

"What do you mean 'it depends'?"

"Whether the body is a man or a woman. It could be fun, you know."

"Oh, quit it, Viola." Ida started laughing softly as Viola snickered like a little girl.

"Who knows? They just might bring a man in here shortly after he dies and he might still be warm. I'd love to be a fly on the wall watching to see how you would handle a man's warm body, particularly at your age." She was laughing so hard, her legs bounced around on the settee.

"You still dream a lot, don't you, Viola?" Ida asked through her laughter.

"Well, tell me. Is he going to put you on salary?

"Oh, heavens. We haven't even discussed that part of the deal yet."

"So it's just a deal?"

"Well, not exactly. I think he knows I'll expect to be paid."

"How does a man know that he has to pay if you haven't discussed it with him?"

"You know men expect to pay when you do something for him." Ida laughed aloud. "I do believe, Viola, you're meddling again, and you shouldn't be doing that."

"I'm just inquisitive and..."

Ida interrupted. "Oh, I didn't tell you that I found my money, did I? I told Horace I would like to buy into his funeral business, but he didn't seem interested."

"Well, for goodness sakes, Ida. How much money did you have in that little cloth bag?" Viola swung her feet to the floor and sat erect. "I stopped by the funeral home on my way out here and he didn't mention a word to me about you finding it, or for that matter, your interest in investing it."

Ida moved to her favorite chair, grunting as she sat. "Well, I doubt that he would tell you."

"He tells me lots of things, Ida Ridley". Boasting, she continued. "You'd be surprised what Horace and I talk about. I want to tell you something else," Viola said as she watched Ida squirm on her chair. "He told me about this man he has there that died right here in your parlor. And you know what? His son called while I was there and he's coming to claim his body."

"Who? Adam?"

"Is that his son's name? How did you know that? What in the world would he want to come all the way here when he don't even know his father?"

"All I know is what Horace told me." Ida said without turning her eyes from Viola. "Isn't it strange that they learned all that information about the man so quickly?"

Without hesitation, she said, "I want to talk to you about what happened."

"Well, Carless told me that he thought you knew more about that man than you let them..."

"I do, Viola, and I want to tell you about it. I've only told Mary, so far. You being my best friend and all, I'll tell you about him, but you've gotta promise me that you'll help me figure out the best way to handle things." Ida got up and went to the hall door. She looked back and said, "Sit right there. I'll be back in a minute." She soon returned with a letter. "Here," she said, handing it to Viola. "Read this."

As Viola read, Ida sat there gaping directly at her. She had always respected Viola for not bringing up secrets she had shared with her for so long.

Viola didn't look up after reading the letter. She simply folded it and held it for sometime without saying anything. Ida was crying when she finally lifted her eyes and looked at her. She saw that Viola too, had tears running down her cheek. Neither spoke, but stood and embraced one another. Ida had been perspiring and the dampness on her ear, and at her hairline, felt cool to Viola's neck. They held each other for a few moments. Ida began to sob. "Ida," Viola whispered, "surely there's a way we could turn these tears into laughter. Come on. We've been through many things together, both personal, and private, and everything has been so funny to you. You know what I think? I think, together, we can work this out to our advantage." Viola released her and they sat on the settee together, still holding hands. "May I make a suggestion, Ida?"

Ida tried to laugh. "I've never given much thought when making up my mind about something, but this sudden surprise... my son that no one knows about, is coming. I, I just don't know what I should do." She squeezed Viola's hand and released it.

"Let me go for Mary," Ida said. She rested her hand on Viola's knee, steadying herself, then pushed herself up. She opened the hall door and yelled. "Mary. Come in here a minute." Not hearing a reply, she re-entered the parlor, walked by Viola and patted her shoulder as she crossed over to the door leading to the back porch. She called again.

"I'm out here. Do you need me right now, or may I finish collecting the eggs?" Mary yelled. She came from behind the laying hen's shelf and saw the afternoon sun was well above the trees. Ida saw eggs were bulging in Mary's dress pocket. She watched as Mary opened the barn door.

"We don't have anymore laying mash," Mary yelled.

"I know," Ida replied. Eggs were still plentiful so she wasn't too concerned. Mary closed the door, bolted it and headed toward the porch where Ida was waiting.

"Didn't you collect them a little early?" Ida asked.

"I wanted to get my chores done early 'cause I'm meeting Wilbur at the graveyard. He said he'd be there about an hour before sundown."

Ida saw the afternoon sun was well above the trees.

"Did you say Wilbur?"

"Yes. He wants to visit his papa's grave while the flowers are still fresh. He wanted to know if I could meet him there."

"How do you plan to get there? Surely you don't plan to walk?"

Mary began to unload the eggs into the small blue speckled pan on the pump shelf. Ida watched her carefully as she layered them on top of one another.

Mary lowered her voice to a whisper. "When I saw Viola drive up, I thought she might drop me off on her way home. Wilbur will bring me back."

Ida, also whispering, said, "Does Jeffrey know you're meeting him?"

"No, and I don't intend to tell him. Now, don't you go and let it slip out when you talk to Viola."

"Oh, I won't. You just be nice to Wilbur. You know what I mean. Not like you're nice to Jeffrey."

Wrinkles plowed across Mary's forehead. Ida noticed the quizzical look on her face and turning toward the parlor, said again, "Oh, you know what I mean."

Leaving the pump shelf, Mary strolled toward the barnyard pondering Ida's remark.

Mary stood by the gate of the graveyard and waved as Viola drove away. She shook the iron gate when she closed it and heard the latch fall into place with a quiet thud. Shading her eyes, she looked at the late afternoon sun. It was difficult to estimate the time, since she hadn't worn her wrist watch. Wilbur was not there yet and she thought it was nice that she could be there early enough to visit with her Papa.

The sunlight sifted through the shimmering green foliage of the maples and the pine needles rattled faintly in the light breeze.

Mary crossed over to the west corner of the graveyard and heard a bobolink in the distance as she stood by her papa's grave. "Papa", she said, "I need to talk to you. Why did you have to die? Do you know how alone I feel? I've missed you, Papa. I know it's been only a few days, but so much has happened. I can't talk to Ida." She brushed bits of trash from the top of a flat headstone nearby and sat down. She stared longingly at the grave. She dried her tears and said, "I don't know why I'm crying, Papa." She had developed a deep sense of change in her consciousness and wanted to talk to someone about it. "What should I do, Papa? I've seen Ida change her disposition. She's beginning to mellow toward me and I don't know how to handle it. You know that once she makes up her mind, no power on earth could change her."

There was a cracking sound and Mary saw a piece of dead limb fall from a leaning loblolly pine. It broke into pieces as it struck the iron fence and crashed to the ground. A squirrel crept under the fence surrounding the graveyard and scratched through the broken debris.

"Papa," she paused a moment, "Ida sometimes can smile as if to beg for forgiveness. I know she's trying to sway my feelings and I know I must give in. She isn't as self-centered as she used to be. We're getting along with one another a little better now and . . . and I'm beginning to realize that she does love me. I want to be her friend... if for no other reason than... than, well,because she looked after you for so long."

She walked to the fence and stood in the sunshine. Drying her eyes and shading them, she looked up the road. She wondered if Wilbur had forgotten to come. Back at the grave, she stooped and fumbled at the near dried-up homegrown daisies on the mound and longed for the peace of her earlier life with her father. She sat on the headstone again. She thought of the farm and wished there were a way she could buy it back. The banker had offered her an extended date to pay the mortgage, and the deadline was only a few days away.

Mary hadn't thought too much about paying the mortgage off. There was no way she could raise the money, so she'd put the idea behind her.

She listened for awhile to the pine needles softly whispering in the sudden breeze. She shifted her position, and said aloud, "I've met a new friend, Papa. It's someone I have pictured in my soul's vision as to what I've desperately wanted for so long. I don't know him well, but he has an earnest face and I see a wide awake spirit, like the ones we read about in books. I think I might love him, Papa, but I don't know what I should do. There's Jeffrey. I'm falling out of love for him."

She moved to the grave and pulled another flower, first putting it to her nose, then kissing it. She squeezed the flower and held it tightly in the palm of her hand. "I know that I'm a country girl, and I know there should be more to living than being able to make love-- just to feel good. I want to feel like the poets, Papa, when they're inspired to write, or, like, like an artist who can leave something behind for others to enjoy."

Mary squatted and poked her finger into the soft sod on the side of the mound. She buried the flower stem and smoothed out the long petals of the white daisy. "I know you're beyond the grave now, Papa, but if there is a way, please, won't you give me a sign?"

The moment she looked up at the sun, she heard a car approaching. She held her breath until she was sure of the sound. Dusting off her clothes, she moved toward the gate. It was Wilbur. She unlatched the gate and waited.

Wilbur steered the hearse slowly to the edge of the road and waved before stopping the engine. Mary returned his smile. As he strolled toward her, there was some sort of sophisticated breeding in his stride. He was tall, but slender. He stood erect and had a likeness of his father. At nineteen, he had thick black hair that was protruding from his unbuttoned shirt collar. His chin had a dimple just like Rufus had. As he approached, he slightly bowed, smiled, and took her hand. Mary wasn't accustomed to such politeness. They kept smiling at one another.

"Thank you for meeting me out here, Mary. How did you get here? Surely, you didn't walk?"

"My goodness, no." Mary laughed aloud. "A friend of Ida's brought me. You won't mind taking me back, will you?"

"Certainly not. I look forward to it. Have you been here long?"

"Only long enough to talk to Papa." She held to his hand and led him toward his father's grave.

Chapter 33

*U*naware of the time having slipped away, they looked up and saw the sun had dropped behind the tall pines, blanketing the graveyard with its shadow. A bobolink sounded in the distance and they squeezed one another's hands.

Mary said, "I just love that sound."

"You know, we don't hear that where I live. There are plenty of owls, and we hear them hoot all the time, but never the call of a whippoorwill."

"Don't you just love the calls of things from nature? I think my favorite is the call of the mourning dove," Mary said, as the sound of fluttering wings left the overgrown lilac bush over in the corner. She could still detect the smell of the lilac, even though the blooms were gone.

Wilbur's hand tightened around hers. She responded with a light squeeze. She lifted his hand to her cheek and smiled at him. "Nice," she said. "You must not work very hard to have such soft hands."

"They're not as soft as yours," he said.

"They do feel good. What kind of work are you

doing?" Mary asked.

"I have a degree in accounting and I work for a large mail order shipping firm."

"I knew you had to be working at a desk job. Your hands give you away. They're not as rough as this farm gal's," Mary said, as she pulled her hand from his. "Look," she said, pointing to the headstone that had fallen on Wilbur and had sent him to the hospital.

"Oh. That? I don't want to see it. It nearly robbed me of my life." Wilbur laughed and turned his head in the other direction, "I won't look."

"Oh, I'm sorry. I shouldn't have mentioned it."

"Shucks. You know I'm kidding. I'm not that sensitive." He took her hand again and pulled her closer to him.

Standing face to face, they stared into one another's eyes until Mary became embarrassed. She looked away. Wilbur turned her toward him and cupped her face in his hands. "You're too pretty for me not to stare at you. You don't mind, do you?"

They gazed at each other for some time before he kissed her on the mouth. She yielded and pressed hard against him.

They held the embrace until she felt his hand slip to her hips and thighs. She backed away. For a moment she wanted to submit to him but saying, "Not here in the graveyard, Wilbur."

"But I want to be with you more than any girl I've known."

Mary felt a sudden flush come to her face as she stared across the newly plowed hay field. She thought of the barn and the spring harvest of fresh hay stored there.

She wanted to be there with him at this very moment, but that was the special place she had enjoyed with Jeffrey. Even though she had met Wilbur such a short time ago, there was a strong and strange feeling causing her to cling to him. She had yearned to have this feeling for Jeffrey, but it was never strong enough for her to make a full commitment to him. He didn't really seem to care, anyway. She couldn't think of him, not with the feelings she had developed for Wilbur. Her new friend was the one controlling her mind now, and she wanted to be stretched out in the hay with him.

Mary knew that Wilbur's stay had been extended beyond his original intentions. The accident in the graveyard and the couple of days in the hospital had kept him from returning and he would be there a few days longer. She dreaded the time when he would be leaving. Their acquaintance had been short and she didn't want to feel deprived. She knew, too, that standing with his arms around her, and having been kissed, wondered how far she should go when he made his advances.

Wilbur released her and walked to a flat top marble headstone and sat on it, swinging his feet. She went to him and stood between his knees. He grasped her hands between both of his and smiled. "I have something to tell you," he said quietly as he pulled her face close to his. "Uncle Horace has offered to take me into the business with him. Said my father would want it that way and that he was aging and would need someone eventually to take over. He wants me to consider going to mortuary school."

Excitedly, Mary asked, "You're going to consider

his proposition, aren't you?"

Avoiding the question, he said, "You know, I had a strange experience the day I was alone with Papa in the hearse. I realized that his death was so sudden, there must have been things he wanted to accomplish that were left undone. My being away from him for so long..."

Mary interrupted, "If you don't mind me asking, why didn't you come to see your father more often?"

"It's too complicated and too long a story to tell you now. But I will tell you." He swallowed hard. "Maybe, before I leave."

"One misses so much when you lose a parent early in life," Mary said.

"Since I didn't know my father well, I sat in the hearse the day I arrived and felt that I could sorta make it up to him in some way." He shifted and Mary stepped back. Wilbur stood and walked ahead, toward the gate. "Uncle Horace and I had a lengthy conversation about how hard Papa worked and about the things he wanted to do. They were making plans to up-date the furnishings in the funeral home. They also had their eyes on some property across the river for a new location, but the Depression seem to linger and they didn't think they should take the risk."

"If you're going to decide to stay, are you going to let Horace know... soon?" Mary asked, sounding optimistic. She had learned that each time she sounded positive, his eyes brightened. His feelings were not too hard to read, as she could easily detect the tremor in his voice when he spoke of going home. She had to find a way to keep him from leaving.

"Yes. I've got to let him know soon. I understand that he's asked Ida to work whenever he really gets busy."

They were passing Seth's grave when Mary noticed the short stem daisy she'd planted on the mound. It had sprung back to life, its petals lifting upward. Stopping abruptly, she removed the flower and lifted it to her face. It was strange that the fragrance of the lilacs saturated the air.

"Do you smell lilacs, Wilbur?"

He sniffed, turning his head a number of times. "No, I can't say that I do."

"You can't smell that sweet aroma?" She placed the fresh daisy to his nose. "Take a sniff."

"Can't smell a thing."

Mary couldn't believe the daisy had taken on a new life and a different fragrance just by being stuck into the soft dry ground. The *sign*. That's what it was. The *sign*. Her papa had given it to her. The flower was alive. "Thank you, Papa," she whispered to herself.

Wilbur was unlatching the gate. "What did you say, Mary?"

"Oh, nothing." Her hand went to her chin. She glanced upward and Wilbur saw her lips move. "Just wishing you would decide to stay here and take over your papa's share of the business."

She approached the gate, Wilbur stepped in front of her. He picked a dried pine needle from her shoulder. Passing his hand over her shining honey-colored hair, he said, "You really would like for me to stay, wouldn't you?"

She was slow to reply, and before she could

speak, he lifted her long hair and kissed her on the back of the neck.

"You know I'd love for you to stay--- forever, in fact," Mary said, clinging to him. With her hand behind his back, she squeezed the daisy in the palm of her hand and waited for his response. She felt her papa's presence as if he stood with them. She relaxed and withdrawing her hand, she saw her palm was wet and the daisy fresh and uncrushed. She was assured this was a *sign* she wanted from her papa. She squeezed it tightly again. Opening her hand, she watched the petals unfold as if the flower was blooming for the first time. "Thank you, Papa."

"What did you say?" asked Wilbur.

She held the unbruised flower for him to see. "Oh, in my silly way, I guess I just thanked Papa for the flower I removed from his grave."

"How could that one seem so fresh after five or six days, especially without rain, and the few on my Papa's grave are only a couple days old and they seem to be all dried up?"

Mary smiled warmly, not sharing her secret with him.

"Are you ready to go?" Wilbur asked as he pushed the graveyard's iron gate open. "I must return the hearse. Uncle Horace may need it."

"Let me go back to Papa's grave just for a minute. I won't be long."

Wilbur closed the gate and leaned against it as he watched Mary walk briskly away from him, her hair bouncing on her shoulders. The faint rays of the sun reflected on her hair as the light beams sifted through the leaves. He felt his heart open and close with each beat, feeling that a bit of Mary's life and charm was creeping in. He felt, for the first time, a closeness for her that he had never experienced with a girl before. He knew little about her past, but it didn't matter. He began to feel that her happiness depended on him and he not only wanted to please her, but also to satisfy himself. Although he had to go away soon, he knew too well his feeling for her would not leave him. This would not be the end, but the beginning. He refused to wrestle with his thoughts. He knew he loved her.

He noticed her wiping away tears as she approached and he took her hand and led her through the gate. A dove fluttered away at the sound of the iron latch falling into place.

She turned her head to hide her tears and softly said, "I hope I didn't delay you too long and..."

"I would wait for you regardless of the time you wanted to spend there."

"Papa was such a support for me." She reached for the handle of the hearse door, but decided to let him open it for her. She hesitated a moment, looking in the back. "This will be my first time riding in a hearse and I'm..."

"Oh, just pretend it's a huge limousine."

"You reckon anyone will see us sporting around and wonder what's going on?"

"It's the only vehicle Uncle Horace has and it's used all the time. No one bothers to even notice anymore."

Mary stood silently.

Wilbur continued, "And, if they notice, I'd be

proud to be seen escorting you about town."

They laughed together. "Then we won't have to take the back streets?" Mary asked.

"Certainly not. I'd like to take you right through town, just to show you off."

"Oh, you can't do that."

"Why not?"

Teasing, she said, "If someone sees me they might be sending flowers to the house."

"That popular, huh?"

"Maybe, I should get in the back and lie down so I won't be seen."

"I'd have to pull the curtains."

"Well, in that case, no one would know I was riding so I might as well get in the front seat." She slid in on the passenger side.

Wilbur walked around toward the back. Pausing at the back doors of the hearse, he peeped in at Mary, then slapped the doors with the palm of his hand. The thunderous sound echoed and he saw Mary open the door and quickly jump to the ground. He laughed and went to her and swept her up in his arms. Her golden hair floated against his cheek. He laughed gleefully.

Feeling secure in his arms, Mary laughed, too. At the time she didn't care if the whole world saw her as he lifted her to the seat.

Still smiling as he settled himself under the wheel, Wilbur reached for her hand and caressed it, then pulled her next to him.

The sun was setting and Mary looked back toward the graveyard and saw the crimson light reflected on the headstones.

Chapter 34

Mary looked neither right or left as Wilbur drove down main street. She saw Ellen Grace crossing the street in front of them.

"Isn't that someone we know?" asked Wilbur.

"Where?" Mary pretended not to see.

"There," Wilbur said, pointing to the young lady crossing the street at the corner. "Don't we know her?"

"Yes. You met her at the funeral," she said reluctantly.

"Would you like to stop and talk to her a moment?"

"I thought you had to get the hearse back to Horace."

Wilbur glanced at his gold wrist watch. "I think we have time to pull over and say hello."

Mary hastened to say, "I talked to her this morning and she told me she was coming to town and would be in a rush to get back home. I think she has a date tonight. I doubt that she'd have time to talk to us."

The stoplight changed and before he put the hearse in gear, Wilbur watched Ellen Grace finish crossing the street. As they passed the intersection, Mary looked in the other direction to avoid her.

The sun was nearly down when Wilbur stopped in front of Mary's house. He jumpedsprang from his seat and rushed around to open the door for her. She was already standing by the hearse gazing at the purple, red and orange clouds as they were slowly blended by the wind. As he touched her shoulder, she pointed toward the sky and asked, "Have you ever seen anything so beautiful?"

"I certainly have," he answered.

"What on earth could be more beautiful than that?"

He only said, "You."

"Oh, quit your teasing, Wilbur."

He glanced around to see if anyone was looking, then kissed her swiftly on the cheek. She too, looked around and not seeing anyone, asked, "Can't you do better than that?"

He folded her in his arms and kissed her repeatedly. Though the embrace was short, he continued to squeeze her hand when he released her. "May I see you tomorrow?" he asked.

"As surely as these clouds fade away and the sun comes up in the morning."

"You mean, I can see you early?"

She nodded and smiled. He said good-by and entered the hearse, turned it around and headed east.

"I can hardly wait," she whispered to herself. She watched the now amber colored sunset reflecting on the back window of the hearse until it rounded the bend.

Mary swung her arms and sang cheerfully as she walked toward the house.

Ida, standing on the porch looked up. "You're happy, I see," she said as Mary came up the steps. Mary could only smile. Ida shook her head. "I'm also happy!"

"Why are you so happy?" Mary asked.

"I did something this afternoon that I feel so good about."

Drawing her words out slowly and childlike, Mary smiled and said, "You can't feel as good about anything as I feel at the moment."

"Oh yes I can. I did something we both can feel good about," Ida said in a tone of voice Mary had never heard before. "After my nap, Viola came and I told her about a dream I'd had about seeing this farm covered with nothing but white daises. The whole field was white with 'em. They were blooming everywhere. I dreamed I ran through them as if I were a little girl again. They were only for me to see, and I felt they were all mine." Ida slapped her knees and laughed happily. "I felt so good, I had Viola to take me into town and without too much thought. You know how much I love this farm." She paused for a deep breath. "I went straight over to the bank with my savings and bought the mortgage they held on the farm."

Mary gasped for breath and covered her mouth with both hands. "You did what?"

"Yes I did. I used the money that I had saved and, after Mr. Crusade figured the amount and the interest, I even had a little left over."

Mary gasped again.

"Don't worry. I bought it back in your name. That's the only way I could do it. He told me that he would have you come in and sign the papers."

Mary stood frozen for a moment. Gaining her composure, she rushed to Ida and threw her arms around her. "I can't believe it. So many good things have happened to me today." She released Ida and they sat very close together on the porch bench.

Mary breathed heavily for a few minutes, then said, "I talked to Papa today while I was at the graveyard. I told him some of my problems that I'd never mentioned to him before. I poured out my heart to him, Ida." Mary began to cry. Ida placed her arm around her shoulder. "I suggested things I wanted to happen in my life, Ida, and somehow, I felt that he heard me. I pleaded with him, that if he would only give me a sign, I'd consider it the best advice I had ever gotten from him. I told him specific things... my... my dilemmas, the things I had been struggling with." She put her hand deep into her pocket and fumbled the flower she had placed there when she left the graveyard. "Here's something I want to show you." She pulled it out. "Look at this," she said, holding it in front of Ida.

"It's a white daisy."

"Look how fresh it is."

Ida took the flower from her, viewed it from several angles and handed it back to Mary. "Where did you get it? Only the flower shops have daisies this time of year."

"It's from Papa's grave. It's the only fresh one there. I found it after I asked Papa to give me a sign. Can't you see? After all these days, it's still fresh."

She took it from Mary again. "It's the kind I dreamed about this afternoon. It's gotta be a sign, Mary. It's gotta be a sign!"

Mary woke the following morning to a foggy damp day. She hadn't seen a dreary day in a long time. She stretched and rolled to the edge of the bed. She immediately thought of Wilbur's visit. The wall clock struck one gong and she checked the time. Only six-thirty. She had plenty of time before Wilbur was to arrive, so she lay there, planning her day. "Why have good things begun to happen to me?" she asked herself aloud. "Maybe it's because I'm in love and I'm looking at things a little differently now. The fresh flower has to be a *sign* from Papa."

She got out of bed and crossed the room and stood staring out the window. She leaned her forehead on her hands and a tear slid down and rested on her chin. She began to pray. "Dear God, will I ever see him again after he leaves?" She crossed over to the bed. "I may never see him again. He's become dearer to me than my own life and I question how I can let him go." The tear dropped from her chin. "What must I do to keep him? I want to make love to him, but if I do, I realize the chance I would be taking. I feel that he wants to make love to me also, and if I lose control of myself, please God, don't think of it as sinning."

Mary threw herself across the bed. She wiped her eyes and did not open them. She slept.

She saw images of the dried flowers on Wilbur's papa's grave and the one live daisy. The smell of lilac was distinct. She heard the hoot of an owl and the latch on the iron gate fall. She saw and heard the flight of morning doves fleeing from the lilac bush. Their wings lifted her high above the farm and she saw a blanket of white flowers below.

The hearse stopped in front of the house and she saw Wilbur walking toward the barn. She watched as he peeped inside and call her name. She followed him and closed the barn door behind them. They gathered fresh clean straw and piled it high in a make-shift bed.

"Ten minutes with you is like being in haven," she said as they lay naked and relaxed beside one another.

As she lay in his arms, she felt his rocking body against her and felt his deep breathing and saw the working of his face muscles. He picked straw from her hair and kissed the back of her neck. She rolled and faced him. "If I could look into your face every day for the rest of my life, I would be the happiest girl on earth and in heaven," she told him.

"That would be heaven for me, too."

She folded her arms around his firm body and held her breath. He made no attempt to wipe away the tears that rolled down her cheek.

He suddenly stood, reached for his clothes and began brushing the straw from them. She was lost in thought. She lay on her back, partly covered, looking up at him as he dressed. "*Your visit here has been so short. Is there any way you could stay longer?*"

"*I'll be leaving tomorrow. I want to go and talk to your step-mother, Ida. Uncle Horace told me I should spend some time with her before I leave.*"

Mary wanted him to go right away. "*Why don't you go now? She may have secrets to tell you, some that she's never uttered to me.*"

"*If I leave tomorrow, frankly, I don't know when I'd have time to go, if not today.*"

As Mary finished dressing, Wilbur moved toward her and picked the straw from her skirt. He pressed his body hard against hers, then rushed from the barn, slamming the door. The noise sounded more like Ida clanging pots and pans in the kitchen.

Mary sat up in bed, rubbed her eyes and gathered her thoughts. The clock struck seven. She jumped from the bed, knowing Wilbur would be there most any time now.

Chapter 35

Both Mary and Ida usually slept late on Saturday mornings, but neither could sleep after the excitement from the day before. It had rained during the night and the sun had not broken through the thick clouds. Mary felt the day was going to be another rainy one. She dressed and headed for the kitchen. Ida had nearly finished her bread baking and the first loaves were cooling on the shelf above the sink.

"We'll have breakfast shortly," Ida told Mary. "We'll just have some freshly made bread and pear preserves. There may be some cream in the ice box on the porch if you'd like to check," Ida told Mary.

"That sounds good." The screen door slammed about the time she opened the ice box, calling to Ida if she should also bring in the butter.

"I have the butter, already."

They ate leisurely, and afterwards, didn't bother to hurry with the dish washing.

Mary sat gazing at Ida as she picked up the few

scattered bread crumbs around her plate. "Do you still feel good about yesterday?" she asked Ida.

"It's strange. I woke up this morning rather early. It wasn't quite daylight so I got up and started baking bread. When light came, the sky was murky gray but I felt even better than yesterday."

Mary thought Ida might have felt a little different about paying the mortgage off since she did it in such haste. Many times she'd known her to take quick action and regret it later.

"Then you aren't sorry you did what you did about the farm?" Mary asked as she held her plate at the edge of the table and brushed crumbs from the table cloth.

"No. I feel even better about that, too," Ida said.

"I lay awake most of the night thinking what a memorable day I had yesterday at the graveyard," Mary said.

"When will you see Wilbur again?" Ida asked as she began gathering the few dishes from the table.

"Oh, he's coming out this morning."

"Why didn't you ask him to come for breakfast? Wouldn't it have nice to have him eat with us? Horace wants us to get to know him better."

Mary interrupted. "He didn't say he just wanted you to get to know him better?"

"He probably figured you two had spent enough time together and knew one another pretty well already," Ida said, turning to the sink.

Mary smiled.

At nine o'clock the hearse stopped in front of the house. Ida and Mary watched curiously from the parlor window as Horace and a chubby young boy walked halfway to the porch. They paused and said a few words to one another.

Ida stood behind Mary and tried to say something, but her words were jumbled. Mary wondered if she was having a stroke.

"Are you all right, Ida?"

"It's... I... Ah... You go to... to... to the door and I'll go for a drink of water." She stumbled toward the back porch, steadying herself on the furniture as she walked.

Mary watched her until she was sure Ida could make it to the porch on her own. She smoothed her dress, pushed the hair from her face and cleared her throat before opening the door.

"Is Ida home?" Horace asked.

"Yes. Come on in. I'll go for her." She held the door for them to enter. She stared at the young man and as he passed she caught a whiff of Bay Rum. He didn't look old enough to be shaving and she wanted to question why he was so doused in aftershave lotion.

Mary called to Ida from the back parlor door and went toward her when she saw her sitting on the steps. They sat together for a moment. Mary noticed the sweat on Ida's brow and asked again, "Are you sure you're all right?"

"I will be in a minute. Just let me get my breath." Ida breathed deeply several times, then grasped the railing along the side of the steps. Mary stood and held her hand until she got to her feet, then opened the parlor door for her and left for the kitchen.

"Hello Horace," Ida said, smiling all the while, not

taking her eyes off him. "What brings you out so early?"

"Hello, Ida. They have come for Rufus' body. Viola told me you would like to know."

"Who? When?" Ida had not seen the boy standing on the other side of the room until she saw Horace's eyes turn toward him.

"Oh my God!" Her quivering right hand went to her mouth as she reached behind her in search of a chair. She collapsed into it. Horace watched as color drained from her face and neck. The boy stared at her.

"This is Adam Millbrook," Horace siad. "He came with his mother to arrange shipment of Rufus' body back to Tennessee. He wanted to come out and see where his father died. I told him all about you and how nice you were and that you had planned to work some for me." He seemed to be rushing through his remarks as he shuffled his hat from hand to hand.

Trying not to seem alarmed, Ida struggled for words of greetings, but blundered through by asking, "So this . . . is Adam?"

The room fell silent. No one said anything until Adam finally asked, "Are you Ida Stacy?"

No sooner than the sound of "No" came from her lips, Ida rushed to say, "Yes! I mean, I've been known for some time as Ida Ridley, but I was Ida Stacy before..." She paused, "before I came to live with Mr. Ridley." If Adam knew who she really was, Ida was impressed by his calmness, but was unable to detect his interest, or lack of it, at her being his mother. They stared earnestly at one another and after a moment he dropped his head and gazed at the floor.

Not looking at her, the boy asked, "Then you are

Ida Stacy?"

Holding out her arms to him, she only said, "Yes. Yes." Her arms fell to her lap when he didn't move toward her.

Adam slowly looked up and walked to her, leaned over the chair and gave her a big hug. She tried to get up, but sank back as if some hand had pushed her into the chair. She wrapped her arms around him as far as they would reach. The waiting was over. The burden of her secret seem to melt away as Adam's arms became tighter and tighter around her.

Without speaking, Adam released her and went across the room and stood by the settee. Ida gazed at him. He had Rufus' grey eyes and even his physique. His belt was buckled beneath his bulging little belly, just like his father wore his. His hair and profile resembled hers. Ida felt the same love as the day she gave birth to him. "It's finally over," she said aloud.

"What?" Horace asked, looking at her with a probing glance.

"I . . . I've finally met Rufus' son." A strong desire was there to say "our son," but not knowing how much Adam knew, she didn't want to lend more confusion in the event the whole story was not known.

Adam stood quietly and made no further inquiry about her and she volunteered no further explanation. She could not avoid silently congratulating herself for remaining calm. She was well aware the wrong question, or the wrong statement, could possibly give her feelings away and her secret would be out. She'd bare her soul to the Lord when she was alone and everything will be fine.

She continued to stare at the young boy. "So you're Adam? What a nice name. Is it a family name?"

"I don't know," the boy said. "Guess it's because I was their first child and "Adam" seemed to fit."

Everyone remained silent. Ida was searching for words and the only thing that came to mind was, "Maybe you'll grow up to marry an Eve, someday." She laughed and glanced at Horace. He tightened his lips and when he wrinkled his forehead and squinted his eyes to keep from laughing, his shaggy eyebrows met.

Adam laughed. Ida continued laughing and Horace joined in.

They were still laughing when Mary entered the room. Ida did not introduce Adam.

Finally, Horace said, "Mary, this is Adam Millbrook. He's the son of the man who died here in your parlor."

"I knew it must be," Mary said. "He resembles him."

"Glad to meet you, Miss Mary."

"Thank you, and I'm glad to meet you, too."

Adam stepped forward to shake her hand, but she patted him on the head instead. Adam backed away.

"How do you like riding in a hearse?" Mary asked.

Adam was a little jittery, but said, "It's all right, I guess."

"I find it sorta fun. In fact, Wilbur is coming and we're going for a ride in it sometime this morning." She made it sound rather emphatic, hoping Horace would get her message and soon take the hearse back to the funeral home.

Adam turned to Horace and asked, "Isn't he the man who told you before we left that he'd decided to stay and work at the funeral home?"

Mary fastened her eyes on Horace, waiting for him to speak. When he remained silent, she moved toward him. Not wanting to sound too enthusiastic, she said, "Oh yes. I think I heard him mention that he might like to be in the undertaking business."

Horace didn't seem to want to confirm Wilbur's staying and turned to Ida. "You, too, will be coming to help me from time to time, won't you, Ida?"

Mary heard 'You too' and immediately thought Horace was confirming Wilbur's stay.

"You know I will, Horace. I'm willing to start anytime," Ida said.

Mary left the room through the hall, certain that Wilbur would be staying. From the back entrance, she called, "Ida. Will you come here a minute? I have something to ask you. It's rather urgent."

She heard Ida say to Horace, "I don't know what could be so urgent, but let me go see what she wants. I'll be back in a moment." She pulled the door shut behind her and joined Mary on the back porch.

She grabbed Mary's hand, swinging them as if she wanted to dance. "It happened! I'll be going to work with Horace, and Wilbur'll be staying! Oh, what a glorious day." She swung Mary around until the porch began creaking. Both were out of breath.

"We'd better stop before the porch caves in," Mary said, hoping Horace and Adam didn't hear them.

When they reentered the hall, Ida saw the cradle Mary had removed from the closet and placed so Ida would be sure to see it. Before she could speak, Mary asked in a soft voice, "Don't you think we can give this to Adam?"

Ida whispered, "When did you have it repaired? The last time I looked at it, it was still broken. One of the slats was left on the pump shelf and when I went for it, I figured the wind had blown it away."

"I know. It had Adam's birthdate written on it and we made sure that particular slat was used when Jeffrey and I had it fixed."

"Oh, Mary. How can I, right out of the blue, give it to him? What would I say? I wouldn't know what I'd say to him. I don't know that I can say anything."

"You'll feel good about it, once you give it to him. He'll accept it, and maybe learn later in life to appreciate it.."

"The timing is all wrong, Mary. Don't ask me to do it right now. I've had more excitement in the last few day than I can handle."

"Oh, come on, Ida. You can handle this. It's no good anymore. It's time you rid yourself of all your doubt, your indecision, and deceiving yourself. Just give it to him, please. You'll be glad."

"What will I say to him?"

"Now, you know you've never been lost for words. I'm sure you'll think of something."

Mary picked up the cradle and held it as Ida pondered her next move. Finally, she nodded and turned to follow Mary to the parlor.

Chapter 36

Mary bumped the walls and door facings with the cradle as she struggled toward the parlor. She entered the room. Horace moved a chair so Mary could get to the middle of the floor. She set the cradle down with a thud, rattling the trinkets on the what-not.

Ida did not follow Mary, but continued down the hall and to the front porch. She heard Horace tell Mary, "Let me help you with that," and Mary's reply, "Oh, I can handle it."

The early haze had disappeared and Ida saw the morning sun had filled the sky and was caressing the pines, maples and oak trees across the road in front of the house. Birds sang and Ida's spirit was renewed. "Why am I out here when I could be in there getting to know my son?" she whispered to herself. She entered the hall, pausing at the parlor door. She took a deep breath and walked in, smiling.

The three were looking at the cradle in the middle of the floor. Adam was slightly rocking it back and forth with his foot.

Assuming Mary had told Adam it was being given to him, Ida asked, "How do you like it, Adam?"

"It's nice. We still have the one my folks bought for me when I was a baby, but this one is home-made and I like it better." He patted his stomach and jokingly said, "I'm a little too big for it now, but I would like to have it, as a keepsake." Everyone laughed. "When I do marry Eve, maybe I'll be able to use it." They laughed again.

Ida wasn't sure if Adam recognized it as an antique, or not, and wondered if Mary had told him that it was bought especially for him during her pregnancy. She remember Rufus had offered to pay for it, but when he refused to talk seriously about marriage, she refused to take his money. Deep down in her heart, she hated to part with it, and if she should never see Adam again the final link of her past to reality would be over. She had her secrets, up until the last few days, but having revealed them, her mind was, at least, at ease, so she reckoned she might as well part with the cradle. She watched as he gently rocked it and felt a large tear creep from beneath her eye lashes.

She thought how much Adam looked like his father. He was big for his age, but his father had been a tall, robust man. Now as she looked at him she felt an impulse to gather him in her arms and ask for at least friendship of him. "I do have some lovable qualities somewhere within me," she wanted to tell him, "and I'll shower them all on you."

Time was standing still for Ida. The soft rug was quieting the rocking cradle and the ticking of the small clock on the mantle was the only audible thing in the room.

Mary heard Ida sniffle and understood the troubled look on her face. She went to her and took one of her hands in hers and hugged her around the waist. Ida sniffled again and Mary tightened her arm.

Adam continued rocking the cradle, he bent over and rubbed a crack on the small side-rails. He said to Ida, "I thought it was broken. I sure do like it. Are you sure I may have it?"

"You will take care of it, won't you? You just might have a real need for it someday," Ida teased.

"I hope so", he replied. So anxious to have it for his own, he picked it up and turned to Horace. "I'm ready to go whenever you are."

Ida pulled herself from Mary and walked toward Adam. He set the cradle down and wrapped his short arms around her as far as they could reach. He kissed her on the cheek. "Thank you."

"Please be sure to take care of it. It's been around a long time," Ida whispered in his ear. She cradled him in her arms and held him for sometime. Horace cleared his throat and Ida released the boy.

"Thank you for bringing him out to see me and," through her tears she said, "I'll get to the funeral home as soon as I can."

They turned to leave and Ida started to her room. "Wait", she heard Adam say. "I want to hug you again."

They rushed toward one another and met midway the hall. Adam cushioned himself against Ida and with tears in his eyes, said, "I love you." Before she could ask, 'When will I see you again', he turned and ran to the porch. She stood alone, weeping. As far back as she could remember, no one had ever told her 'I love you', and the hot tears blinded her eyes.

From her bedroom window, she saw the hearse drive away. Although it was early in the morning, she fell across her unmade bed and cried aloud for the first time in years.

Mary was standing in the kitchen and heard crying coming from Ida's bedroom. She turned the burner down on the oil cook stove and went to her. Opening the door, she saw Ida lying across the bed.

"Ida", she said, "I think I know the hurt you're going through and I want to help you get over it. Please don't cry." She sat on the bed and stroked Ida's hair. "It's about time for Viola to make her morning visit. You don't want to be crying when she comes. She thinks you are such a happy person now."

Ida turned on her back and dried her eyes on the sheet. "Don't think I want to see her this morning," she whimpered. Sniffing a couple of time, she asked, "I can smell coffee. Did you make some more?"

"Yes. You know how Viola likes her second cup in the morning. I made a fresh pot. Why don't you come and have some?"

After helping Ida straighten the covers, Mary left for the kitchen. Ida opened the chiffrobe to select a dress to wear on her first day of work at the funeral home.

Entering the kitchen, Ida pulled the corner of the bench from beneath the table. Mary watched her lower herself down slowly on the bench. "Are you having trouble again with your back?"

"No. Just old age, I reckon." As the steam

spewed from the rusty coffee pot, Ida rose from the table and poured herself a cup and returned to the table. "You know, Viola sure drinks lots of this stuff. Guess she wants to keep the Luzianne Company in business."

Mary moved to the window, sipping her cup. "We can't complain about how much of ours she drinks. She's brought many pounds over here through the years and ..."

Ida interrupted. "I'm not complaining about how much she drinks, but she never brings any sugar and never uses less that three spoonfuls each time she drinks a cup."

"Now that you're going to work with Horace, don't you think we can afford to buy a little more sugar?" Mary laughed, trying to cheer her. "What is it now? Twenty-four cents for five pounds?"

She turned from the window when Ida asked, "How does this dress look for my first day at work?"

"It's nice. Isn't it your newest one?"

"Yes, and I hope Horace will like it."

"When Viola gets here, are you going to ask her to drive you over there?"

Ida moved and stood in front of the long tarnished mirror over the buffet server and checked her appearance. "Oh, I'm sure she will." She pulled one of her eye lids down. "My goodness, look how blood shot my eyes are. And look at these swollen bags under them."

Mary wished Viola would come right away and they would leave for the funeral home. She and Wilbur would have more time alone.

"I declare. That's a pretty dress," Mary said.

Ida twisted and turned, admiring herself. She rubbed the front of her dress and then her hips, trying to appear thinner. "Don't you think I've lost a few pounds, Mary?"

Mary put her hand to her chin, tilted her head. "I definitely think so. Maybe . . . let me see."

Ida backed away from the mirror and Mary walked around her. "Maybe, four or five pounds." Ida's face exploded with a broad smile. Mary saw that her strategy was working. Flattering her was changing her mood.

Ida left Mary in the kitchen and went to the back porch to wait for Viola. She stood on the steps and leaned her head against the post and gazed at the nail still protruding from the pump shelf. She didn't care about the damage it had done to the dress she had worn earlier. It was not important now. Deep in her consciousness she knew there was a sense of change coming over her. She reasoned too, that such small things were not worth worrying bout.

She thought of Adam. For years, she had tried to put the thoughts of motherhood out of her mind. Hearing him talk and touching him rekindled her motherly instinct and she wanted the feeling to last forever.

Engaged with her thoughts, Ida didn't hear Viola pull up in the side yard, nor did she see the dust from the car swish around the corner when it stopped. Viola waited for the dust to settle, then walked toward Ida.

"Ida. You're all dressed up."

"Viola, you nearly scared the be-Jesus out of me. I didn't hear you drive up." She pulled on the step's railing and stood, dusting the seat of her dress.

"I heard you're going to work at the funeral home for awhile this morning. I was afraid you'd be gone before I got here to get my second cup of coffee, and here you are all dressed up and ready to go." Without pausing long enough for Ida to respond, she asked, "After I drink my coffee, would you like for me to drive you over there? I stopped by to see Horace on my way out here and they were loading the hearse, so I just started to drive off, but he waved me back. There was a young woman standing near the hearse with a child, watching. You know, Horace didn't bother introducing us and I swore to myself that I had seen that boy before. He sure looked familiar." She was talking so fast, she didn't bother to sip the coffee Mary had brought to the porch for her. She moved closer to Ida and whispered, "While driving out here, it all came to me. He looked so much like you, I knew he had to be your child." She paused. Ida thought it best to keep silent.

Things had been in such a whirl lately, Ida couldn't remember how much she had told Viola about Rufus, or anything that had recently happened. If she kept listening, eventually, Viola would let her know everything she knew. Keeping silent right now would be to her advantage, she reasoned.

The kitchen door slammed and they saw Mary coming, bringing another cup of coffee to Viola. "Another cup, just like you like it," she said. "Lots of sugar."

"My dear," Viola said, "This will make three cups this morning. Why don't you drink it? If I have another, I'll pee all the way back to town. Now wouldn't that be something, me stopping on the side of the road?" But she took the cup. She thanked her and Mary reentered the kitchen.

Viola sat on the porch bench with Ida and they talked quietly about Rufus. No more than she said, Ida couldn't tell just how much her friend knew.

Having finished the coffee, Viola put the empty cup on the pump shelf. "Thanks, Mary," she called, then turned to Ida. "What time do you have to be at the funeral home? I'll take you 'cause I've got other things I want to do this morning."

"I told Horace I'd get there as soon as I could."

"Well, we'll go now, if you're ready. You sure look nice. Have I seen that dress before? I don't think I have. How long have you had this one?"

"It isn't exactly new. I bought it a week or two before Seth died."

"My Lord. That's been less than six weeks ago. That really bothers me, Ida. You buried Seth in that old faded suit and here you are sporting a new frock and ..."

"We've been through this before, Viola, and I'm not going to listen to it anymore."

Viola walked on ahead toward her car. Ida followed and before she got in, she said, "I'm sorry, Viola." She opened the door on the passenger side and a portion of the stuffing fell from the seat. Picking it up, she crammed it back into the cavity under the seat cushion. She settled herself comfortably and Viola started the car.

Ida saw the hearse approaching. "Wait right here a minute, Viola."

They watched until the hearse came to a stop in

front of the house. "You reckon he wants me to ride to the train station with him?" Ida asked.

Horace came walking toward the car. "Were you all going to the funeral home?"

"Yeah," Viola said, not giving Ida a chance to answer.

"Good," Horace said, looking at Ida. "I left Wilbur there with Adam and they will wait until you get over there. We shouldn't be too long. Even if the train isn't on time, we won't have to wait. We should be back within the hour."

As Horace walked back to the hearse, the glare of the morning sun reflecting on the windshield prevented them from seeing who was riding to Tuckersville with him. Watching the hearse drive away, Ida asked, "Who was that riding with him?"

"I have no idea, but it looked like a woman. Who do you think it could have been?"

"I couldn't tell, but we'll ask Wilbur when we get over there."

"Let's go on right now. I'm anxious to know," Viola said.

It wasn't like her friend not to ask personal questions when they were alone, but Viola drove without saying anything. Ida became curious. Had her friend learned something that she didn't feel free to discuss with her, she wondered.

Before entering the driveway at the funeral home, Viola broke the silence and said, "I've figured it all out, Ida." Waiting for a response, she kept staring straight ahead.

Ida said nothing.

Chapter 37

After making several trips to the front yard and looking up the road toward town, Mary returned to the porch and picked up the small rocking chair and bounced it several time on the floor to clean off the dust. She rubbed her hands over her shapely hips and smoothed out her dress before sitting down. She stroked the strands of hair that had fallen about her face and she went to the back porch.

She looked in the small oval mirror hanging over the pump shelf that her father had used for shaving only a few weeks ago. On her way back to the front porch, the mantle clock struck as she passed the parlor. It was eleven-thirty and Wilbur should have been there. He hadn't kept his promise and it was nearly midday.
More and more her confidence in men was being shattered. Often, Jeffrey didn't come through with his promises, either.

The whole morning was wasted and she wished now she had gone to the bank to sign the repossession papers for the farm. At least she would have been doing something productive. She thought of waving down the next car heading toward town and asking for a ride. If Wilbur couldn't keep his word, she wasn't going to hang around and waste her afternoon.

Mary went to the edge of the yard and waited. A dust trail was visible up the road before a car came into sight. As it came nearer, she recognized it as Viola's old green Ford, so she turned and started toward the porch. A branch from the butterfly bush brushed against her face. Stripping a hand full of the tiny late lavender blossoms from its spike, she tossed them in the air and watched them drift to the ground. A few butterflies fluttered around, waiting to alight again on the bush in search of nectar.

Before Mary sat in the homemade wooden swing on the end of the porch, the car came to a stop and Wilbur yelled, "Hi there."

Surprised, Mary left the swing holding out her arms and smiled. They met halfway the yard. "I was about to give you out," she said.

He took her by the hands. "Uncle Horace had to take a body to the train station over in Tuckersville. I was concerned about not having a way out here to see you, so Ida insisted that I use Viola's car to drive out."

"Ida volunteered Viola's car?"

"Yeah, but Viola didn't seem to mind. She cautioned me about pushing the clutch all the way to the bottom. If not, she said I'd have trouble getting it in gear. Sorry I couldn't have gotten here earlier."

"Oh, that's all right. Viola does so many nice things for us," Mary said.

"She didn't seem to mind," Wilbur said.

"She is a very pleasant woman. She and Ida are the best of friends, you know," Mary said, leading him to the swing.

"Adam's mother went to the train station with Uncle Horace, leaving me with Adam. We had a nice long talk before Ida and Viola got there. The things that kid tells me . . . well, I thought he was just talking, as some kids do. But when he said he was adopted, and seemed to know all about the man who died out here, I began to believe him. Said the man was his real father."

"I asked him if he wanted to ride out here with me, but he wanted to stay and talk with Ida. I helped him unload a cradle from the hearse, and listened awhile to him talk to Ida about it."

"Did he tell you that he liked it?"

"Yeah. You've seen it?"

"It was here and Ida gave it to him."

"It looked like an antique."

Mary shook her head, paused and pondered whether she should explain why he had it.

As they swung, Wilbur watched her long golden hair as it left her neck and fell softly back into place as the swing went back and forth. Mary watched the butterflies circling the bush by the gate.

"You want to know a secret?" Mary asked.

"You mean just between you and me?"

"Now, it wouldn't be secret if we told anyone else, would it?"

"I promise I will keep it," Wilbur assured her.

Mary placed her hand on his leg, turned to whisper in his ear and saw Jeffrey's car approaching.

She paused, then said, "See the car coming? It's an old friend of mine. I understand that he's dating Ellen Grace. Remember the girl we saw in town crossing the street? I think you met her at the graveyard."

Before Wilbur replied, Mary left the swing, hoping Jeffrey hadn't noticed her sitting so close to Wilbur.

She walked to the gate and stood by the butterfly bush and waited for Jeffrey to stop. "Hello, Jeffrey," she said cheerfully, noticing the scowl on his face when he got out of the car. "Glad to see you."

Jeffrey's jaw tightened. "What's all this, `glad to see you' stuff?"

Wilbur left the swing and stood on the steps. Jeffrey asked, "Isn't he the fellow who just came into town? What's he here for?"

"Please keep your voice down. He's no more than a friend. He's Horace's nephew."

"What's he doing driving Viola's car? Doesn't he have one of his own?"

"Jeffrey, please keep your voice down," she pleaded, turning her back to the porch.

Suddenly, she felt Wilbur's arm go around her waist. For a minute she froze, but managed to say, "Wilbur, this is Jeffrey." Wilbur extended his hand. Jeffrey only looked at him momentarily, turned quickly and got back in the car. The car sped away, leaving them in a cloud of dust.

Mary squinted her eyes and covered her nose, waiting for the dust to settle. She didn't look at Wilbur until she had brushed her clothes. Wilbur stooped and wiped her shoes with his hands, then cleared the dust from his own shoes.

"What was that all about?" Wilbur asked.

Mary became nervous and didn't respond immediately.

"Why are you so shaken by his sudden leaving? Is there something you want to tell me?" he asked. She took him by the hand and led him to the swing. Mary nudged the floor with her foot and the swing swayed. "Oh, it's nothing. Jeffrey is that way."

In the face of her past, she recalled other incidents in which she was never prepared for Jeffrey's abrupt behavior. Today, she wasn't pretending and really didn't care how he acted and she was not going to let it bother her.

Wilbur put his arm around her shoulder and touched her face. She turned gently toward him and wished with all her heart the matter could be forgotten.

"But I thought he was . . . "

Mary put her finger to his lips. "He isn't that important. Frankly, I just don't want to talk, or even think about him and his ugly ways, when you and I are together."

Her remark must have pleased him. He kissed her on the cheek. She shifted in the swing and her hand went behind his neck and she pulled his face to her. During their kiss, the roar of Jeffrey's car caused her to pull away. They watched him pass. Mary had never known Jeffrey to drive at such speed.

The roar faded in the distance and when the dust had settled, Wilbur asked, "After driving by here earlier, he couldn't have gotten very far down the road before turning around and coming back. Isn't he a bit too old to be showing off?"

Mary didn't want to stir his curiosity further and tried to choose her words carefully. "He's that way. I've known him for a long time and I've seen him behave like this before. But, we don't have to concentrate on him." She laughed and after a moment, turned back to him and said, "Where were we?"

"You were about to tell me a secret."

Remembering his kiss, she was disappointed that he didn't kiss her again. "Oh yes. Now, I want you to promise me that you won't say anything about what I'm gonna tell you."

"Come on now. You can trust me." Wilbur said, patting her on the thigh. She slipped close to him. "For the last few weeks I have been observing Ida's behavior and I've tried to piece a few things together." She noticed the puzzled expression on his face and wondered if she should continue. "So much has happened since Papa died and I can't seem to make any sense out of anything."

Mary heard the roar of Jeffrey's car coming up the road again and saw the dust rising higher and higher as the car came into sight. Approaching the house, the beat-up old Hudson slowed and came to a stop directly at the front gate. Jeffrey's old dog Spike, that she didn't care for, had his head stuck through the rear window and was trying to crawl out. She saw Jeffrey grab the dog's back legs, slap him on his rump and throw him into the seat. She had never seen him so violent with his dog before.

Wilbur left the swing and started toward Jeffrey. Mary followed until Wilbur was in the middle of the yard. Taking his arm and slightly pulling him back, she said, "Please don't go near him. It's not a good time to talk to him," Wilbur stopped. Jeffrey shook his fist at them and accelerated the engine. They watched as he drove away, disappearing in a cloud of dust.

"He'll never make that curve at that speed," Wilbur told her.

Trying not to sound too concerned, Mary replied, "Oh, don't worry," and by the time she had said, "He's a good driver," there was a thunderous crash. From the gate they saw a huge cloud of dust rising and drifting across the field.

There was silence.

"Wilbur!" she yelled. "We gotta go to him!"

"I'll take you and I'll go for help."

By the time their car stopped at the wreck, and before Mary could get out, Spike was pawing at the door on the passenger side. She pushed her door open and forced the dog away. He ran around and around Mary, making it impossible for her to walk. She patted him on the head and he rubbed himself against her, causing her to stumble.

Jeffrey's car had rolled over in the ditch and had thrown him through the door. He lay face down in the edge of the field. Wilbur jumped the shallow ditch, reached for Mary's hand and pulled her across.

They rolled Jeffrey over. His eyes were closed and his mouth partly open. His head fell to one side. "My God, his neck is broken," Wilbur whispered.

Mary gasped and looked away.

Spike sniffed around his master's head, licked his face, then lay next to his limp body and whined. Wilbur felt for a pulse and Mary caressed Jeffrey's head in her hands.

"I hear a car. Let me go and stop it," Wilbur said.

"Don't you think they'll see the wreck and stop anyway?" Mary said, releasing Jeffrey's head. When she looked up, Wilbur was already in the middle of the road waving his arms. She tried to force Spike out of the way.

Pushing him, she saw a letter protruding from Jeffrey's shirt pocket. She stared, trying to decide whether she should take it or not. A portion of the return address was visible and it was from Ellen Grace. She reached for it with the feeling that any time Jeffrey was going to slap her hand away or snatch it from her. Slowly pulling the letter from his pocket, she quickly stuck it inside her blouse.

"It's Uncle Horace," Wilbur yelled from the road. "Maybe he can help us."

Mary looked at Jeffrey again and tears welled in her eyes and she felt sorry for him as she walked to the edge of the ditch. She didn't look back as she waited for Wilbur to help Horace across the ditch, then said, "Give me your hand and help me back across and I'll wait with the woman in the hearse."

Mary and Mrs. Millbrook watched Horace struggling to get Jeffrey on Wilbur's shoulders.

"Let me go and get Spike out of the way," Mary said. She sizedup the width of the ditch and decided to go a few yards down and cross at the narrow section. From the other side of the ditch, Spike ran along the bank to meet her. They looked at one another and just as Mary leaped, Spike sprang from his side of the ditch at the same instant and collided with Mary, pushing her backward into the ditch. Mrs. Millbrook came to Mary's rescue. The dog ran playfully to her and she kicked him just before he leaped toward her. He rolled over a couple times, growled, and ran toward Mary as she lay on her back. He sniffed at her, then rushed back toward Jeffrey.

Mrs. Millbrook helped Mary get to her feet and they brushed the dirt from her clothes. Mary felt for the letter, making sure it was still there.

Horace and Wilbur had given up trying to get Jeffrey across the ditch and had laid him on the soft mound of dirt that had been plowed up by the tumbling car. Mary stood by the hearse, still brushing her dress.

Horace yelled, "Mary, get that sheet from the back of the hearse and bring it to us, please."

She opened the back doors and retrieved the sheet and tossed it across the ditch to Wilbur. She watched as they spread it, then turned away when they began to roll Jeffrey over.

Horace yelled at Mary, "You go for the coroner and we'll wait here until you get back."

"I don't want to leave," Mary said.

Horace cupped his right ear with his hand and asked, "What did you say?"

"I don't want to go," she yelled back. "I want to stay here with Jeffrey."

Wilbur stared so intently at her, she knew he must be puzzled as to why she didn't want to leave. Just a little while ago she had convinced him that she wasn't interested in Jeffrey. He stared at her for so long, she finally said, "I'll go with you." He smiled and took her by the hand.

They glanced back as they drove away and saw

another car had pulled up and had parked in front of the hearse.

Mary spoke little and sat gazing out the side window. Wilbur reached for her hand and pulled her to him. His arm went around her shoulder, almost caressing her.

"Do you mind dropping me off at the house so I may change my dress?"

"On my way back, may I stop and pick you up?"

"Sure. Just give me enough time to spruce up a little."

Wilbur stopped in front of the house, got out and opened her door. He kissed her on the cheek and left her at the gate. She waved until the car was out of sight, then strolled toward the back porch. She glanced at the barn and thought of the straw bed she had shared with Jeffrey. She had to forget about him now. It was over.

As she pulled the screen door open, a section of the rotten screen fell to the floor. Maybe Wilbur would mend it. Jeffrey had promised Ida that he would repair it, but never did. She couldn't think of trivial things now, not at a time like this. Not going inside the kitchen, she let go of the screen door and sat on the bench, watching more of the rotten screenwire fall to the floor.

She reached inside her blouse and pulled out the letter and removed it from the envelope. She began to read.

My dear Jeffrey,
The thing that we feared has happened.
Last Wednesday morning I awoke with a

strange sickness I had never felt before. I must talk to you about it. Please come by and take me for a ride.

With love,
Ellen Grace

The letter was brief and had been opened so she knew that Jeffrey had read it. She looked up and saw the barn. Lifting her damp eyes toward the sky, she whispered, "Thank you Lord for sending me Wilbur."

Chapter 38

Mary pondered the letter Ellen Grace had written Jeffrey. Yet she thought it strange she didn't feel sorry for her, or even care about her situation. She thanked the Lord that it hadn't happened to her. She always made sure that Jeffrey was not too eager to rush things and insisted that he be careful. Mary remembered her times of fear, and she knew all about anxiety, but she couldn't become too concerned about Ellen Grace. She would just have to wait out the moon change as she once did. . . and pray a lot. She was glad it wasn't her responsibility to tell her the news of Jeffrey's death.

After changing her dress, Mary carried Ellen Grace's letter to the barn. She had her hiding place for things she didn't want anyone to find. Everything was kept in a small tin box above the rafters over the barn door.

She reached for the box she had hidden away and opened it. Cautiously she removed the dried-up daisy she had taken from her papa's grave. Removing the birth certificate she found the day that Spike tore the cradle mattress to pieces, she read it again. Now, she wished she had shown surprise when Ida told her about a son born to her thirteen years ago.

She put the letter from Ellen Grace beneath the other items, closed the box and shoved it far back on the shelf.

Just as she stepped outside, she saw Wilbur standing by the sheriff's car. She leaned against the barn door until the sheriff drove away.

Wilbur spoke to her, but the only thing she heard was that Jeffrey was indeed dead. Mary turned away and sat in the open door. She lowered her head to her knees and covered her face with her hands. Wilbur sat beside her and pulled her close and whispered, "It's bad to lose a friend . . . "

"He's more than a friend," she interrupted.

Mary felt his body relax. He removed his arm from her shoulder and took her hand. "I don't understand," he said.

"I mean, he's been around a long time." She sniffled and rocked her head on her knees. "He was somewhat of a fixture. You know. . . always there when you need someone, I guess that's what I'm trying to say."

Still holding hands, they walked into the sunlight. She led him to the edge of the garden and leaned against a fence post.

Staring out across the garden she noticed that some of the tomato vines were withered and the stunted squash vines were yellowing. The uncut cabbage heads were splitting for lack rain and the bean vines were gray with dust from the road.

Wilbur stood gazing at her. "Do you have any idea how pretty your hair is, glistening in the sun?" he asked.

"Come to think of it, I don't think I have ever seen it in the sunlight. Glad you like it, though," she said. Mary was proud of her hair, but she had never been flattered by anyone as often as she had been by Wilbur.

She meticulously smoothed her hair, turned toward him and rubbed the back of his neck and said, "Your hair is the color of a, of a, what's that black bird that seems to strut when he walks? You know, the one that's a dark purple color when he's in the sun. I think it's a starling, isn't it?" She ran her fingers through his hair. Trying to smile, she said, "I bet you put dye on yours."

"At my age? Never!" He laughed aloud and she just smiled. They held to one another and walked toward the car.

Before entering, Mary asked, "Do you mind if we don't go back to the wreck? Don't you think we should return Viola's car?"

"The sheriff said the coroner was out there and had declared that Jeffrey's neck was broken. We'll go on to the funeral home, if you prefer."

Mary squeezed his hand and smiled. "Oh, wait a minute. I've gotta run in and get my lipstick. I won't be a minute."

Wilbur waited patiently and opened the car door when he saw her coming from the house. She was clutching a small purse.

Ida and Viola watched from their rocking chairs on the funeral home porch until the car had stopped and the dust had settled. Ida saw the disturbed expression on Mary's face as she got out. She had seen this grave look before and immediately knew something was wrong. She dropped her cardboard fan beside her rocker, grabbed the arm of Viola's chair and by the time she had pulled herself up, Mary and Wilbur were on the porch.

"What in the world is wrong, honey?" Ida asked, placing her arm around her. Mary began crying. Ida, waiting for a reply, embraced her. Mary relaxed in her arms and before she spoke, Wilbur said, "There was a wreck not to far from your house and Jeffrey was killed."

"Jeffrey? Oh my Lord!"

"It seems he was speeding and lost control of his car."

"My Lord! Who was with him?" Ida asked, releasing Mary.

"Only his dog. Mary and I rushed to the site when we heard the crash and soon afterwards Horace came by, on his way back from the train station with the hearse. The coroner is out there now. I just talked to the sheriff and he seems to think there's no need to go by the doctor's office, so they'll bring him directly here."

Ida turned to Viola. "Did you hear that? Jeffrey dead?"

Viola shook her head and went to Mary. They both cried, clinging to one another. Mary knew that Ida could deal with death better than Viola, but Viola had a better understanding of people's feelings at a time like this. She could always count on her being there for support.

"Come on, Viola. Let's see if we need to do

anything inside before they bring the body," Ida said, sounding more like an order that a request.

Mary released Viola and motioned for her to follow Ida.

"Will you be all right, honey?" Viola asked.

"I'll be fine."

"Sure she will," Wilbur said. "I'll stay with her."

Viola patted him on the arm and whispered a soft 'Thank you' and followed Ida. She looked back before entering the parlor and smiled when she saw them embracing.

Adam had the cradle turned upside down in the middle of the floor when Ida and Viola stepped inside the room. Seeing them, he pointed to the pencil scribbling on the middle slat. He wanted to be sure that Ida was who he thought she was, and said, "This is my birth date written on the bottom." He waited for a response, and not getting one, he asked, "Why is it on here?"

Blushing and stammering for words, Ida said, "It's just a coincidence, I guess." She knew Adam was going to press her for an explanation and she had to find a way to put him off for a while. "Viola and I have to make preparations for a body to be brought in. I'll talk to you later."

"But isn't this why you gave the cradle to me, 'cause it has this date on it?" he asked.

Ida waved Viola toward her, smiled at Adam and said, "Your mother will be here shortly. Why don't you go on the porch and wait for her while Viola and I do a little work for Horace? Mary and Wilbur are sitting out there."

"Yes. Why don't you go out there and tell Wilbur that I want to see him," Viola said.

Adam left for the porch.

"Viola, what must we do? Is there anything we can do before Horace gets here?" Ida asked.

"I don't know one thing but to wait. You're new on the job, you know. Can't expect you to jump right into embalming somebody." Ida heard a trace of teasing in Viola's voice. "You know what, Ida Ridley? You've always said you like to fondle men, now here's your chance. You can do it and not have them rejecting you."

"Oh, cut your mess out, Viola. This is serious business."

"When did you decide you were gonna be serious about funerals and such?" inquired Viola.

Just as Viola began laughing, Wilbur entered and said, "You wanted to see me, Viola?"

She took his arm and asked, "Why don't you use my car and take Mary for a drive and come back after they have brought Jeffrey here? I think it would be better if she wasn't around when they arrive with him."

"Thank you. That's a good idea. She seems to be broken up a bit, but she's trying not to show it. We'll be back in a little while."

They waved to Adam as they drove away, but before they were out of sight of the funeral home, the hearse passed them. Mary looked, turned around and watched as it entered the back driveway.

When Ida heard the hearse approaching, she stuck her head through the door and asked Adam if he would come and remove the cradle from the parlor. She held the door open for him and felt hot tears flushing her eyes as he maneuvered it through the door. Ida closed the door quickly and went to meet the hearse as it backed up to the rear entrance.

As soon as Horace got out, Ida said, "You know I'm here to help, so tell me what I can do."

"Where's Wilbur?" Horace asked.

"He just left. They'll be back shortly."

"Then you'll have to help us. You hold the doors open. Maybe the coroner and I can get the body unloaded." Horace was out of breath, but said to the coroner, "The sheriff was following us." He looked around. "Where did he go? We'll wait a minute and he'll be here and can help."

"It isn't that much of a job," the coroner said, "We can handle it."

Mrs. Millbroke had gotten out of the hearse and was on her way to the front yard when she saw the sheriff drive up. She turned and yelled, "He's here!"

Adam had started toward the hearse when his mother stopped him. "Don't go back there, son. I think it's best that you stay with me."

"Come look at the cradle. Got something to show you," Adam told his mother.

Horace had undressed Jeffrey's body. It lay on the white porcelain table in the small room with a sheet pulled up to the chin. Ida was alone. She could detect a strong smell of coffee as she stood with the shaving mug in one hand and the lathered brush in the other.

Horace didn't have to discuss the procedure of shaving with her. She was already experienced after shaving Seth every three days after he had the stroke.

"Yes, sir. I've got experience shaving a man," she said to herself and began lathering Jeffrey's face. She picked up the straight razor and with the first stroke, the flesh was set so tightly around the jaw that she couldn't move it. "Relax, young man, or you'll not get a close shave," she said to the dead man. Pressing a little harder with the razor, she had trouble getting rid of his five o'clock shadow. After a few extra strokes, she decided to shave beneath his chin.

She became suddenly aware that here she stood with a straight razor at Jeffrey's throat. She remembered some of the words Seth struggled to say while being driven to the hospital after his last stroke. It was all becoming clearer to her at last. That's what it was. He had seen Mary and Jeffrey making love in the garden the afternoon he was stricken.

Ida's pulse quickened when she thought of her chance to finally get even with Jeffrey. She cleaned the razor on the sheet, while looking at him over the top of her glasses. As she held her breath and gritted her teeth, she heard a soft knock on the door.

Viola asked quietly, "May I come in?"

Ida opened the door just wide enough for her to squeeze through.

"I must say Ida, you're a brave soul. I just couldn't shave a dead man," pointing to Jeffrey's body, "and I can't let you stay all closed up in here by your self, either, not the way you have felt about him all these years."

"You don't think I can handle a job like this? You just had to come in and check on me, didn't you?"

"Oh, you've always been able to handle a man by

yourself, all right. Guess I'd better take that back. I know you'd rather have a live one any time."

Ida began wiping the lather from Jeffrey's face.

"At least, I'm not scared of a dead one," she said, watching Viola walking nervously around the porcelain tables, wringing her hands. She lifted the sheet and lowered it. "Yes sir, this is going to be interesting work," Ida said. She peeped under the sheet again. "Look, Viola. Let me show you something." She jerked the sheet from Jeffrey's body.

"My goodness!" Viola exclaimed. "Is that what all the young gals around here is . . ., was excited about?"

Chapter 39

"*I*'m enjoying this ride, Wilbur," Mary said, "but while we're away, would you mind taking me by the bank? This may not be the right time to go, with Jeffrey's death, and everything, but I have some papers to sign."

"Sure. You have an appointment?"

"No. Mr.Crusade said that I could come in at any time and that it wouldn't take but a minute or two. It has to do with the farm. I'll tell you all about it later."

It was a little past noon and Main Street dozed in the hot silence of a slow afternoon. Wilbur found a parking space right in front of the bank.

After he parked the car, Mary sat there, primping, waiting for him to open the car for her. If the people in the bank were watching, she wanted them to see what a gentleman Wilbur was.

Before entering the bank, she caught a glimpse of her disheveled hair reflected in the glass door panel. She smoothed it and straightened her shoulders.

Wilbur held the bank door for her to enter. "Thank you," she said.

Mr. Crusade was standing in the doorway of his office watching Mary smiling broadly. She was greeting the girls at the service windows. He called out, "Hello, Mary. Nice day we're having, isn't it?" . Before she could reply, he asked, "Won't you please come in?"

Mary signaled for Wilbur to have a seat before she entered the banker's private office.

Mr. Crusade pulled up an oversized leather office chair, its arms too wide apart for Mary to rest comfortably. She sat very erect, clutching her small purse tightly with both hands. His desk was huge but his chair appeared too small when he shoved his immense body into it.

The banker reached into the desk drawer and removed a folder. He opened it and drew out several papers. Glancing quickly over them, he turned them around so Mary could read them from her side of the desk.

"I have marked the lines on which you are to sign."

Anxious to leave the stuffy office, she didn't spend much time reading, skipping over the fine print. She and the banker reached for the ink pen at the same time, their hands touching. He grasped her wrist and held it for a moment. Their eyes met and she let the pen drop to the desk top. Not taking her eyes off him, she stood and picked up the papers with her free hand. He released his hold and handed her the pen.

Mary remembered how he had sat next to her and pressed his leg against her thigh the day her papa's will was read. She got up and moved to the window and began reading the papers more carefully.

"If there's anything you don't understand, I'll explain it to you," the banker said.

Not looking at him, she said, "I can read, Mr. Crusade."

"No doubt, Mary, but just in case." He moved from behind his desk toward her.

Mary stepped to the office door and opened it. He went back behind his desk. "You seem in a hurry."

"Yes," was all she said.

He stared at her and said, "Since you are in such a hurry, it was nice that Ida came in and did all the preliminary work. All you have to do is just sign."

There were a few minor statements that she wanted to ask about, but decided they were not that important. She moved to the desk, flipped the pages and signed them cautiously. She pushed them in his direction and turned to leave.

"Mary," he called.

She turned and looked at him, not acknowledging his, 'I'm sorry,' and left his office.

The three bank tellers, wearing shocked expressions, watched as Mary approached Wilbur. They didn't try to keep their voices down and she knew Wilbur must have told them of Jeffrey's death. Wilbur took her hand and as they were saying good bye to the tellers, Ellen Grace entered the bank.

"Why, hello, Mary. Isn't this a gorgeous day?" and hardly taking a breath, she added, "And hello to you, Wilbur. Gorgeous day. A very gorgeous day!"

As Ellen Grace turned to greet the tellers, Mary

whispered to Wilbur, "She doesn't know about Jeffrey. Maybe you should tell her."

"Why don't you tell her? I don't think it's my place to let her know. It would seem strange coming from me. I barely know her."

"Well, I'm not gonna be the first one to tell her."

"Good Lord!" they heard Ellen Grace say. "Oh no! It can't be!" The girls at the windows had told her.

Mary looked in time to see Ellen Grace's hands go to her stomach, then move quickly to her face. She turned toward them. "Did you hear that, Mary? Jeffrey's dead! Oh, Mary! I'm so sorry." Looking at Wilbur, she directed her remarks to him. "You just don't know how much he cared for my friend, Mary."

At the moment, Mary was more embarrassed than concerned. She squeezed Wilbur's hand and began to cry. He led her toward the door.

They had turned off Main street before Wilbur asked, "Why are you still crying?"

She shifted on the car seat and looked out the side window. "Ellen Grace had no business making that remark to you. She's such a busybody. You're the one I care for, but she's always trying to . . ."

Wilbur slowed the car. "Now, now, now. I'm not interested in her. You're mine and I'm yours. Let's just pretend that we didn't hear her. She doesn't mean a thing to me."

Mary looked at him, patted his thigh and only said, "Thank you," returning his smile.

The tall dried daylilies stalks along the road lightened her heart, and she smiled, as she remembered the orange colored trumpet flowers that topped them earlier in the spring. She knew she didn't possess the tenderness she thought he saw in her, but she was willing to change. She wanted her smile to show him the joyous side of her.

She gazed at this man with his powerful personality for a long time, and wondered what he was thinking. No way did Mary want him to see her as a lonely, broken hearted woman.

"Why do you look at me so long at times?"

"Your face never seems to show anger. It always reflects your gentle nature. I wish I could be that way."

"You're a far greater woman that I am a man."

"You want to explain that?"

"Well," he said, pulling off the road and stopping beneath the drooping branches of an overgrown willow tree. "Lately, you have handled all these deaths like no other person I know. You've been so calm and seem to be in such control."

"Oh, stop it, Wilbur," she said, gesturing with her hand as if to say, you must be teasing.

"A real mark of a stable person . . ."

She interrupted. "There are moments in my life that I feel I'm alone and I have to deal with my frustration all by myself. But it's always been that way." The smile left her face. "Had my stepmother. . ., Ida. . . . , if she had been a little different toward me, I could have dealt with things a little easier." Mary opened the car door and stood outside. It had been unusually hot, that is, until they left the bank. A slight wind poured under the branches and she breathed in the cool air and watched as Wilbur came walking toward her. The breeze tangled his soft black hair.

"Let's walk in the edge of the woods. Wouldn't you like that? It's cooler," Mary asked. She took his hand and they meshed their fingers.

Mary wasn't too eager to leave the cool shade of the trees. There were no blossoms on the wild hibiscus that grew on the edge of the woods but their leaves were curled up for lack of rain. She stripped a handful from their stems, crumpled them and threw them in the air. "Do you think it's gonna rain? I can't stand this weather."

"You mean, you can go through all the things that's happened in the last few weeks, and you don't think you can handle a little hot weather?"

She stopped. He turned to her.

"Kiss me," she said.

"I can't do anything about changing the weather, but I can do this." He enveloped her in his arms and held her tightly until she struggled to loose herself. He held her at arm's length. "You know, Mary Ridley. I love you." Again he pulled her to him. "May I ask you something?"

"If you have to ask, maybe I should say no."

"Please don't say no. Not until I ask."

Giving herself to Jeffrey was easy, but Wilbur was so different from him. The answer would be "no" if he expected her to yield to him the way she had to Jeffrey. Mary pulled from his embrace and backed slowly away. She saw a ready smile, which always seemed to be there, and stepped back within his reach.

He took her hand. "I want to marry you, Mary."

Her facial expression became a frozen stare. Surprised, she asked, "Marry me?" She waited for his answer.

"Yes. Will you marry me?" he asked as he dropped on his knees in the dust, right there in front of her. She saw a trace of dust rise slightly and resettle around him. He knelt there with both hands stretched out to her.

She dropped to her knees and they embraced.

"Does this mean, you will?" he asked.

"Isn't it a bit early in our relationship to talk of marriage?"

"I don't think so, since we're in love."

"But we have known one another for . . . for such a short while."

"Are we going to feel any different tomorrow than we do today?"

"I don't think I can love you more than I do right now," Mary said, pulling him against her.

"Then, what's your answer?"

"I've got to think about it."

"You need more time, then?"

Mary rose to her feet, leaving Wilbur sitting with his legs under him. "Maybe within a day or two I'll have an answer for you."

"You sound a little uncertain."

"Since you'll be working with your Uncle Horace, you won't be leaving, so, just give me a little time. I promise, well . . . , maybe by tomorrow before the sun goes down I will have made up my mind." She leaned and kissed him on the mouth. He sat there transfixed.

"Give me your hands." She pulled him to his feet and slipped her arm around his waist.

"I can't lose you, Mary!" Wilbur said with tears in his eyes.

Mary had never seen a man so moved and didn't think she could stand to see him cry. Stirred by the emotion in his eyes, she folded her arms tightly around him. If she could be convinced that he loved her with any degree of the feeling that she held for him, there would be no doubt in her mind that her answer right now would be "yes".

Wilbur said with assurance, "Holding me like this gives me a lot of courage. I love you and I want you to remember, I'll always be good to you. Please don't doubt that,"

"I'll let you know tomorrow. Right now, I think we should go."

"I want to kiss you again," he said, and before the words were out of his mouth, their lips fused.

Chapter 40

Spike, Jeffrey's dog, was lying on the back stoop of the funeral home when Mary and Wilbur drove up. He didn't bother to look at Wilbur when he got out of Viola's car, but the minute he saw Mary, he sprang from his prone position and ran to her, wagging his tail slowly. Mary couldn't stand the pitiful whining and rather that ignore him, she stooped and rubbed his head.

"Oh, you poor doggie. I know how you must feel."

She stood and let him walk around her several times before she attempted to move. There were characteristics about the dog she hadn't seen before, and for the first time she began to realize why Jeffrey thought so much of him.

Wilbur stood nearby, his dark eyes fixed on Mary and lingered for a moment. She tossed her head and her blond hair, perfumed and soft, fell about her face when she looked down at the dog. Wilbur grinned. "You're showing a bit of interest in that dog you said you didn't care for." In only a few days he had gotten to know Mary well and had learned to read her expressions, and often was right when he contemplated her remarks.

"I feel sorry for Spike," Mary said. "Jeffrey told me that his family didn't care for the dog and had nothing to do with him. That's the reason he hauled him around all the time." She sighed a little as she continued stroking the dog. "Now I wonder what will happen to him?"

"He's taken a liking to you, for sure."

"You are implying that I take him in and care for him are you?" she asked, not taking her eyes off the dog.

"No. But he'll have to have someone."

"Do you like dogs? I've never heard you say."

"Oh, I like dogs. He certainly is obedient."

"Do you really think I could handle him?" she asked, glancing up at Wilbur.

"Well, between the two of us, I think we could manage."

Mary knew Wilbur was thinking that her response to his proposal would be `yes', and maybe that's why he suggested such. She didn't know anything about dogs, only that they were pests and required a lot of attention. But, if that is what Wilbur thought she should do, maybe she could arrange to keep Spike. She patted the dog and pushed him away. Wilbur took her hand and they went up the back steps and into the funeral home.

Before the door closed behind them, Mary heard Ida laughing softly with Viola in another room. She approached the closed door and waited a moment before knocking. The laughter stopped.

"May we come in?" Mary asked, her head close

to the door. She hadn't noticed the faded sign on the door until Wilbur pulled her back and pointed. "Look," he said.

"Embalming Room? I don't think I want to go in there," she said, and immediately walked down the hall.

Viola came from the room and followed them. On her way to the parlor, she met Horace carrying a pail, a small brush and a small rubber hose attached to a large glass bottle. Mary heard her say to Horace, "Ida is waiting in the embalming room for you."

"Ida," Horace said, while moving slowly about, fumbling for the items he needed and placing them on the small side table near the window. "There are certain things we morticians do in the embalming process that aren't very pleasant. Since you have agreed to help me, you may want to look the other way during some of the procedures."

"Oh, you know me," she said, hoping to impress him. "I can take most anything. Remember the time I went to the country with you to embalm that old man? It was before I went to keep house for Seth, you know. Well, I helped you some then, and I didn't mind."

"Yeah. But I also remember that you sat facing the wall much of the time, too," Horace said in his usual loud voice. He tried to hook the empty bottle to a metal stand beside the porcelain table holding Jeffrey's body.

Ida peeped again under the sheet at the corpse. "I'm stronger now after having gone through all these deaths recently."

"But you only saw the glamorous side of our work." Still trying to hang the bottle, he asked Ida,

"Would you mind getting that large roll of cotton from that cabinet and putting it over here?"

Ida opened several cabinets before finding the roll. "This one with the grey wrapper?"

"Yes. And step over here and help me lift this jug of solution and pour it in the bottle." He pulled the stopper from the jug and a smell, unfamiliar to Ida, filled the room.

"What's that stuff?" she asked.

"It's formaldehyde. Other chemicals are mixed with it to preserve the body."

"Why, I've never smelled such an odor."

"If you stay in here, there will be things you've never smelled, or even seen before."

"I'm gonna stick it out," Ida whispered.

Horace walked round the table, squeezed past Ida and accidently pulled some of the sheet off the body. Ida was pulling the sheet back over the corpse when Horace turned toward her with a straight razor.

"That's another thing, Ida. We never leave a naked body uncovered during the process of embalming. That's one of the ethical rules we try to follow in this business."

Ida knew better. She recalled the time, years ago when she and Viola were on their walk and peeped in the window of the embalming room and saw the two naked men stretched out on the table. Horace interrupted her thought.

"I will shave him first."

Ida's eyes grew big watching Horace raise the blade from the razor handle. She had never seen a razor so large The one she used to shave Seth was smaller.

The shaving brush clanged against the mug until the right consistency of lather suited Horace.

"I've already shaved him," Ida said, "Scraping a dead face with a razor didn't sound at all like I remembered when I was shaving Seth. The sound was more like scraping dead wood with fingernails."

Horace set the mug aside and closed the razor. "You did a nice job," he said. "After we scrub the body, I'll find the artery," pointing at Jeffrey's neck with the razor, "and I'll cut it so we can insert that rubber hose there on the bottle. The solution will replace the blood that will be forced out through the opening in the groin. The last thing we'll do is scrub the corpse again with the bacterial solution over there on the shelf. Will you hand it to me, please?"

Horace filled the pail with water and poured a small bottle of liquid in and stirred the solution with the brush. He scrubbed the upper body and handed Ida a towel. She turned her back while he used the brush to scrubbed the lower part. She wanted to sneak a peep to see how thorough he was scrubbing, but decided he might see her looking.

"Now that we've cleaned him, we'll rub his body in this Ponds Cream. Here. Take this jar and rub it on all parts of his upper body while I rub the lower part."

Ida hesitated. "Is this necessary?" she asked, not wanting to touch the corpse. She had only touched two other dead folk and she remembered how cold and clammy they were.

"It keeps the skin from drying out during the embalming," he said.

After the body was rubbed with cream, Horace

pulled the cover up, leaving only the head and neck exposed. Ida watched him force open the partly closed eyelids and drop in a thick liquid, then pressed them shut. She didn't ask about the coins he placed on them. She'd always heard they were to hold them shut.

Ida handed the other razor that she had cleaned for him. He took it and walked to the leather strap hanging by the door and ran it across it several times to sharpen it. Ida pulled the sheet down a little further and folded it neatly across the dead man's chest.

Horace began cutting a two-inch incision on the left side of Jeffrey's neck. Ida turned her head. Horace stopped and said, "If you plan to learn the trade, you've got to watch."

"But I'll never have to do that, will I?" She tried not to show her fear. She kept looking. Now that she had seen the rubber hose attached to the exposed artery, she continued watching the process for about thirty minutes. Finally, she had taken about as much as she could stand. She asked, "Are we about through?" When she saw blood, she let go of the tubing she was holding in the neck of the bottle and it fell to the floor. She picked it up quickly, squeezed the end to stop the flow of the liquid and stuck the end back into the bottle.

She watched Horace remove the coins from Jeffrey's eyelids and put them back in his pocket. "The fluid is nearly all gone. What do I do now?" she asked.

Horace leaned across the corpse to clamp off the tube to prevent air from seeping into the body. Suddenly, a large puff of air escaped. Ida jumped back and grabbed her nose. "What in the . . . ?"

"It's only air escaping from the body," Horace

said. "It will do that until the cavities are filled with the solution. Hand me the Trocar, please.

"The Trocar? What's that?" Ida asked.

"It's that sharp-pointed instrument over there on the table."

Still holding her nose, she lifted the metal rod carefully. Stretching across the corpse, she handed it to Horace. She watched him use it until she became sick. She told Horace she had to leave the room.

"I can handle the rest alone," he said. "I do want you to watch me sometime though, as I stitch the openings back together and stuff the rectum." He turned the stiff body over and reached for the cotton and began pulling it apart.

Ida had turned pale and he knew she was about to throwup. "Why don't you go out for some fresh air? You'll feel better soon. I'll be out after scrubbing the body again."

Ida rushed from the room, heaving as she pulled the door shut. Mary, Wilbur and Viola heard her and rushed down the hall toward her. Ida's clothes were reeking with formaldehyde.

Chapter 41

The night was long, Mary's sleep was disturbed by the squeaking of Ida's bed. She thought about Jeffrey, but she told herself to stop it. Jeffrey was dead. So many deaths: her papa, Dudley, Rufus. She tossed restlessly.

She would think about her love for Wilbur. Nothing else mattered. Dudley's death didn't seem to disturb Wilbur, since he hardly knew his father, and Mary understood his feelings. But through the years, there was much she had learned about Wilbur's father, and someday maybe Wilbur would want to ask her about him. After all, if they were to marry, she would want to tell her children about their grandfather.

During those quiet hours before daybreak, Mary's life took on new meaning. Her feelings toward her friends had changed. Now that Ellen Grace had let herself get in that 'particular way', Mary began to feel sorry for her. Maybe she should go to her after the funeral and offer help. But, there was the letter she had taken from Jeffrey's shirt pocket that no one knew she had. No, she would wait until she had heard the news from someone else. There were no secrets between her closest friends and surely someone would tell her. If she waited she wouldn't have to reveal that she had taken the letter from Jeffrey's pocket.

A mockingbird warbled in a tree just outside her bedroom window. Dawn had come while she was busy with her thoughts. She sat up to raised the shade to discover it had rained. She fell back across the end of the bed. In spite of her sleepless night, she hadn't heard drumming on the tin roof or splattering on the window pane. The morning was fair. Not a leaf quivered on the trees. She hesitated a moment before sitting up. Ida was in the hall humming. Mary opened her bedroom door and saw her removing the artificial flowers from some of her old summer hats. "What are you doing? Trying to find something to wear to the funeral?" she asked.

"Trying to find something to make a wreath of flowers." Ida held up several flowers she had torn from the hats.

"Surely, you're not going to use those old faded flowers for an arrangement."

"Well, why put good money in fresh flowers to dry up in a day or two? There's nothing in the yard we can use. These old hats aren't worth wearing out in public, anyway. After I take the flowers off, I can wear them to work in the garden."

"If the hats are not worth wearing out in the public, don't you think it's because of those faded flowers? Wouldn't it be embarrassing to put them in a wreath and put them on display for everyone to see?"

Mary asked.

"Well, we could save some money."

Mary just stood there looking at her. Ida continued to remove the flowers.

"How do you think I saved the money to buy the farm back?" Ida went on. "I scraped every cent I could and saved it, knowing full-well that someday we would need it."

Mary knew it was useless to argue with her. Furthermore, she didn't want to hear everytime money was mentioned how Ida had bought the farm back. "I'll make the coffee," she said, and left for the kitchen.

Ida soon entered carrying her apron full of the artificial flowers. "I'll be back in a minute," she said, heading for the back door.

Mary murmured softly, "I'll see to it that you'll never put them on the grave."

Ida stopped and looked back. "What did you say?"

"Nothing. I started to tell you that there'll be lots of people at the grave. I heard late yesterday there would only be graveside services. He didn't go to church, anyway."

Ida stopped for a moment and looked toward the barn. "Might as well. The devil will get him anyway for all that whoring around he did."

Mary wasn't surprised at Ida's harsh remarks. They were no different this time, in spite of Jeffrey's death. Everytime his name was mentioned, Ida had never failed to remind her of the fact that he wouldn't amount to a row of beans and would never have anything to leave behind to show for living on this earth.

Maybe he didn't have anything, Mary thought, but if Ellen Grace is pregnant, he certainly would leave something behind.

Everyone was quiet as Viola drove to the graveyard. Ida sat on the front seat and Mary rode in the back, holding the wreath of artificial flowers, wondering how she could get rid of them before they arrived at the graveyard.

Viola stopped the car along the roadside and they walked toward the grave, weaving around the tombstones. Everyone had gathered near the grave. Ida pushed her way through those standing behind the family and stood at the foot of the coffin, observing everyone. She noticed the young women far outnumbered the other mourners, several of them wiping their eyes. She tried to figure out which ones would miss him most.

Jeffrey was such a rascal and at first she hadn't understood why the girls were so crazy about him. It came clear to her when she and Viola were alone in the embalming room and they had peeped under the sheet at his body.

The preacher raised his hands. There was silence. The air was still and the bark of a fox sounded in the edge of the woods. Mary thought it might have been Spike and looked across the narrow field.

"Sometime we wonder if there is justice in this world," the preacher said as he began his remarks. "Sudden death stirs the soul of each of us as we wonder why anyone so young is snatched so quickly from this life, even before there is a chance to really live."

Ida nudged Beulah and leaned nearer. She

whispered, "If he didn't have a chance to live with all his goings on, I don't know who had."

Beulah straightened, turned her head and pretended not to have heard the remark. Ida moved a short distance away.

Mary saw several of her girl friends grouped together, crying. Touching Viola's arm, she whispered, "I'm going to join them. I'll meet you after the service." No one seemed to be listening to the preacher's comments, but were more interested in watching the single girls as they huddled aside from the crowd. Ellen Grace was grieving more than the rest so Mary went directly to her and circled her waist with her arm. Ellen Grace laid her head on Mary's shoulder.

"I understand," Mary said in a sympathetic voice. She tightened her arm around her. "All of us will miss him," she said, trying to sound sincere.

"Oh, Mary, I've gotta talk to you," Ellen Grace whispered in her ear, not wanting the others to hear.

"Sure, sure," was all Mary said.

"Can it be as soon as tomorrow?"

"I'll find time to see you any time, Ellen Grace."

Mary released her and gave her the lace handkerchief Wilbur had given her. Ellen Grace wiped her swollen, bloodshot eyes and offered it back. "Oh, keep it for the time being. You can return it later," Mary said. The Evening In Paris perfume from the handkerchief lingered on Mary's hands.

Mary was anxious to get back to the funeral home to see Wilbur. He had stayed there to give Ida a chance to attend the graveside services. When the crowd began to disperse, Mary went immediately to Viola's car.

There, on the back seat, lay the wreath of flowers. She was glad Ida had forgotten to take it to the graveside. She placed it in the foot of the car but when she saw Ida coming toward her, she put it back on the seat. If she was coming for it, Mary was glad she hadn't lingered at the grave.

"I need those flowers," Ida said, reaching through the window for them. Mary reluctantly handed the wreath to her. By the time Ida had stopped to pick up the flowers that had dropped from the wreath, nearly everyone had left the grave. Mary was glad. She watched from the car as Ida placed the wreath on the end of the coffin. Two ladies returned to the grave and while talking to Ida, they fumbled and examined the wreath closely. Mary watched them walk away, chatting and smiling at one another.

Ida waved Viola toward her and they headed for the car.

CHAPTER 42

Mary was deciding on the answer she would give to Wilbur's wedding proposal as she rode toward the funeral home. The quietness she had left at Jeffrey's graveside gave way to the chatter from the front seat of Viola's car. The conversation, dominated by Ida, didn't interest Mary as she kept busy with her own thoughts.

She thought of the excitement Wilbur must be feeling now that he was officially part owner of the funeral business. For days the whole community had been talking about the possibilities of the partnership between Wilbur and his Uncle Horace. She had not seen, or talked to him today, and was anxious to see his reaction to the excitement.

Although she had promised her answer to his proposal today, she wanted to relish his enthusiasm at being a businessman. Yes, that's what she would do. She would wait, unless he insisted that she give an answer.

Ida and Viola continued to chatter about

unimportant things as they got out of the car. Mary waited until they were on the porch of the funeral home before she left the back seat of Viola's car. She looked around, wondering if Wilbur might have seen them drive up. As she slammed the car door and looked at the front entrance of the building, she was surprised to see Wilbur come from around the building straight to her. As he approached, she smiled so he could see the small dimple, that he liked so much, appear at the corner of her mouth.

Wilbur did not smile back. His stern face relaxed but his eyes were unreadable. He took her by the hand and led her into the shadow of the elm tree. She could not see past the little frown that formed a line between his dark eyes. Without speaking, she found herself pressed against him. She pulled away and rubbed the lines between his eyes with her finger and watched them disappear. There was silence for a time.

For a moment she thought he was going to press his lips against her upturned face, but he held her at arm's length and stared deep into her pale blue eyes. She felt him trembling.

Finally she said, "I'm so happy for you."

"Then your answer is yes?" he asked.

"I'm talking about your being part owner of the funeral home."

"I'm not interested in that right now. First things first. You are going to marry me, aren't you?"

"Don't you want to enjoy the excitement of being in business for a while before we decide? "

"No," he said quickly. "You are the most important thing in my life right now. Should your answer be no, I'd just as soon not have a part of the business."

"Then I'll have to give you my answer." Mary turned and saw Viola and Ida coming toward them.

"We're happy for you," Ida said, almost shouting before getting near them.

"Yeah," Viola said. "There's nothing like being in business for yourself . . . " her words trailing off into silence when she saw them in an embrace.

Ida took Viola by the hand, and leading her toward the car, said, "They didn't even know we were there."

Mary knew that Ida and Viola had gotten in the car when she heard the two doors slam. She released her hold on Wilbur, stared into his dark eyes and asked teasingly, "So you want to marry me, do you?"

"Yes, yes. I've waited all my life for someone like you to share the rest of my life and you're the girl to make me happy."

As she parted her lips to speak again, Wilbur tightened his arms around her and planted a hard kiss on her mouth. She did not struggle against his tight embrace in spite of Ida's and Viola's staring. The feeling was contentment and she wanted it to last forever.

When he released her she said, "I'll marry you Wilbur, but there are so many things we must work out first."

"Nothing's impossible when two people are in love. I promise I'll work hard to please you. . ."

Mary interrupted, "Oh, you know I'm not hard to please. Just love me and everything will be just fine," she assured him.

"Here. Give me your hand as a promise that you'll love me as much as I love you." He took her left hand in both of his and lifted it to his lips. After kissing the palm of her hand, he slipped a diamond ring on her finger. "Take this as a solemn promise that I will love you forever and ever and I will never hurt you as long as I live."

Mary looked at the ring. "It's gorgeous," she said. "Look how it sparkles. It must have cost you a fortune. It's so large. When did you get it? How did you know I was going to say 'yes'?"

"It belonged to my grandmother. I have carried it in my pocket for years hoping that one day I would run into a pretty girl whose finger it would fit," he said, teasing her.

Mary went along with him. "I'm so glad my fingers are dainty. I bet you tried it on a hundred fingers." She stepped from under the elm tree and held it out into the sunlight. It sparkled like nothing she had ever seen before. She hugged him and was kissing his cheek tenderly when Viola blew the car horn. "Thank you, my love," was all she could say. She turned and started walking away. Turning to look back, she saw tears were in his eyes. She hurried to him and kissed him again, then rushed toward the waiting car, concealing the ring from Ida and Viola.

As she entered the back seat of the car, Viola said, "I saw you kissing that handsome fellow." Ida kept quiet. Any minute Mary knew Ida would pipe in some remark, but she sat silently.

Feeling exciting, Mary turned the ring round and round on her finger, wanting to tell them about it, but decided to wait until she and Ida were alone.

It was after eleven o'clock when Mary went to her room. She undressed, but she had no desire to sleep. The whole day had been exciting. Tomorrow would be a new day in her life, now that she had decided to marry Wilbur. "Mary Dunlock" she thought. "Ah. That name doesn't sound bad at all," she whispered to herself, admiring the ring on her finger.

Mary had difficulty getting to sleep. Twice in the night she woke up, remembering the disturbing dream in which she had been left at the altar. Unable to get back to sleep, she raised the shade and the window higher and placed her pillow at the foot of the bed. She lay with her head near the window and felt the soft cool air blowing against her face. For a long time she lay listening to the night. Many of the pleasant sounds were drowned by the scraping and tapping at the window by the branches of the tree that grew nearby. She listened, wishing it were Wilbur wanting to come inside.

Chapter 43

*I*t was very late. The mantel clock struck two. The night was unusually cool for mid-August. She was cold and got up to lower the window. She breathed in the perfume of the honeysuckle and was glad now that she had never had time in the spring to pull its vines from the fence that surrounded the vegetable garden.

Still trying to relax, she thought of her youth and how much she missed her papa. She thought of her first dolls, and immediately her mind drifted to Ellen Grace. She wondered how long her friend had been pregnant. Maybe tomorrow, when they meet, Ellen Grace would tell her and she would offer her help.

She heard a gentle knock on her door. She sat up in bed as Ida entered with the lamp. "Do you mind my coming in for a minute?" she asked.

"You can't sleep, either?"

"I lay awake thinking about your papa. Today is

his birthday, you know, and I had so many things on my mind, I just couldn't sleep." Ida placed the kerosene lamp in front of the mirror on the low dresser and it brightened the room. She sat on the foot of Mary's bed and it sagged slightly. "I heard you pull the window down and figured you were awake."

"I can't sleep either. So many things have happened today. In spite of the sad things, there is something exciting that I haven't told you."

"Oh, I know about the funeral home deal," Ida said nonchalantly.

"This is something that you don't know yet."

Ida saw Mary's broad smile and, although the room was dimly lighted, she saw happiness in her face.

Mary hesitated for only a minute before she spoke. "Wilbur," she said softly, "gave me an engagement ring today. He wants to marry me right away."

"My goodness, he acts fast. What has it been? Just a week or two since you met him?"

"Time doesn't matter when you're in love."

Ida took her hand and looked at the ring.

"I know he loves me," Mary assured her, "and he's so tender with his feelings." She squeezed Ida's hand. "And do you know what? Yesterday, he said all the folks congratulating him for taking over his papa's share of the funeral business, but he said it just didn't seem to excite him as much as my telling him that I would accept his proposal."

Ida leaned toward Mary to hug her. Her weight shifted and the bed collapsed. They lay there laughing. As Ida struggled to get up, Mary got out of bed and tugged at her until she could stand. "I'll never lose this weight," Ida grunted. They continued laughing.

"How old are you now, Ida?" Mary asked.

"Now honey, you know I'm only fifty-one."

"At that age, you don't have to worry about your size. You've got plenty . . . "

Ida interrupted, "of time to loose it?"

"No. You've got plenty time to enjoy every minute of your life. Being fat . . .," a slow flush spread over Mary's face, "I mean, being your size is so much a part of you. Horace is certainly not worrying about your weight."

"Sure. But he doesn't have to drag it around with him all the time, either." Ida said as she patted her rear. They laughed again.

Ida picked up the lamp. "Try to get some sleep now so you'll look fresh in the morning when we begin telling folks about your engagement. I'm very happy for you and I want to say I think Wilbur will make you a mighty fine husband." Holding the lamp high, the light reflecting on her face softened her expression. Mary even thought it softened her voice. From the door, Ida paused and said. "I surely do like your ring. We'll talk about wedding plans over breakfast." Ida pulled the door shut behind her and the room became dark.

Mary turned her face to the wall, covered her

head with the pillow. "I've got to get some sleep," she said aloud. She hadn't heard the clock strike for sometime and wondered if Ida might have forgotten to wind it.

She could not relax. She thought of how her relationship with her stepmother was changing and how pleasant she had become. During the last few weeks, lots of things had taken place in Ida's life. Her close association with Horace, her liking Wilbur and being asked to work at the funeral home had caused her to show a certain amount of happiness she hadn't shown before. Maybe Horace would propose to her, Mary thought, but there would be no way she could reach the point of happiness that she had found in Wilbur's love.

Her thoughts were disturbed by a mockingbird turning up for his early morning songs. Daybreak had not yet come and she thought she heard rain on the tin roof. She raised her head from the pillow and listened closely. Deciding it was a mouse running about in the attic, she turned over and faced the door and pulled the sheet over her.

The morning air was crisp and clear and the sun was still behind the pine trees that lined the other side of the road. A perfect morning for all good things to happen. Nothing could spoil her day in spite of her sleepless night. As she stood on the front porch glancing around, she noticed how the pine trees cast purple shadows across the road, broken only by a few rays of sunlight. The sound of a car broke the silence.

The car stopped at the gate and Mary started to it when Ellen Grace emerged from the passenger side. She could not see the driver before Ellen Grace waved the car off.

Meeting her in the middle of the yard, Mary reached out to take her hands, but her friend embraced her instead. After releasing one another, Ellen Grace turned her head slightly. Their eyes did not meet. What was she thinking, Mary wondered? She hesitated only for a minute before she asked, "Are you all right?" her voice sounding sincere rather than curious.

"I guess I'm all right," she told Mary. She began to cry. They walked to the porch and sat on the edge. Mary reached to remove a small pebble from her shoes and in the process, Ellen Grace saw her ring. She immediately took her hand. "When did you get that?" she asked as she wiped away her tears.

"Only yesterday. Isn't it beautiful?" Mary flashed it in the sunlight which was beginning to seep in under the porch roof.

"Oh, how I wish it were mine." Ellen Grace said, wiping her eyes and continued to cry. "If only I had waited. Why . . . why do I do such foolish things, Mary? I've got to talk to you about it. How can I say it, other than I'm . . . I'm pregnant? Its Jeffrey's. I'm sure if things hadn't happened the way it did, I would have no fears." She leaned against Mary and asked, "What must I do? Oh, what must I do?"

Mary cradled her in her arms and hugged her

tightly. "When did you learn?"

"More than a month ago."

"Does anyone else know?"

"No." Ellen Grace pulled away and walked away from the porch. "Only Jeffrey. I guess he knew. I sent him a letter a couple of days before he . . ." She stopped short, gasped for breath, "was killed . . . Oh Mary. I don't know what I'm going to do. You gotta help me decide." She turned toward her. "Please help me," she begged. "I've never needed help like I need it now." She walked back to the porch and sat close to Mary.

The screen door opened and Ida stepped on the porch. "Why, hello, Ellen Grace. I'm surprised to see you out so early. What brings . . ." She saw her crying and let her voice trail off to a mere whisper.

Ellen Grace only held tightly to Mary and cried even louder. She did not answer.

"Ellen Grace is deeply hurt about Jeffrey's death and how unconcerned everyone else seemed to be," Mary told Ida. She shook her head at Ida as a signal for her not to talk about Jeffrey's death. She wondered if her remark was convincing enough to keep her from asking more questions.

Ida understood and patted Ellen Grace on the head and went back inside to begin breakfast.

The aroma of country sausage frying on the Comfort Range in the kitchen floated through the hall to the front porch. Mary asked, "Have you eaten anything?"

"I haven't eaten since early yesterday. I can hardly stand the odor of food." Ellen Grace turned her head and covered her face with her hands.

"You must eat something." She wanted to add that she must eat for two now, but decided against it. "Come go to the kitchen with me. Dry your eyes and come along." Mary rose to leave but Ellen Grace held to her arm.

"My ride will be back in a minute or two so I'll just wait here on the steps. You run along and eat."

"You know I'm not going to leave you alone after you came out here to see me. In a day or two we'll talk some more. Maybe between us we can come up with a plan."

Before Ida came to say breakfast was ready, Geraldine drove up to pick up Ellen Grace. Mary asked Ellen Grace to wipe her eyes and put on a smile to avoid questions from Geraldine, that the secret would remain only between them. Ellen Grace thanked her and they walked to the car together. The three chatted briefly about Mary's engagement, admired the ring and waved to one another as the car drove off.

Viola arrived at noon for her daily visit. She had heard about Mary's ring through the grapevine and came out to find out all she could about their plans for marriage.

"We haven't talked about setting a date yet," Mary said. "We got to wait and see when the church will be available, anyway. Wilbur doesn't want to wait. Said he didn't think he could run a new business and at the same time do heavy courting." They laughed.

"Time is running out for all of us gals, so we'd better hurry. I'd marry that cute young thing tomorrow if he'd asked me. Wouldn't you, Ida?"

"I would have married Horace yesterday if he had asked me." Ida pointed her finger at Viola. "First, you've gotta find you a boy friend," she said jokingly. "Horace is mine so you better leave him alone. You don't want a big fight on your hands, do you?"

Mary laughed and went to the back porch, leaving them in the kitchen teasing one another. She sat on the bench near the open window listening. She heard Viola tell Ida about a rumor she'd heard only today that Horace wanted Ida to move into the funeral home when Wilbur was married and moved out.

"You know I'd move in the minute he asked me," she heard Ida reply.

"I'm surprised you didn't the day you started working there."

"Why, that was only a few days ago. Or was it yesterday?"

"I don't see why you don't just go on and move right in before Wilbur gets out."

"I'd start packing my personal things right now if I thought it would rush Mary's marriage."

Hearing Ida's remark, Mary slid down the bench nearer the window. She knew Ida was giving her approval for an early wedding, and it pleased her.

CHAPTER 44

Mary watched the clouds and the wind as it angrily shook the trees. She was afraid the weather would not set the mood she wanted when she talked to Ellen Grace. Bad weather always affected her, and today, after thinking about what she would do if she were in the same condition, she just didn't have a good feeling about talking to her friend.

They were to go for a long walk at Ellen Grace's suggestion. Maybe a walk around the farm and into the meadow that stretched all the way to the little hill where her papa never wanted the tall pines to be cut. Mary had found solitude when she visited that area. But today, she knew they wouldn't be able to go there unless the approaching storm blew away soon.

She sat on the wash bench near the well in the back yard and watched the wind twisting and shaking the trees. Maybe they would go to the graveyard, she thought. But, no, that is where Jeffrey is buried and there was no way it could create the mood needed for her to talk to Ellen Grace about her problem. Besides, the graveyard was the place where she went to talk to her papa whenever she felt burdened. It was her private place and she couldn't take someone else there to talk.

She left the bench and went to the front porch. No sooner than she sat in the swing, Geraldine drove up. When Ellen Grace got out of the car, Mary heard Geraldine say, "I'll be back in about an hour. I only have a few things to pick up in town." She waved at Mary and called, "Y'all take care, now," and drove off.

The wind had calmed down. Mary looked at the sky. The clouds were silver-lined and were moving rapidly toward the east. She met Ellen Grace at the gate, smiled and took her hand.

Still watching the sky and discussing the weather, they entered the meadow. They pulled the farm gate shut behind them and said little as they walked. The wind had ceased. Mary pointed out to Ellen Grace the giant dead black walnut tree she once played in. Its twisted arms reached high into the air as if still begging the sun to warm them enough to bring forth the new growth that failed to come in the spring. Ellen Grace stopped and studied the old tree.

They came to the opening on the side of the little hill that had only a few scraggly trees with some old abandoned bird nests.

Ellen Grace turned and looked back at the dead walnut tree. "You know, Mary, I feel just like that old tree, reaching out for help. I'm scared and I don't know which way to turn." She began to cry.

"Please don't cry," Mary said, placing her arm

around her. "Let's talk about what would be the best thing to do."

"I can't get rid of the baby. My conscience won't let me even think about it." She let go of Mary's hand and kicked a pine cone from the path. "What other alternatives do I have? I can't stay here and have the baby. Oh, if Jeffrey had only lived." She tried to stifle her sobbing. Taking several deep breaths, she walked a little ahead of Mary and reached a dense shady spot on the slope and threw herself on the grass. "Mary, I'm only nineteen years old and here I have ruined my life."

Mary did not comment. She wanted her friend to talk, hoping she would suggest what should be done before she made her own suggestions. Moments passed. "Ellen Grace, you know I'm to marry Wilbur in a few days and I have been thinking thoughts that might sound a bit wild to you."

"If it will help my situation, Mary, I don't care how wild they might sound." She continued sobbing. "Talk to me Mary. Tell me what to do." She rolled over on the grass, sat up and faced Mary. Her lips parted as if to speak, but something kept the words back. She only stared, waiting for Mary to speak.

Finally, Mary spoke. "My first suggestion is, if you don't mind me stating it quite frankly, that you find an excuse to go someplace for a long visit. Lets say, you're going to live with a relative in another state to go to school. I think it will work. If you'll consider putting the baby up for adoption, I will do all in my power to persuade Wilbur that he and I should take it. I'll talk to him and I'm sure he'll want to do it."

"Oh, Mary. My going away will require so much

lying. I can't put you through that."

"Wilbur loves children. He's told me many times that after we're married he didn't know if he could wait nine months before we had our first baby."

"But the lies we'll have to tell."

"Well," Mary paused as if she hadn't given thought to an alternative. "Maybe you can go someplace and after giving birth, give it up to someone whom you'll never know or even . . . "

"I can't bear to even think about doing that."

"Then let's say we'll take the baby, boy or girl. Wilbur wouldn't mind which."

"Would you really take the child and raise it?"

For a moment there was silence as the two looked at each other. Ellen Grace sat there with wide, interested eyes. Mary did not look away, but stared earnestly at her, assuring her that she was sincere.

A light wind blew up again and the thunder began to roll in from the east. "Maybe we should start back before it begins to rain," Mary suggested, rising and brushing the back of her skirt. "We wouldn't want you to catch cold in your condition." Taking Ellen Grace by the hand, she pulled her to her feet. "I'm a believer that nothing is so big that given a little thought, it can't be overcome."

"Mary, you've tried so many times to convince me that that's the way life is and I do want to have that assurance." She stared at the dead tree. "I promise you I'll think about what you have offered and let you know as soon as I decide where I can go for a few months." She hugged Mary and said, "You are my friend, and oh, the dearest one.

"You've gotta stop crying. Between us, we'll work things out."

"But you don't know how I feel deep inside."

"You've got to say to yourself, 'I'm going to be all right'. Say it over and over to yourself. Go ahead. Say it and see if you don't feel better."

Ellen Grace barely whispered the words.

"Say it loudly. You got to convince yourself. No one but you can bring it about."

Ellen Grace kept repeating, "I'll be all right. I'll be all right."

The wind shifted and chilled them. They walked toward the farm gate that separated the little grove of trees and the meadow. A carpet of blooming clover spread out before them.

As they passed the old dead walnut tree, Ellen Grace stopped and leaned back against the huge trunk that had been warmed by the sun. "Look how this old tree is begging out for new life. I wish I could die and start my life all over again," she cried.

"Don't say that," Mary begged. She took her hand and they walked to the house, occasionally smiling at one another.

Chapter 45

Viola's old Ford pulled up and stopped almost against the garden fence in Ida's back yard. Viola yelled, "What are you doing out there so early?"

Ida, still holding the hoe, yelled from the backside of the garden, "Although it isn't time yet, I gotta get those row fixed to plant winter salad seeds. I thought I felt a touch of fall yesterday, and with the wedding coming up right away, I had to get it fixed." Ida wiped her brow with the back of her hand. "You do want some greens this winter, don't you?"

She was fighting her habit of complaining, so she added, "There's so many things to do around this place I'm glad you came to help me," she yelled.

Viola went to meet her at the garden gate. Spike was at her heels. She tried pushing the dog with her foot, but he continued to lick her ankles. She removed the stick from the gate that Ida used to prop it and the gate fell from its only hinge and hit Viola on the hip. She took a swing at Spike with the stick and he ran yapping off toward the house.

"Ida, you have nothing but booby traps out here

and that damn dog. Why did you bring him home with you?" Not giving Ida a chance to answer, she continued, "I know you'll be glad when Wilbur moves in and can keep the place up for . . ."

Ida interrupted, "I'm getting older, but I can still keep my chores going."

"You want me to take that dog off someplace and kill him for you?" Viola looked toward the house and saw Spike lying on his stomach wagging his tail and gazing at her. "You sorry rascal," she yelled. "You better not come back out here."

Ida struggled with the gate and gave up trying to get it back on the hinge. She leaned it against the fence.

"Why don't you fix this old gate like it should be? And look at this old rusty, broken down wire fence you've got around this garden. How do you keep the varmints out? Surprised you even have a thing growing."

Ida only smiled. "I can manage. Figured that next spring, if there's a garden out here, Wilbur and Mary will tend it."

Viola looked her over. "And look at those hands and fingernails of yours. You'll never get them clean for the wedding."

Wiping the sweat from the back of her neck, Ida said, "Oh, don't worry about me. I'll just wear gloves." She raised her hand to slap her friend on the back as she had done so many times, but Viola jerked away and said, "Don't you dare rub those dirty hands on my dress."

"Well, aren't you touchy this morning. What's wrong? You get up too early? You should have stayed in bed. You need your beauty sleep more now than ever, anyway."

Viola turned and walked disgustedly to her car. Grasping the door handle she turned and said, "I came out to tell you something, but you're so ugly to me I think I'll just go back home and let you find it out the best way you can."

"Oh, come on now, Viola. You know I'm just teasing."

"Well, I'll just tell you and leave." She blared it out. "Old Lady Crabstein died suddenly last night."

"Good Lord. What happened?" Ida asked. She leaned the hoe against the fence and walked toward her.

"Just died at the table while they were feeding her."

"When do they plan to bury her?"

"The same day as the wedding."

"How in the world can we have a wedding with the whole wedding party tied up with a funeral? There's no way we can handle it. They'll have to bury her another day. Mary will never agree to postpone her wedding," Ida said. "They'll just have to keep her out until the wedding's over."

"Don't worry about it. I understand everything is being handled by the funeral home in Tuckersville."

"Well. Thank the Lord," Ida breathed a sigh of relief. She reached for the hoe. "Here. Take this. I'll get another one from under the shelter over there," she said, pointing to the nearly collapsed shed next to the barn. "You can help me. That way, it'll only take us another ten or fifteen minutes. I've gotta get these seeds in if you're gonna come over here and help us eat greens this winter."

"Why don't you forget the garden? Let Wilbur and Mary worry about it. You'll be eating with Horace, anyway."

"Now, Viola, you know how young folks are about things. Do you think for one minute they'll be interested in growing things?"

"Well. We both know that Mary will be interesting in only one 'growing thing' and that won't be green." They giggled.

Viola tossed aside the hoe she had taken from Ida. She waved and said, "Just wanted you to know about Mrs. Crabstein. See you later." She got in her car and drove off.

Wilbur dressed for the wedding in the embalming room of the funeral home. He put on his highly polished black leather shoes and thrust his hands deep in the pockets of the pant of his new black suit. He had once thought of borrowing a tuxedo, but decided to invest in a wedding suit that he could also use for funeral services.

He became suddenly aware that his lifestyle would be drastically changed after his marriage today and his hands shook.

There was no air circulation in the embalming room. As he dressed he realized it wasn't the heat, but his nervousness that caused sweat beads to drop from the ends of his hair onto his new white shirt.

He carefully removed his new black string tie from the celluloid box. Fumbling, he finally got it tied, but it was too tight. He loosened it.

Wilbur wasn't happy with Mary's selection of her

maid of honor. He couldn't understand her picking Ellen Grace over some of her more attractive girl friends. The last time he saw them together, he noticed how quiet and secretive they were and wondered what was going on. He brushed it off when Mary confirmed that their friendship had lasted over the years.

Wilbur headed toward the front porch. He stopped and gazed at himself in the tall tarnished mirror in the hall. The ends of the string tie were uneven so he stopped and retied it. Now he was able to breathe a little more comfortably.

As he passed the empty parlor, he glanced through the open door and was glad that he had hauled Mrs. Crabstein's body to the Tuckersville Funeral Home early in the day. He was glad too that they were handling the funeral service. He hadn't wanted to help his Uncle Horace with the embalming and suggested that Ida help him, but she was busy with last minute plans for the wedding.

The morning was a busy one and he had been anxious to get dressed. Although the church was only a short distance away, he now wished he hadn't dressed so early. The humidity had changed so quickly that his shirt was wet with sweat. He went to the porch and sat in a rocker where a light breeze was blowing.

There was no breeze blowing through the window of Mary's room. As she glanced toward her wedding dress spread out smoothly on her bed, she debated if she should apply her make-up before or after she put the dress on. Her friends had spent two weeks cutting, sewing and fitting it and she didn't want to smudge it with lipstick and rouge while pulling it over her head. She knew a solid white wedding dress denoted purity and she thought of another color in the beginning, but she wasn't about to let her close friends smile as she walked down the aisle.

There were no parking places near the church when the wedding party arrived. Mary had never seen so many cars at the church before. At her request, the preacher had invited the congregation to her wedding, but she had never given thought to such a large attendance. Cars were everywhere, even both sides of the road were lined with vehicles.

Riding up the driveway, Viola saw a space in front of the church which she assumed was left for the bride to park. Viola pulled her old Ford in the space. She saw Mary on the edge of her seat and smiled at her through the rear view mirror. "Aren't we lucky?" she asked.

Getting out of the vehicle, Mary noticed a hearse was parked at the side entrance of the church with a few men standing around.

Wilbur, Horace, Ellen Grace and the preacher stood near the steps. Everyone else had entered.

Wilbur went to meet Mary as she rushed to get out of the car. "For a minute there, I thought you weren't going to get here on time," Wilbur said.

"I wouldn't have missed this day for anything under the sun," Mary said, smiling while trying to catch her breath.

"You're beautiful," was all Wilbur said as he took her hand and led her up the steps.

The preacher, clutching his prayer book, said,

"When you hear the organ began to play, I want you two to come slowly down the aisle together, pause at the altar and I will proceed." Before he opened the church doors he instructed Ellen Grace to follow him and stand near the altar facing the congregation. He held the door open for Ida and Viola. When he saw they were seated, he entered, followed by Ellen Grace.

The doors closed behind them, shutting out the soft chattering of the crowd. Wilbur and Mary waited nervously for the music to begin. "The Preacher's instructions sounded simple enough," Wilbur said, watching Mary smooth the front of her dress to remove the wrinkles.

At the first note of music, he kissed her lightly on the lips. She pushed up the black hair on Wilbur's forehead and rubbed away the sweat that glistened on his cheekbones. As they waited to enter the church, she gazed into his blue eyes and could only think of her desire to have a baby that mirrored an image of him. But, there was Ellen Grace. There would be time to discuss with Wilbur about taking her baby. But what if the child resembled its father? Mary put the thought from her mind.

Holding hands, neither of them looked ahead when they entered the sanctuary. Ignoring the huge crowd that had packed the church, they slowly made their way down the center aisle, occasionally bumping into the pews.

Mary heard the rustling of her floor length satin wedding dress and slightly lifted the skirt and glanced around. Her eyes fell upon the flower arrangements centered around the altar. She gasped for breath and said aloud, "Funeral flowers!" She looked at Wilbur. He was still staring at her and smiling broadly. She tugged at his arm and they stopped halfway down the aisle. She didn't see Ellen Grace, but heard her crying.

"Something is wrong," Mary whispered to Wilbur. Her voice trembled and she wasn't sure that he understood her. "I knew something was wrong when I heard the first notes of that song. What are we going . . . what are we going to do? Why are all those folks standing up front?"

Wilbur pulled her close and said gently, "Just wait right here." He released her and she leaned against the end of the pew. She began to cry as Wilbur pulled away and started walking alone toward the altar where he joined the preacher and the undertaker from Tuckersville. A lady whom she had never seen put her arm around her.

Mary's view of the side entrance to the sanctuary was obscured by the many hats the ladies were wearing but she was able to see the six pallbearers who had entered with Mrs. Crabstein's coffin, their faces contorted from the weight.

As the men began to back up with the coffin, silence fell over the crowd. Mary saw several wreaths of flowers topple over and she thought she heard the sound of water splattering. The excitement caused the crowd to stir. Many Sundays she had heard members of the congregation talking before church services, but never like this. She covered her face with her hands.

The lady removed her arm from around Mary and shoved her hips hard against the woman sitting beside her. "Tighten up a little, please," she said, and suddenly there was room for Mary to squeeze in on the pew. The lady was fanning with the fan provided by the funeral home. Mary lifted her face and dried her tears. Her pulse quickened when she saw flashes of Jesus crossing back and forth in front of her.

"What are they going to do?" she kept asking the lady over and over.

Finally, the gentle lady said, "It will be all right, honey. The men at the front are talking it over and they'll get things straightened out. Now don't you worry your poor little head," the lady said, patting Mary on the thigh.

Suddenly there was extra room on the pew. Mary was glad. She could spread out on the pew to avoid getting more wrinkles in her dress. She knew the man who left his seat and was walking down the side aisle toward those who were still in discussion. He was the church steward and a highly respected member and she was confident that he could straighten things out.

She couldn't stand the mumbling any longer. She stood. Leaning toward the lady beside her, she said, "This is my day and I'm not going to sit here hiding in the crowd." She left the pew and started walking toward the altar.

Wilbur met her halfway the aisle. He took her hand and led her to the front entrance. When they faced the altar front they saw the pallbearers struggling to get Mrs. Crabstein's coffin back through the door. After several maneuvers to take the coffin back outside, the preacher motioned for it to be pushed against the wall. "But don't move it too far forward," he warned. "The floor is a little weak over there."

Four ladies left the congregation and began picking up the flower arrangements and carrying them from the church through the side entrance. The preacher stopped them. He raised his arms above the congregation and said, "My friends, there's been a little confusion. There was a misunderstanding about scheduling things here at the church today and we apologize. If everyone will remain calm, and be seated, we will soon get the services underway."

Just as the preacher had settled everyone down, a commotion erupted near the side entrance. A few of the folks got to their feet to see what had happened. Others just sat there. Mary could see that one end of Mrs. Crabstein's coffin had crashed through the termite-eaten floor. Standing at the rear of the church, she and Wilbur could see the end tilting upward. The pallbearers tugged until they were able to pull it from the hole. Several of the flower arrangements were overturned again and they heard one lady say, "Don't tromp on them there flowers. I done that arrangement."

"Please settle down," the preacher begged. "We'll have things going in a few minutes."

A few sighs came from the congregation. Some stretched their necks to see the activity over by the side door. The coffin was placed against the wall and the four ladies stood in front of it holding sprays of flowers.

Wilbur whispered to Mary, "Aren't we lucky to have so many flowers to decorate the church?"

Mary felt he was teasing and she answered nervously, "Yes, but had we known, we could have saved lots of time bringing in all those home-grown larkspur, sunflowers, and zinnias." She caught her breath, then whispered, "I hope they don't tear up those ferns Beulah loaned us."

Wilbur gazed into Mary's eyes, and despite all the pleasure of looking at her, he saw beauty he had never seen before. Even at this tense moment, she looked as if heaven were even now present in her thoughts.

Ida, sitting three pews from the front, kept watching one of the pallbearers who didn't appear satisfied with the way Mrs. Crabstein's coffin was turned. He continued tugging at the foot of the coffin until his hands slipped. He fell back into the lap of the granddaughter of the deceased and the young lady screamed. Viola was more interested in what Wilbur and Mary were doing and missed the incident. Ida nudged her just in time for her to see the pallbearer struggling to get to his feet. After a moment of snickering, Ida tried not to laugh, but the pew continued to shake. All those around her began to stare. Viola didn't think it was funny. She became embarrassed and turned her head.

Ida threw her head back, trying to control her laughter, and her hat fell behind her pew. She placed her arm around Viola's shoulder and lowered her hand to feel for the hat. Her hand fell on the knee of the man sitting directly behind her. Suddenly she felt a slap on her wrist. She shifted on the pew, glanced back to see the man's wife looking disgustedly at her. Trying to stifle her snickering, Ida whispered that she was sorry and took the hat from the woman, but didn't put it back on.

Viola slipped close to her and whispered, "Ida Ridley, I'm never going to get out in public with you again. In fact, I don't even want to sit next to you." She pushed against the lady sitting on her right, but the lady shoved her back toward Ida.

The music began. Ida saw Ellen Grace stand as 'Amazing Grace' rang out from the old pump organ. She watched the girl's face turn red from embarrassment and saw her quickly sit back down. She'd always teased Ellen Grace about standing at attention when she heard that particular song played. Afterwards, Ida had always referred to it as Ellen Grace's personal anthem.

The preacher walked over to the organist and whispered some instructions to her. She abruptly stopped the hymn and switched her music books. She bowed to the couple at the rear of the church and began playing the 'Wedding March'. The preacher stopped her and waved to the couple to wait as he strolled to the altar shaking his head. He grasped the edge of the pulpit. His lips were trembling. "I am truly sorry for the mix-up that has occurred here today, my friends, and I sincerely apologize. I have the assurance that the Good Lord knows that we are not perfect and will understand our frailties, and He will be patient with us. I'm sure all of you will be just as patient and understanding as we conduct the services we now seem to have finally straightened out." He looked at the organist and nodded. She began to play 'Amazing Grace' again. The preacher shook his head at her, but she wasn't looking at him. Again he walked over and asked her to play the wedding music. They smiled at each other. As she resumed "The Wedding March" he grasped his prayer book and stood in front of the pulpit and motioned for the bride and groom to come forward. Everyone turned and watched Mary and Wilbur move slowly down the aisle. Wilbur was still gazing at his bride-to-be and saw her perplexed expression. They stopped in front of the altar and faced one another.

The preacher opened his prayer book and cleared his throat. He looked at the congregation and said, "Dearly beloved, we have gathered here to pay our last respects to this . . . " He adjusted his tiny horn rimmed glasses, flipped a few pages in his prayer book and began again. "Dearly beloved, we have gathered here to join this man and this woman in Holy Matrimony."

At certain times Ida's laughter had a way of setting the mood for other people. She could not keep still on the pew and the people sitting around her also began to chuckle.

Mary stood facing Wilbur during the vows and dared not look past him for fear she would gaze upon the coffin of Mrs. Crabstein. She was nervous enough already and knew if she caught sight of the felt covered coffin she might forget to repeat the vows and she didn't want to concentrate on anything but becoming Mrs. Dunlock.

Before the preacher finished asking Wilbur if he would take Mary to be his wedded wife, Wilbur responded, "I do, I do, I do." Mary squeezed his hand each time he said 'I do'.

Wilbur didn't wait for the preacher to finish pronouncing them man and wife, but kissed Mary during the announcement and began leading her toward the exit. No sooner had they turned to leave, Mary saw Ida and Viola getting from their seats to follow them out. She was glad because she was afraid if they waited for those attending the wedding to file out ahead of them, there was a possibility of them missing the train. At the sanctuary doors, Mary glanced back and saw them trailing close behind.

When they were in the vestibule, and as soon as the doors swung shut, Ida heard the preacher say, "Those of you who came to attend the wedding may now leave with the wedding party before we begin the funeral service." Ida rushed back to the altar and picked up the vase of bright red gladiolus that she had arranged for the wedding. Holding the flowers above her head and pushing through the crowd to join the married couple, she sloshed water on the people who had gathered in the aisle.

After saying good-bye to those standing around on the church porch, Mary descended the steps and looked up. She had never seen a day so perfect. The silver lined clouds shut out most of the early afternoon sun. Her white satin wedding gown glistened and glowed like the outlines of the clouds. Two nearby mockingbirds were singing in harmony. What a nice omen, she thought.

Before Mary had a chance to say good-bye to everyone, she heard Ida call out, "We gotta hurry if you're going to catch that train to Richmond." She wondered how Ida knew they were going to Richmond, but decided it really didn't matter.

Mary rushed to hug her friends then entered the car and they rode away. The crowd continued to wave as the noise from Viola's old car drowned out the funeral music coming from the church.

Viola stopped at Mary's house for the couple to change clothes and pick up their luggage before she drove them to the train station in Tuckersville.

Ida held one of Mary's suitcases on her lap. Mary and Wilbur sat in the back of the car, their feet propped on the other suitcases they were taking on the trip.

"Wasn't there room back there for that handgrip?" Viola asked Ida. "The weight of you and that bag is going to mash the rest of that stuffing out of my car seat."

"I'm gonna re-stuff it for you if it's the last thing I do," Ida responded, "and I'm going to do it with big wads of stuff that won't flutter out every time I sit on the darn thing." Ida was shifting on the seat like an old hen settling in her nest. Mary knew she was trying to rowel Viola. She thought Wilbur would question her about Ida and Viola's jabbing one another, so she whispered to him, "Don't give it a thought. You'll have plenty of time to get to know them. I've been hearing this for years and I seem to think it's the only way they can remain friends." Wilbur only raised his eyebrows.

They sat there listening to Viola and Ida talking until they were approaching Tuckersville Train Station. The women were not interested in them, so Wilbur spoke softly and told Mary that he was planning to buy a car when they arrived in Richmond. She squeezed his hand and kissed him on the cheek.

Viola, looking through the rear view mirror said, "I saw that."

Ida looked back. "What did I miss?" she asked. They laughed.

They came in sight of the train station before Ida started talking again. She finally asked, "What did you all see back there? Apparently I missed out on something."

"Well," Viola said. "If you must know, there was this handsome man running, trying to catch up with us and he . . ."

Ida slapped Viola on the leg and said, "Oh, cut it out, Viola. If there was a man running behind us, I know he was chasing me. Not you."

"That's what you think," Viola replied, and stepped on the gas.

The time of arrival for the next train was written on a blackboard which hung beneath the old railroad clock on the side of the train depot. If the train was on time, they had twenty minutes before it was to arrive. Wilbur had purchased their tickets in advance so they began unloading the suitcases from the car and placing them on the edge of the platform. Ida and Viola had left the couple alone and walked over to talk to friends who were waiting for the train's arrival.

"Guess what?" Wilbur asked Mary. "Uncle Horace gave us money to buy the car."

"He did what?" she asked surprisingly.

"Said we would need one if we were to live out on the farm."

"Oh, that's great. I'm so excited!"

"He said he wanted us to get a new one and that it would be our wedding present."

"Oh, I can't take much more excitement today," she said.

"Oh, but I can excite you more."

Mary was about to ask him how, but felt a flush come suddenly to her face. She smiled and glanced away.

Wilbur couldn't keep his eyes off her. In front of all the people standing around, he folded her in his arms. "I love you," he said and held her until he heard the train whistle in the distance.

The train came to a swoshing stop and the steam whisked around them. Wilbur and Mary were in front of the snake-like line of passengers that haphazardly stood on the platform a few yards away. It moved toward the door of the train when the steam drifted off.

Everyone watched and waited for the passengers as they struggled to get off the train with their heavy suitcases. When Wilbur thought everyone was off, he started to help Mary aboard, but the conductor asked them to wait and to step back a little. They watched as a trunk, two large suitcases and a cradle were placed on the platform.

Mary called excitedly to Ida. Ida rushed to her. "Isn't that the cradle you gave to Adam?" she asked. Ida gasped. She looked up and saw Adam descending the steps. She pushed her way toward him with outstretched arms. Adam ran into them and began to cry. He pressed his chubby frame against her and she tightened her arms around him.

"Oh my God! My God! You've come home!"

"Yes. I . . . I ran away to be with my real... real mama," was all Adam said and continued crying.

Ida kissed him on the face and neck repeatedly and she sobbed. Sobbing - not like a child, painful or heartrending, but like an old woman.

THE END

For a personal autographed copy of **Cradle in the Back of the Hall**, complete the information below.

Ship to: (please print)

    Name _____

    Address _____

    City, State, Zip _____

    Day phone _____

_____ copies of *Cradle...* @ \$9.95 + 60¢ tax each   \$ _____

Postage and handling @ \$2.50 per book   \$ _____

Total amount enclosed   \$ _____

Make checks payable to: *Lenward Thomas*

Send to: **Offshore Publishing**
P.O. Box 4325 • Emerald Isle, NC 28594

For a personal autographed copy of **Cradle in the Back of the Hall**, complete the information below.

Ship to: (please print)

    Name _____

    Address _____

    City, State, Zip _____

    Day phone _____

_____ copies of *Cradle...* @ \$9.95 + 60¢ tax each   \$ _____

Postage and handling @ \$2.50 per book   \$ _____

Total amount enclosed   \$ _____

Make checks payable to: *Lenward Thomas*

Send to: **Offshore Publishing**
P.O. Box 4325 • Emerald Isle, NC 28594